CREED

WANTED

BRYCE HARTE

BERKLEY BOOKS, NEW YORK

**To the Honorable Donn H. Dahlke,
with admiration and gratitude**

CREED: WANTED

A Berkley Book / published by arrangement with
the author

PRINTING HISTORY
Berkley edition / May 1991

ISBN: 0-425-12727-3

10 9 8 7 6 5 4 3 2 1

FIGHTING FOR A CAUSE

CLETE SLATER—a forgotten hero of the Confederacy, he rides south to Mexico with a new name, Slate Creed, and a fiery passion for revenge.

JIM KINDRED—two-bit cattle rustler and part-time gunslinger, he leads the Thicket Gang in a reign of terror over the Southwest.

THE GOLIHAR BROTHERS—shiftless members of Kindred's band, they follow the orders of a bloody family vendetta and shadow Creed's every move.

SEÑORITA SILVERIA ABEYTIA—the breathtaking Mexican beauty who is the woman of Creed's dreams—and the only woman who may tear him away from the woman of his heart who waits in Texas.

COLONEL FRANÇOIS DUPIN—sadistic leader of Emperor Maximilian's Contre-Guerrillas, ''the butcher'' has the power to make Creed a reluctant soldier once more.

CLAIRE MOUNET—a more powerful enemy than any man, this sultry schemer holds the key to Creed's fate in her cold and calculating hands.

CREED

Berkley Books by Bryce Harte

The CREED series

CREED
WANTED

REAL HISTORY

The author has woven a few fictional characters into the real history of the Mexican Civil War, while continuing the story of Clete Slater who has now taken the name of Slate Creed.

The history of the Mexican Civil War was a bloody struggle between the Mexican people and an army of merciless European mercenaries. Many Americans fought and died on both sides of this conflict. The battle for Matamoras was only a small chapter in that terrible war, but it was a real event, involving real people on both sides.

In this tale that takes Creed below the Rio Grande, every geographical item, meaning every town, river, creek, hill, street name, etc., existed at the time of the story depicted herein. All spellings of places, particularly that of Matamoras, were those that were in use in 1865, the time of the story. Rancho Abeytia Tres Palmes existed, although under a different name.

Of the people in this story, Colonel François Achille Dupin of the Imperial Army of Mexico under Maximilian was the founder of the Contre-Guerrillas who fought the Juaristas without mercy. Dupin was known as the "Tiger of the Tropics".

General Juan Cortina was known as the Red Bandit when

he was robbing and rustling in Texas, but he was a hero of the Mexican people.

John Hunter and Frank Newhouse were Americans who fought for the Juaristas.

And, of course, Benito Juarez was the president of Mexico.

The Battle of Matamoras did occur at the time of Creed's adventure in Mexico, and it was fought much as described herein.

James Kindred and his gang of outlaws did go to Mexico to avoid prosecution in Lavaca County, and the Golihar brothers were draft-dodgers who used Somer's Thicket as their hideout.

The units of the American army mentioned in the story were sent to the Rio Grande as a threat to Emperor Maximilian.

Prologue

"What will you do after you leave here?" she asked softly.

"Hide for a while, I guess," said Slater. "After that, I don't know. Go to Mexico after Kindred and his bunch, maybe. Or I might go looking for those polecats that said I led that raid in Mississippi. I don't know for sure, but I do know this much. Until I can clear my name and live up to my family's motto, I can't call myself Clete Slater. My granddaddy said that I should always be proud to be a Slater and that I should always do my best to uphold the Slater creed: 'Steadfast in honor and loyalty and justice.' That's exactly what I intend to do, but I'm going to do it as ... as ... I don't know. Maybe I'll just call myself that. Slater Creed ... or maybe just Slate Creed, as a kind of constant reminder of what my life has to be."

Texada's tears cascaded over her cheeks as she said, "Will we ever be together again?"

"Yes, of course, we will, darling."

"When?" she asked hopefully.

Slater didn't have an answer for her. He heard a cock crow in the distance and realized that dawn would be coming soon. "I have to go, Texada," he said.

"When?" she cried.

"I . . ."

"When, Clete? When will we be together again?" she sobbed.

"I . . . I don't know the answer to that."

Texada wrenched herself away from Slater, turned her back to him, and moved away two short steps. "Then go! Go before it gets light out!" Slater moved toward her and put his hands on her shoulders, but she rejected his touch. "No, don't. Just go, Clete, and leave me be."

"Texada," he said softly.

"Go!" she screamed as all the anguish of love rendered her soul into spectral shreds.

With tears in his own eyes, Slater whispered, "I love you," then turned and headed down the tunnel toward the well house.

Texada spun around to look at him one last time, but he was gone. "I love you, Clete darling," she said as if he were standing there with her. "I'll always love you, and I know we'll be together again. Someday."

By the time he crossed the property line of Glengarry Plantation, Clete Slater had made up his mind that he would be known as Slate Creed from that moment until the time that he could clear his given name and return to his native home as a free man. Until then, he would be a fugitive from the injustice of being accused and convicted of a crime he didn't commit.

1

Nimbus was a horse easily recognized as belonging to Clete Slater, fugitive from justice, albeit Yankee justice. Everyone in or about Lavaca County, Texas, who knew Slater knew his gray Appaloosa. See one—man or beast—and you usually saw the other. One might forget Slater's face or his horse but not both. Each was identified with the other, and that was that.

If Slater had taken this fact under serious consideration when he lit out from Glengarry, he might have saved himself a great deal of trouble later on.

When the first glow of daylight shone in the east, Slater figured that traveling by day was not in his best interests. Too many Yankee patrols looking for him; that much was certain. And who knew how many civilians there might be on the roads who were also out to get him for the inevitable price that would be placed on his head? But where to hide until dark came again? He pondered this question for a moment before coming up with an answer, then swam Nimbus across the Lavaca River below the old Zumwalt Settlement near the mouth of Rocky Creek. He rode southeast from there, past old Kent's place, across the former county line, until he came to Somer's Thicket in the bottoms along the Lavaca just west of Beardsden. It was in his head that he might hole up for a day or two or maybe three until he could sort out his thoughts and decide where to go from here. After all, Somer's thicket had been the perfect hiding place for Unionists, draft dodgers, deserters, and all sorts of outlaws during the recent War Between the States. Why wouldn't it suit his purpose now?

Slater eased Nimbus down the steep bluff into the densely timbered maze of underbrush, vines, hackberries, and live oaks that was the thicket. In the distance, he saw a wisp of blue smoke lazily curlicuing skyward from a grove of cottonwoods. Dying campfire, he thought. Better see with whom he might be sharing his temporary residence before deciding whether to stay or not. He nudged the Appaloosa in the direction of the smoke.

After a dozen or more twists, turns, and dead ends, man and horse came to a clearing and stopped. Slater scanned the area with the trained eye of a military veteran. He felt his mount stiffen beneath him; a sure sign of danger, said the experience of three-plus years of combat. Instinctively, he glanced up at the spreading branches of the cottonwoods and saw a man asleep, legs astraddle a large limb, back against the trunk, rifle resting in the crook of his left arm, and his right hand tucked in the lever of the Henry, ready for action, supposedly. Guard, thought Slater. He squeezed Nimbus with his knees, and the stallion went ahead in a careful walk, knowing that his master wanted him to move with all the stealth of a cat on the hunt, until they were directly beneath the slumbering man. Slater straightened his legs, and Nimbus halted there. Reaching up, Slater grabbed the barrel of the Henry and pulled down hard.

Feeling his gun suddenly being jerked away from him, the guard came awake, startled but reacting. He tried to hold on to his weapon but only managed to get himself unseated. ''Ai-ee-ee-'' slipped through his lips, followed by *clunk* as he hit the ground at the Appaloosa's feet. He rolled over and started to scramble to an upright position but was halted by the sight of the Henry's muzzle staring him between his pale blue eyes.

"Not another sound!" hissed Slater through clenched teeth.

The man related his willingness to cooperate by making a series of little nods and by shifting his frightened eyes back and forth between the rifle barrel and Slater, who was glaring hard at him.

"I don't mean you any harm," whispered Slater, "but I don't want you doing anything foolish either . . . like maybe shooting me first and asking questions last. Understood?"

Again, the nods and shifting eyes.

"Name is . . . Creed. Slate Creed." There! He'd done it! He'd taken the name he'd told himself he would take until he could clear his real name. He'd told Texada he might do it, and now he had. There was no turning back now. He would be Slate Creed until he righted the wrong done to him or he died—whichever came first. "I know about this place," he continued. "I know about the kind of men who hide out here. I need to hide out here, too. For a while, leastways. That's all you need to know about me. Understood?"

Once more, the nods and shifting eyes.

"Good enough. Now how about you leading me into camp so none of the others who are hiding out here mistake me for a John Law and go to shooting at me before asking me to stay for a cup of coffee?" Creed raised the rifle away from the man's nose.

The man swallowed hard, sighed, and said, "Sure thing, Mr. Creed." Then he turned and led the way into camp.

Creed followed but at a safe distance.

The outlaw camp at Somer's Thicket wasn't much to look at: a score of brush-covered lean-tos scattered about a clearing beneath more cottonwoods. Most of the structures were unoccupied at the moment. Evidently, the regulars who hid here were off somewhere, probably up to no good. Creed saw only two other men besides himself and the guard. Both of them were sleeping, each in a separate hut.

"What's your name?" Creed asked the guard.

"Bateman Bell," he answered with a long-toothed smile. "Most everybody calls me Bats though, Mr. Creed. That's 'cause they say I got bats in my bell tower." He chortled, sounding like a pig rooting at the trough.

"Well, Bats," said Creed, slipping into a down-home brand of dialect, "I've been up all night, and I'm all done in right now. I'd take it kindly if you were to see to it that I ain't bothered by no one until I wake up later today. Do you think you could do that for me, Bats?" He handed the Henry back to Bell.

Accepting the rifle with a big smile of surprise, Bell said, "Sure thing, Mr. Creed. I'll do 'er. I'll even feed and water your horse, if you want me to."

"That would be real nice of you, Bats." Creed slid down from the saddle and handed the reins to Bell. "His name is Nimbus. You take good care of him, and I'll show you my appreciation when I wake up."

"Yes, sir, Mr. Creed."

Creed couldn't figure out why Bell, who had to be five to ten years older than he was, kept calling him *Mister* Creed. Then he saw his long shadow on the ground and realized that he was still wearing his grandfather's hat, the chapeau of an older man, a brown felt sloucher. He touched his face and was reminded that he hadn't shaved in three days; his thick, full mustache and whisker stubble of auburn and black sprinkled with white gave him the appearance of a man much older than his twenty-three years. No wonder Bell called him *Mister*.

When planning his escape from the Yankees, Texada had thought of everything he might need for a trip. She had

packed his saddlebags with an extra shirt, a change of socks
and underwear, his razor, shaving mug and soap, and had
even included a face towel. Just like a cowboy or cavalryman would do, she had rolled two thin blankets inside a
rain slicker and had tied them tight to the back of his saddle.
Creed shook his head in amazement. Texada was everything
he wanted in a woman and maybe more. He truly loved
her, and although they had only been apart a few hours, he
already missed her.

Creed took down the bedroll and started to loosen the
strings but stopped when he saw a piece of paper poking
out from between the blankets. He pulled at it, and it came
free easily. The page was folded in quarters. He opened it
and read:

My Darling Clete,
    If you have to open your own bedroll, then it means
that we are apart. I will not know how far or for how
long, but I will know that wherever you go my love
will always go with you. I love you, my darling. Take
good care of yourself and come back to me as soon as
you can.
    With All My Heart,
        Your Darling,
            Texada

As Creed recalled how soft she felt in his arms and how
tender her lips were when they touched his, one of the
sleeping men began to stir, having heard voices in the camp.
He rolled over, sat up, and gazed through blurry eyes at
Nimbus and Creed. Rubbing the sleep from his orbs, he
yawned and looked again. Muttering ''Holy Christ,'' he
began to scramble through his bedding, searching for his
weapon. Finding it, he propped himself on one dirty long-
johned knee, raised a Colt's Navy into a firing position,

cocked the hammer with his thumb, and took deliberate aim
at Creed's head. He squeezed the trigger, and the barrel of
the six-gun belched loud and clear with a flash of gunpow-
der, spitting out a lethal .36-caliber ball.

Neither Creed nor Bell had noticed the man's movements
before the booming report of the revolver shocked them into
instant reaction. As the flying lead passed over their heads,
both men dropped to their knees, each turning in the direction of the shooter, Bell with his Henry coming ready for
action and Creed with his Colt's Army pulled from his belt,
cocked, and prepared to kill—if necessary.

Seeing who was doing the shooting, Bell swore, "Good
Lord, Champ! What in hell's gotten into you?"

"That's him!" shouted Champ as he pulled back on the
hammer again and tried to take aim for a second shot.

Suddenly, Creed recognized him. He was Champ Golihar, one of the dirty outlaws who had tried to rustle his
cattle and in the process had killed his younger brother,
Dent Slater. The fury of hate glazed Creed's eyes with
fearless abandon as he dropped the bedroll, stood, and
started walking at Golihar, his gun hand filled with death
and extended toward the youthful outlaw.

"You murdering son of a bitch!" swore Creed just before
he squeezed off a round.

The bullet tore harmlessly into Golihar's bedding, now
all balled up in front of him. Golihar felt a sting in the
quadriceps above the knee on which he knelt. He looked
down at it, fearing he would see his own blood spewing
forth. He saw none and was relieved enough to fire a second
shot, his aim being poorer this time because his hand shook
so badly.

As he kept moving ahead, closing the gap between them
to less than ten paces, Creed bent his arm so that the Colt's
was aimed straight overhead. His thumb pulled back the
hammer, and as the cylinder rotated, the expended cap on

the fired chamber fell away. With the gun cocked again, he extended his arm once more, took aim, and squeezed off another round. Like the first shot, the second failed to strike its intended victim. As he marched through the black powder smoke into plain view of his target, he prepared to shoot a third round.

''I didn't kill him, Slater!'' shouted Golihar, fear dripping from his words. He popped erect, fright bulging his eyes, and ran off toward the thicket.

Seeing Golihar run, Creed stopped, suddenly regaining his senses. He knew he would never catch Golihar if the outlaw made it to the brush. He turned and dashed back to Nimbus. Snatching the reins from Bell, he leaped into the saddle, then spurred the Appaloosa into a charge. The stallion burst into full speed with all the instinct of a thoroughbred racer. With his Colt's still at the ready, Creed rode toward the retreating Golihar and was upon him within seconds.

Golihar glanced back and up at Creed. The hate in Creed's eyes bore into his soul, and in his own mind, Golihar saw the muzzle of Creed's gun as the black mouth of Satan opening wide to spew eternal hellfire and brimstone at him. ''Oh, God, no!'' he screamed as he tried in vain to shoot over his shoulder at Creed, the ball never coming within five feet of its intended victim.

Unflinching, Creed lowered his Colt's and aimed at the fleeing coward's yellow spine. The distance between target and gun was only a few inches when Creed fired the fatal round.

Golihar dropped in a heap, still alive but only for the moment. The bullet had severed his spinal cord, then tumbled down into his chest cavity. Blood bubbled between his lips as he looked at the morning sky one last time through glassy eyes.

Creed reined in Nimbus, turned him around, and rode

back to the dying man. Still in the saddle, he aimed at
Golihar once more, taking no chances until he was certain
the outlaw would never shoot at another man again. Finally
satisfied that Golihar could do nothing to harm anyone,
Creed dismounted and knelt down beside him.

"You'll be dead soon, Champ," said Creed frankly and
honestly, "but I want you to know this before you die. I'm
sorry that I had to kill you. I would've preferred it to be
otherwise, but it's too late to change that now. What's done
is done. This would never have happened if you hadn't
joined up with Jim Kindred and killed my brother. I blame
him, not you. You're just a boy led astray. It's Kindred
who should be lying here instead of you. But he isn't, and
you are. It's all a shame, Champ." Then with true sincerity,
he added, "May the good Lord have mercy on your soul,
Champ Golihar."

2

"You killed him, Mr. Creed!" cried Bell excitedly.

"He was one of them that killed my brother," said Creed as he turned away from Golihar's body.

"But you shot him in the back! That ain't right to shoot a man in the back."

Creed ignored Bell's remark, not wishing to take the time to justify himself any further to this simpleton. He began walking away from the corpse, then halted again as the third man in the camp came running up in his stockinged feet and long johns and with a six-gun in his hand. Creed glared at him, then at his weapon.

"What's going on here, Bats?" the newcomer to the scene demanded. He looked at Creed, suspicion casting an ominous shadow over his blue eyes. "Who's this?" he asked.

"This is Mr. Creed," said Bell, "and he just killed Champ." Then turning to Creed, he added, "Mr. Creed, this here is Kit Haynes."

Haynes peered behind Creed and saw the dead man. He cocked his piece and started to raise it at Creed, but he was too slow. Creed had his Colt's pointed directly at Haynes's mouth within a heartbeat of the click of the hammer of Haynes's gun.

"Now I've got no argument with you, Mr. Haynes," said Creed, "but I can make one . . . if that's your pleasure."

Haynes stared at the gaping muzzle of the six-gun, eased back the hammer on his own weapon, and said, "Champ Golihar wasn't nothing to me, Mr. Creed. It makes me no-never-mind that he's dead, but it's sure as hell going to rile up his brothers when they get back."

Creed lowered the Colt's a bit and asked, "And who might his brothers be?"

"Crit and Charlie Golihar," said Bell. "They're sure to be mad as hell when they find out what you did here, Mr. Creed."

"Yes, sir, that's right," said Haynes. "Crit and Charlie will sure as hell want to kill you outright as soon as they get back here and find out what you did."

Creed's mind was suddenly filled with unexpected thoughts as he glared at Haynes and sized up the situation. He had killed the younger brother of two outlaws that he didn't know and with whom he had no quarrel. The Golihars would certainly be unwilling to accept his reason for killing Champ and would wish to avenge their brother. This was a fight Creed didn't need or want but was sure to get if he stayed at Somer's Thicket. The Golihars would call him out, bullets would fly, and someone would be killed for sure—maybe him, maybe one or both of the Golihars, maybe all three of them. And what of the other men with Crit and Charlie? They would surely side with their friends. Most likely, such a fight would result in Creed's death. Dying held no fear for him; he had proven that much on several battlefields during the recent war. It was dying without avenging his own brother's murder that concerned Creed the most. He would probably have to face the Golihars sooner or later, but he wished it to be later—after he had finished with Kindred and his gang of outlaws.

"They're coming back here?" queried Creed. "Where are they now?"

"They're off taking care of a little freighting business right now," said Bell, snickering over his own joke.

"That's right," said Haynes with a giggle. "Crit's sort of the leader around here, if you get my drift. We was beginning to run low on supplies, so he and the rest of the boys went off to do some trading with Teddy Johnson."

"With Teddy Johnson?" queried Creed. "Like Jim Kindred and that bunch of his did a few months back?"

"You got it," said Bell. "Champ there rode with Kindred on that one."

"I know," said Creed. "He rode with him when he tried to rustle the Double Star outfit's herd over in Louisiana. That's when they killed my brother."

"I remember hearing something about that," said Haynes. "Wasn't Dent Slater the one who was killed that day?"

"The same," said Creed.

Bell spoke up, saying, "Then you must be—"

Creed stopped him by saying, "The name is Creed. Slate Creed." He aimed the Colt's at Haynes's nose for emphasis. "You remember that when you tell Crit and Charlie Golihar who it was that killed their little brother. And remind them what the Bible says about an eye for an eye and a tooth for a tooth. Tell them this business is finished now as far as I'm concerned, but if they want to make more of it than it already is, then they can come looking for me down to Mexico. That's where I hear Jim Kindred and the rest of that mangy bunch of his lit out for, so that's where I'm going. Did you get all that, Bats?"

"Yes, sir, Mr. Creed."

"What about you, Mr. Haynes? Did I make myself clear to you as well?"

"Yes, sir, Mr. Creed."

"That's good. Now I'd take it kindly if both of you was to drop your guns right here." He paused while they dropped their weapons. "Now let's take a walk over to that big tree there." He pointed at a cottonwood with the Colt's. The trio marched to the tree and when they reached it, Creed asked, "Have you got any rope around this place, Bats?"

"Yes, sir, Mr. Creed," said Bell. "Over there by the picket line."

"You go and fetch it back here, Bats," said Creed, "while Mr. Haynes here pretends he's a bear with a real bad itch in the middle of his back and starts scratching himself on that tree trunk."

Bell retrieved the rope as ordered, and Haynes began rubbing his back on the cottonwood's bark like a bear would. Bell returned in less than a minute and handed the rope to Creed.

"Bats, you hold out your left hand," said Creed, "and Mr. Haynes, you hold out your right. Put them together knuckle to knuckle."

Bell and Haynes did as they were told, and still holding his gun on them, Creed used his free hand to wrap their wrists with the line.

"Now both of you stand with your backs to the tree," said Creed. As soon as they complied, he said, "Now reach out with your other hand until you touch each other." When they did this, he tied their hands together, Bell's right to Haynes's left, encircling the trunk with the two men. For good measure, he wrapped the remaining line around them and the tree.

"Now I don't like doing this to you boys," said Creed, "but I don't know either of you well enough to trust you not to shoot me in the back when I ride out of here. You can understand that, can't you?"

"Sure can, Mr. Creed," said Bell.

"You don't have to worry none about us," said Haynes.

Creed grabbed Haynes by the lower jaw, squeezed it in his hand, and forced Haynes's head back against the tree. Getting as close to Haynes as he could without touching noses with him, Creed said through gritted teeth, "You're missing my point, Mr. Haynes. I know the kind of vermin that lives in this place. Not one of you can be trusted any more than a rattlesnake can be trusted. You just be thankful that I'm leaving you alive to tell Crit Golihar what happened here this morning, instead of me pinning a note to him on your dead body." Creed relaxed his grip and said, "Now do you understand me, Mr. Haynes?"

"Yessir, Mr. Creed. Yessir."

And with that, Creed took his leave of them.

3

The Thicket Gang had been thrown together haphazardly as a direct result of the War Between the States, but the war wasn't responsible or the cause for all of them turning outlaw. Many of the desperadoes who inhabited Somer's Thicket had been living outside of the law before the Confederate Conscription Act of April 6, 1862. Prior to that date, these seedy characters had used a place on Crooked Creek in the northeast sector of Lavaca County as their point of rendezvous. When pressure from the military headquarters at nearby Columbus became too great for them, they were forced to find a more suitable location. The thicket along the Lavaca River in the southern part of the county suited them perfectly.

At one time, the gang consisted of over thirty of the hardest looking men in that part of Texas, most of them draft dodgers and deserters from the Confederate Army. A few were professed Unionists, but these men left the area for Mexico or the Far West as soon as travel was convenient and safe. Among those who remained in Somer's Thicket through the duration of the war were Bateman Bell, Shep Colbath, Bill Colbath, Bill Terry, Lou Bishop, Kit Haynes, and Crit, Charlie, and Champ Golihar.

Crit Golihar became the official leader of the gang because

he was the smartest, the boldest, and the bossiest. Also because his two younger brothers backed his play when someone got up the nerve to challenge his authority.

When the war ended and Jim Kindred—the county enrolling officer—and the Home Guards were no longer pursuing the men in the thicket, some of them made an attempt to rejoin society. Champ Golihar, the youngest of the three brothers, was one of these, and he only left because it was his mother's wish. Even so, he couldn't resist the temptation to join Kindred and the Detchen brothers in the raid on Teddy Johnson's freight wagons, and he was a participant in the fouled-up attempt at rustling the herd of cattle being driven to New Orleans by the Double Star Ranch vaqueros. Crit and Charlie advised Champ against riding with Kindred, telling him that Kindred was bad luck and that no good would come of anything that the deputy sheriff was part and parcel to. They were only right and found out how right they had been that early autumn day when they returned from raiding Teddy Johnson's freight wagons themselves.

The Thicket Gang rode into camp loaded down with the booty from their morning's work on the Victoria Road. They were heady with the spirit of success until they saw the long faces on Bell and Haynes.

"What's troubling you two?" asked Crit Golihar from atop his chestnut mount. Tall and lean but not skinny, Crit Golihar looked born to the saddle. Had his character only been as straight as his spine, he could have made a dashing, handsome cavalry officer with his sandy hair, blue eyes, and square chin. "You look like you're going to a funeral . . . or worse."

"Yeah, they do look like a couple of mourners, don't they?" said Charlie Golihar with a giggle. Charlie had the same sort of look to him as Crit did but on a little smaller and darker scale. Not quite as tall as Crit, hair a bit browner, and maybe an inch thicker in the middle of his body. The only big difference between the brothers was their eyes: Charlie's were always full of feeling whereas Crit's were serious, cold, all business, even when he was laughing.

Bell and Haynes glanced sideways at each other. Neither of them had been looking forward to this moment.

"Hey!" said dark-haired and bearded Shep Colbath, pointing at the lean-to where Champ Golihar's body lay covered with a blanket from head to ankles, only his bare feet protruding. "Who's that over there?"

All of the mounted outlaws shifted their view in the direction Colbath was indicating.

"You boys have a bit of excitement while we were gone?" asked Crit, thinking the corpse was that of some lawman who had come snooping around.

"You might say that," said Bell, his eyes downcast at a foot that was pawing at the dirt.

Charlie jumped down from his roan and hurried over to the lean-to, eager to see who the dead man was. He whipped back the blanket, expecting to see the face of a stranger, but that was not to be.

"Oh, God, Crit!" cried Charlie, his voice close to a shriek with anguish.

Crit focused on the body, saw that it was Champ, then jumped down from his horse and ran over to where Charlie was kneeling beside their dead brother. He wasn't believing what he was seeing, but the sight was enough to take the sap out of his legs as he dropped onto both knees next to Charlie.

Outlaws though they were, Crit and Charlie Golihar were not without emotions, although Charlie was more likely to show his than Crit ever would. Tears filled their eyes, then flowed copiously down their cheeks. They leaned shoulder to shoulder against each other as they wept openly. Crit touched Champ's cold forehead with a loving hand, then slowly brushed back the tousled golden locks.

"He weren't much more than a boy," said Crit between sobs.

"He was Mama's baby," said Charlie.

"Poor Mama!" said Crit. "How's she going to take this?"

"Aw, Champ!" cried Charlie. "Why'd you have to go and get yourself killed like this?"

That was a good question, thought Crit. He wiped his eyes with the back of a gloved hand. Anger began to rise within him. His head made a calculated turn, shifting his reddened eyes—whether bloodshot or filled with fire, who knew?—on Bell and Haynes. Then he rose. Slowly. An inch, not much more, at a time. And moved toward the two men as if eggs were beneath his boots and he was saving them for a bloody omelet. He came face to face with Haynes. Crit's aspect was frightful, monstrous, appearing hungry for blood, while Haynes feared for his life.

"What son of a bitch did this?" said Crit in a low, beastly, bloodthirsty growl that sent a shiver down Haynes's spine.

Haynes's throat was too dry to talk, but not so Bell's.

"He said his name was Slate Creed," blurted out Bell.

"Creed?" rasped Crit, not knowing the name.

"That's what he's calling himself now," said Haynes, finding his voice. "His real name is Clete Slater."

"Slater?" queried Crit, his head moving backward in tiny, spastic jerks. "The Slater the Yankees are supposed to hang today?"

"That's the one," said Haynes. "He got away from them and now he's on the run."

Crit's grief and anger instantly dissipated as thoughts of tangling with Creed entered his head and brought him back to the cold reality of the situation. "What in the hell was he doing here?" he asked.

''He came here looking for a place to hide out,'' said Bell.

Charlie dried his eyes, and for the first time, he noticed that there were no visible wounds on Champ's head, chest, or gut. He rolled him over for a look at his back and saw the bloody hole along the spine just below the neck.

''Hell, Crit!'' shouted Charlie. ''He was shot in the back!''

Crit turned to his brother and said, ''Shot in the back?''

''Look for yourself,'' said Charlie.

Crit didn't have to. He turned back to Haynes and Bell. His anger returned. ''Do you mean to tell me that son of a bitch came into this camp and just shot my baby brother in the back right under your noses?'' he growled. ''What in the hell were you two doing while he was murdering my baby brother?''

''Bell was the one,'' muttered Haynes, suddenly finding his voice. ''He was the one. He was supposed to be standing guard when it happened.''

''Is that so?'' queried Crit, eyeing Bell sideways.

Haynes continued, saying, ''He let Slater—''

Bell interrupted him, saying, ''He's calling himself Creed now.''

''Creed or Slater, I don't give a horse's ass what his name is!'' roared Crit. ''The son of a bitch murdered my brother, and I want to know why you two let it happen!'' He drew a Colt's Navy .36 from its holster on his left hip and put the muzzle to Haynes's nose in a threatening manner. ''Start talking, Kit, and make it good because I'm in no mood for trifling. You hear me?''

''Sure, Crit! I hear you. Like I was saying, Bell was standing guard and Creed jumped him and forced his way into camp. Then he saw Champ and shot him in the back.''

Crit turned on Bell and aimed the six-gun at his left cheek. ''You got a better story than that, Bats? You best have one because if you don't . . .'' Crit intentionally let his voice trail off as he cocked the hammer on his gun.

"It weren't exactly like that, Crit," said Bell confidently although with caution.

"Then how exactly was it?" asked Crit.

"Like Kit said, I was standing guard when Creed slipped up on me and got the drop on me. He said he didn't want no trouble, just a place to lay low for a while. So I brought him into camp. He and I was talking when poor Champ come awake, saw who it was, and started shooting."

"You say Champ shot first?" queried Charlie. "Then how come he was shot in the back?"

"I was coming to that," said Bell. "Champ got off the first shot, then Creed fired back. Both of them missed each other. Creed started walking toward Champ, and he fired again but missed again. Champ took another shot, then started running for the bushes. Creed jumped on his horse and rode him down and shot him in the back."

"Why didn't you do anything about it?" asked Crit.

"He had my guns," said Bell. "But Haynes could have done something about it. He still had his when he came running up to find out what was going on."

Crit turned on Haynes again. "Now ain't that interesting."

"He was fast, Crit," blurted Haynes. "I swear it. He got the drop on me the same as he did on Bats, and before I knew it we were both tied up to that tree over there."

"He got the drop on you, then tied both of you to that tree?" asked Crit. "Is that what you're telling me?" He was incredulous.

"That's the whole of it, Crit," said Bell. "We got loose just a little while after he rode off and thought it best to stay here until you got back from the raid."

"Well, I'm glad you did, boys," said Crit. "Now I don't have to go looking all over tarnation for the two of you so

I can hang you for letting that son of a bitch murder my baby brother." He turned to the others in the gang who were still mounted and said, "Come on, boys. Let's string them up to that tree."

"Now hold on, Crit," said Colbath. "I don't see that hanging Bats and Kit is going to do a whole lot to bring Champ back to life."

Crit turned his gun on Colbath. "Are you saying no one should pay for Champ's death, Shep?"

"Not no one," said Colbath. "I'm just saying it shouldn't be Bats and Kit. It should be Creed and only Creed. After all, he's the one what killed Champ, ain't he?"

Crit scanned the faces of the other gang members, realized they were in agreement with Colbath, and knew the wiser move now was to direct his revenge at Creed and only Creed. "All right, Shep. I guess you're right. Creed is the one who killed Champ, and he's the one who's going to pay for it." He uncocked his gun, put it away, and turned to Bell and Haynes again. "I'm sorry, boys, but you know how it is."

"Sure, Crit," said Bell. "We know how it is."

"You got any idea where Creed was headed from here?" asked Crit.

"Sure do," said Bell. "We told him you and Charlie would be coming after him, and he said you could go looking for him down to Mexico."

"Is that right?" said Crit with a cunning smile. "Well, I guess we'll just have to do that, won't we, boys?"

The outlaws looked around at each other, exchanging looks that said they weren't exactly keen on the idea. Again, Colbath spoke up for them.

"As much as I liked Champ," said Colbath, "he weren't my kin, so I ain't got no reason to chase all the way to Mexico after Creed."

"You ain't, huh?" said Crit angrily. Then he surveyed the faces of the other men. "And I suppose the rest of you feel like Shep does?"

"Well, yeah," said Bishop. "Champ were your brother, Crit. Not mine. I liked him, too, but I can't see that it needs all of us riding all the way to Mexico to gun down one man when either you or Charlie could do the job just as easy."

"All right," said Crit, "I see how it is. Well, Charlie, I'm going after the son of a bitch. You coming?"

Crit didn't really need to ask.

4

The man she loved had been gone from her life for only two days, but to Texada Ballard, the time seemed more like two centuries; she loved him that much.

After aiding Creed in his escape from the makeshift jail in the cellar of Glengarry mansion, Texada had headed home toward her grandmother's house in Hallettsville but was caught on the road by a Federal cavalry patrol that was out looking for Creed. The young lieutenant leading the unit knew Texada and her relationship with the escapee. He arrested her and took her back to Glengarry, where his commanding officer, Colonel Lucas Markham, could question her. Much to the lieutenant's chagrin, Markham—his left arm in a sling because his fiancée, Creed's sister, Malinda, had shot him through the triceps to prove to him that she wouldn't hesitate to kill him if he didn't let her brother go—released Texada immediately and chastised the junior officer for wasting time on the girl.

Safely home again, Texada put herself back into the busy routine of her life: working in the store that had once been her uncle's and taking care of her aging, ailing grandmother, Mrs. Margaret Hallet, the town's founder and first lady, who was in her eighth decade of living.

The war had been a boon to some people in the South,

but to most, especially those who supported the Confederacy and accepted its paper currency, it was a financial disaster. Collatinus Ballard, Sr., Texada's uncle, was in both categories.

The Ballard fortune, which was directly tied to that of Mrs. Hallet because Collatinus was her son-in-law, grew in the early years of the war because Collatinus expanded his real estate holdings and his various businesses. With the end of the Confederacy, his cash, which was mostly in paper, became worthless and the value of his property dropped dramatically. He was forced into putting up most of his holdings for sale. When few buyers came forward, bankruptcy was the only alternative. He lost the general store where his son and niece worked, but they didn't lose their jobs.

The Ballard cousins' new employers were a trio of Yankees named Posey, Green, and Shoemaker. Not wanting to do anything that might stifle trade, the owners wisely kept Coll Junior and Texada on the payroll and made no waves in local affairs, meaning they minded business instead of politics. Coll was put in charge of buying goods and stocking the shelves, while Texada waited on customers.

Of the three partners who owned the establishment, only Henry Shoemaker worked in it. Shoemaker had fought with the 38th Iowa Infantry during the war. Realizing the South was destitute and in dire need of hard cash, he took his mustering-out pay and found his way to Texas, looking for an opportunity to buy an established business for much less than its real value. Along the way, he found his two partners, and together they discovered Hallettsville, liked the look of the town, and bought Collatinus Ballard's store at the sheriff's auction. Yankees though they were, none of the men bore any hatred or disdain for the Confederacy or its people, slaveholders or not; and this attitude helped them gain a foothold in the local business community.

On the third morning after Creed's escape, Mrs. Lindenberg, the wife of Fritz Lindenberg who owned the only saloon in town, came into the store, looking to buy a bolt of cloth to make a dress for her soon-to-be daughter-in-law. Texada greeted her and was showing her some of the yard goods they had in stock when Gabe Zumwalt entered the establishment.

A powerfully built man in his younger days, Zumwalt had gone to fat in his middle years. He was a man of the land, a farmer but also a rancher because he kept cattle and hogs on his place south of town, on the west bank of the Lavaca River. As usual, he wore the wide brim, low crown black felt hat that was sort of his trademark; he was seldom seen in public without it squarely covering his bald head. He glanced around the store, saw Henry Shoemaker standing behind the service counter, and made straight for him.

"Good morning, sir," said Shoemaker, smiling officiously at Zumwalt as the latter approached him. The storekeeper had a medium build, bald pate, chestnut eyes, auburn hair, hawk nose, and a neatly trimmed mustache—all of which, except for his pale complexion, made him appear to be Mediterranean, which he wasn't. He wore black garter sleeves to protect his collarless white shirt from the incessant Texas dust that seemed to accumulate on everything no matter how many times a day one cleaned.

Zumwalt's gray muttonchops stood out from his jowls like thistles. With his ruddy complexion and the corners of his thin-lipped mouth turned down in what seemed to some to be a permanent frown, he had all the aspect of an Amish farmer marching into a prayer meeting all set to do battle with Satan himself.

"*Guten morgen!*" said Zumwalt in his native tongue, forgetting himself for a moment.

"Ah, *wie gehen sie, mein herr?*" said Shoemaker, being solicitous with the native of the Old World.

Surprised, Zumwalt responded in German. "*Sprechen sie Deutsch, Freund?*"

"*Sehr klein . . . das ist alles,*" said Shoemaker.

"*Ja*, of course," said Zumwalt, switching to English. "You are not German, are you?"

"Actually, I am," said Shoemaker. "My great-grand-father changed the spelling of our family name at the time of the Revolution." Then realizing that Texans had had their own revolution and that Confederates considered the recent war also to have been a revolution, Shoemaker quickly added, "The American Revolution of 1776, I mean."

Zumwalt studied the storekeeper for a second, then smiled and said, "*Ja*, of course. You will do then. I am in need of a new rifle. Those men at Somer's Thicket, they had a shooting there the other day."

Shoemaker's face turned serious at this news. "Was any-one killed?" The way he asked the question was morbid, almost ghoulish in nature.

"*Ja!*" said Zumwalt. "One of the Golihars. Champ, the youngest. A man named Creed shot him in the back."

Although she was supposed to be paying all of her at-tention to Mrs. Lindenberg, Texada was half-listening to the conversation between Zumwalt and Shoemaker. When she heard Creed's name mentioned, she recalled how he had said that he might take that name, and from the sound of things, he had.

"Would you excuse me for a minute, Mrs. Lindenberg?" she asked her customer.

Mrs. Lindenberg saw the worried look on Texada's face and the glow of her own apple-colored cheeks dulled as she said, "*Ja*, of course."

Texada went over to the men and with caution and po-liteness said, "Pardon me, Mr. Zumwalt, but did I hear you say a man named Creed shot Champ Golihar in the back?"

"*Ja!* That is exactly what I said. Two days ago."

"Where did you hear this story?" asked Texada.

Zumwalt peered at her as if he were trying to see inside her soul. "Why do you ask?"

"I know . . . er, knew Champ Golihar," said Texada.

The old man studied her for a half second, then said, "Crit and Charlie Golihar came by my place the day it happened. They were taking their brother's body home to their mama. Crit told me how it happened and how he and Charlie are going to Mexico to kill this Creed who killed their brother."

"I see," said Texada. "Well, thank you, Mr. Zumwalt." She dipped in a half-curtsy before returning to Mrs. Lindenberg.

"As I was saying, Mr. Shoemaker," said Zumwalt, "I need a new rifle to protect my farm and family. You will excuse me for saying this, but with all these Northerners coming around and all the darkies running free now, a man can no longer feel safe in his own bed. Who knows when someone will decide to take what I have worked so long to build? Those men at Somer's Thicket. I thought they would all go home once the war was over. No. Now they ride out at night in a gang, and I don't know what they are doing, but I know it is not good. Wasn't Teddy Johnson robbed again just the other day?"

"Yes, he was," said Shoemaker. "No one knows who did it this time, but one thing's for sure. It wasn't Jim Kindred and that bunch he led to Mexico."

Zumwalt became pensive for a moment, pinching his lower lip between his right thumb and index finger. Then as if a light suddenly went on in his head, his eyes brightened, and he absently waved the digit at Shoemaker. "Wait a minute," he said. "Wasn't Champ Golihar one of those arrested with Kindred for robbing Teddy Johnson back in June?"

Shoemaker stroked his chin in thought, then said, "I believe you're right, Mr. Zumwalt. Seems to me Champ was one of them, and I believe he was also one of those that Clete Slater said was with that bunch that killed his brother."

Zumwalt shrugged and said, "Then Champ deserved to die. I know the Slaters a long time now. Over twenty years. Honest and hardworking. All of them. If Champ was part of the gang that tried to steal the Slaters' cattle and then killed young Dent, then he deserved to die. He was an outlaw. So are his brothers, but they haven't killed anyone yet. At least, not that I have heard about."

"But you said they were going to Mexico to kill this Creed fellow who killed their brother," said Shoemaker.

"That is what Crit Golihar told me," said Zumwalt. "So maybe they will finally kill someone. Who knows?"

Texada had heard enough. As far as she was concerned, too much time had already been lost. Creed needed to be warned that the Golihars were coming after him, and he might need some help stopping them, too. As soon as she finished with Mrs. Lindenberg, she told Shoemaker that she had to go home and see about her grandmother, then left the store without waiting for him to give her permission to go.

Texada hurried home and changed out of her dress and into her riding clothes: men's trousers, shirt, and boots. After a quick word with her grandmother, repeating Zumwalt's story of the shooting at Somer's Thicket to her, she saddled up Pixie and rode out to the Double Star Ranch to tell Jake Flewellyn and the other vaqueros the same tale.

Double Star Ranch was still listed on the tax rolls as the Jess Tate farm, although Jess Tate was dead at the hands of Harlan and Farley Detchen for more than a month now. The ranch now legally belonged to Tate's brother Matt who had gone off to Colorado to prospect for gold back in '59. No one except his late parents had heard a word from him

since then, and all anyone around Hallettsville could remember about him was that Matt was living in Denver.
When Jess was murdered, the county clerk sent a letter to
Matt in Denver with the hope that it would find him. If Matt
couldn't be found in a reasonable time, then the county
judge had the right to order the sheriff to sell the property
for back taxes. Until then, Creed and Jess Tate's other
friends would mind the place—for Matt, for the sake of the
law, but for themselves more than anything.

When Creed was arrested by Colonel Markham for al-
legedly leading a raid on a Federal supply train, he put Jake
Flewellyn in charge of the vaqueros and Double Star Ranch.
Like the good man that he was, Flewellyn set to work
improving the place and getting matters ready for a cattle
drive the following spring. He had the men mending old
fences and putting up new ones, especially around the corrals at the ranch house. They were in the middle of building
a wind shelter when Texada rode up.

Since Texada had become Creed's intended, the Double
Star vaqueros had ceased to consider her to be a pigtailed
tomboy and now thought of her as the grand lady she was
struggling hard to become. Upon seeing her ride into the
yard, Flewellyn left the crew at the wind shelter and went
to greet her. Doffing his hat and smiling, he said, "Good
morning, Miss Texada. Kind of surprising to see you out
here at this time of the day."

Texada was a little out of breath when she said, "Have
you heard about the shooting yet, Jake?"

"What shooting was that, Miss Texada?" asked Jake,
his head cocked quizzically to one side.

"Champ Golihar. I think Clete shot him."

"Clete? When?"

Texada related Zumwalt's story to Flewellyn, then said,
"I'm pretty sure Clete and Creed are one and the same,
Jake. He told me he was thinking about calling himself Slate

Creed until he could clear his real name. I think that's exactly what he's done, and now Crit and Charlie Golihar are riding to Mexico to kill him.''

"But what if it wasn't Clete that killed Champ Golihar? You did say he was shot in the back, didn't you? That don't sound like the Clete Slater I know.''

"Who knows if he was really shot in the back, Jake? The Golihars could be making that up. Everyone knows what liars they are. They're almost as bad as the Detchens and that old biddy Sophia Campbell. I still say it's Clete, and I think you should take some of the boys and ride to Mexico to warn him or stop the Golihars.''

"Miss Texada, that's an awfully tall order,'' said Flewellyn. "Mexico's not exactly across the Lavaca. It's a week or more of hard riding just to get to the Rio Grande. Then after that, who knows where Clete might be? And the Golihars, too. How do we find them?''

"Well, I can tell you this much,'' said Texada. "If you can find Kindred and his gang, you'll find Clete close by.''

"I don't know, Miss Texada. I don't know that Clete would want us butting in like that.''

Texada was angry now. "Butting in? Wouldn't Clete do as much for you if you were in his place?''

Flewellyn was a caught fish and he knew it. No sense fighting her hook any longer. Better to jump in the boat and get prepared for filleting right now than later.

"Well, since you put it that way,'' said Flewellyn, "I suppose I can't rightly refuse, now can I?''

There was no humor in Texada's voice when she said, "No, I guess you can't.''

"All right then, we'll go, but first let me make sure this story about Champ Golihar is one hundred percent on the level.''

"Fair enough,'' said Texada. "But if it is, then you promise to ride to Mexico and help Clete?''

"I promise.''

5

Creed's brother and best friend were dead by the hands of Farley Detchen, Harlan Detchen, Jim Kindred, and twenty-five other men who had tried to rustle the herd he and his brother were driving to New Orleans that summer. Eleven of the outlaws had been killed in the attempted theft, and three more had been captured and hung on Creed's orders. Now he had shot down another, leaving the Detchens, Kindred, and ten members of Kindred's gang.

Harlan and Farley Detchen were hiding behind their foster mother's skirts on her plantation. This much Creed knew for certain. He also knew that Sophia Campbell protected her adopted offspring with the aid of Colonel Markham and the Federal army unit under his command. As long as Harlan and Farley had this much cover, they were out of Creed's reach. Creed knew this, too, but also told himself that sooner or later the Detchens would come into plain sight, and when they did he would be ready to make them pay for their parts in the murders of his brother and his best friend.

Kindred and the men who chose to stick with him had fled across the Rio Grande to avoid prosecution in the Lavaca County court for raiding freighter Teddy Johnson's wagons. That was one reason for them to run. The other

32

was to escape the brand of justice Creed had sworn to administer to all of them, whether as a group or one by one.

Exactly where Kindred and his bunch had gone in Mexico, Creed didn't know for certain, although it was his guess that they had lit out for Matamoros or Bagdad across the Rio Grande from Brownsville or had gone west to Laredo or Eagle Pass and crossed there. No matter; he would find them, even if he had to spend the rest of his life doing it.

With Somer's Thicket no longer a feasible temporary hideout, Creed was forced to ride night and day for a week, dodging Federal cavalry patrols all the way until he reached that wide ribbon of water that separated Texas and Mexico. Both he and Nimbus were near total exhaustion when Creed urged his horse into the cold Rio Grande for the swim to the other side. Once Creed was on Mexican soil he felt safe.

He was sadly mistaken.

Mexico was in turmoil. Creed knew it but didn't care. The civil war between the Imperialists, who supported Emperor Maximilian and were in turn supported by the French Foreign Legion of Louis Napoleon of France, and the Republicans, the followers of the legal president of Mexico, Benito Juárez, who were also called Liberals and Juáristas, was not his affair. He had only one thought in mind when he crossed the border from Texas, and that was to find Kindred and his gang. He would start looking for them in Matamoros. But not yet. Not tonight. *Mañana, por favor.* Tonight, he was too tired to go on. Nimbus was nearly done in, too. He would make camp and rest himself and his horse. Creed owed them both that much.

After unsaddling and picketing Nimbus, Creed rolled out his bedroll, but before he settled down for a good sleep, he read Texada's note one more time. Sort of seed for his dreams. He slipped out of consciousness with her lovely image before his mind's eye. He slept soundly.

The night was over and the next day was well begun

when he was disturbed from his slumber by a booted foot
nudging him in the ribs.

"Eh, gringo, what are you doing here?" asked a Mexican
in very good English.

Creed came awake slowly. His body ached dully all over,
and his stomach clawed at him, demanding to be fed. He
rolled onto his back and opened his eyes to see that he was
surrounded by sombreroed Mexicans, six of them. Like
pallbearers for a funeral. Maybe his. Or maybe the Mexican's, the one who kicked him again and repeated his previous question.

"What are you doing here, gringo? Are you lost? You
must be lost to come to Mexico riding such a fine horse as
that one over there. No gringo brings such an animal into
Mexico. He usually takes it from Mexico; then we have to
steal it back. Eh, *compadres*?"

A round of laughter followed.

"This is a nice thing you do for us, gringo," said the
Mexican. "We are most grateful that you save us the trouble
of crossing the river to steal it from you."

The man's English was too good for him to be a Mexico
Mexican; he had to be a Texas Mexican, which was bad
news for Creed. A Texas Mexican south of the border had
to be a *bandido*, meaning he had no love for Texans, the
usurpers of his native land.

Creed's eyes became accustomed to the morning light.
He saw their faces clearly now, and he didn't like what he
was seeing. These were not peones in white cotton shirts
and trousers. These men were armed with pistols, rifles,
and large knives, identifying them as *bandidos* at the worst
or Juáristas at the best. Either way, they were menacing,
and he was hoping they were only part of a bad dream.
Another kick, this one harder than the first two combined,
dispelled that thought.

"On your feet, gringo," said the Mexican, a touch of
anger in his voice.

Creed wanted to reach for his Colt's beneath his saddle, but he knew that would be a futile gesture that would only lead to his certain demise. Of course, he might be about to die anyway. Why not go down fighting? Better to wait and hope for a chance to escape or defend himself properly. Instead of going for the Colt's, he threw off the top blanket, then rolled over to position himself to rise. As soon as he was on all fours, the Mexican kicked him in the gut, this time as if he meant it, lifting him off the ground and blasting the wind from his chest. Creed collapsed in a heap, then instantly curled himself into a ball, as much for protection against another assault as out of instinct to recover his lost breath.

"You move too slow, gringo. Try again, *por favor*."

I will, you son of a bitch, thought Creed as he went through the same motions again, only a little faster. This time he was ready for the kick, took its full force, but didn't let it affect him as before. He came almost erect, head bowed, pretending to be afraid.

"Eh, *muchachos*, this gringo is a tough one, no?"

All of them began to laugh.

Creed had his opening. He took it. He grabbed the leader by the left hand with his left, spun him around, and pulled him hard against his own body. Then he simultaneously threw his left arm around the Mexican's throat and with his right drew the man's *pistola* and cocked it. In the next instant, he was backing away, dragging the surprised captive with him.

"Now, *muchachos*, just stand your ground," said Creed, waving the gun at the other five *banditos*. "Don't any of you go for your guns or I'll shoot this son of a bitch and then three or four of you. *Comprende, amigos?*" Then he put the muzzle of the revolver to his prisoner's head and growled in his ear, "Tell them to do as I say or I'll put a bullet in your brain right now."

"There's no need to get all excited here, friend," said a man behind Creed. "No one's going to harm you. So why don't you just take it easy and let Miguel go?"

Creed recognized the man's lingo as being Texas English. It sounded good to him, but at the same time, it worried him. Why would a Texan be mixed up with a bunch of Mexican bandits?

"Who the hell are you, mister?" said Creed over his shoulder, reluctant to take his eyes off the Mexicans or to release Miguel.

"Name is John Hunter. From Hopkins County, Texas. Who might you be?"

"Creed. Slate Creed from . . . Lavaca County, Texas."

"I know Lavaca County," said Hunter. "Spent some time up there just last year. Helped some boys out of a predicament they were in and brought them back down here. Most of them signed up with Juárez to fight the French, same as I did and same as Miguel and his boys there. They're part of General Cortina's outfit."

"You say these men are soldiers?" queried Creed.

"Of a kind," replied Hunter. "Look, you let Miguel go and give him back his gun, and I'll see to it that nothing happens to you. I give you my word as a Texan."

Although Creed didn't know Hunter, he knew a Texan when he heard one, and a real Texan never went back on his word; to do so was tantamount to selling one's soul to the Devil and no God-fearing Texan would ever do that.

"I'll accept your word on it, Mr. Hunter," said Creed, "but I would like to take a look in your eyes before I do."

"Fair enough," said Hunter. He walked around in front of Creed and Miguel, stopped between them and Miguel's *compadres*, put his hands on his hips, smiled with genuine friendliness, and said, "Is this close enough for you, Mr. Creed?"

John Hunter was no giant, although the Mexican officer's

uniform he wore did give him the look of a man of stature. He was a bit dark in his complexion with brown eyes and black hair. Put a serape and a big straw sombrero on him and he could almost pass for a Mexican, thought Creed. Little did Creed realize that Hunter had done just that the year before when he ventured back into Texas to retrieve a pair of mules for another man. He would have gotten away with the ruse, too, if a so-called old friend hadn't recognized him and turned him into the Home Guards at Columbus.

Creed studied Hunter's countenance for a moment before answering, "Yes, it is, Mr. Hunter." He lowered Miguel's *pistola* and eased up on the stranglehold. "What are you to these . . . Mexicans, Mr. Hunter?"

"To this bunch you're playing with, not a whole lot. But to those men behind you, I am their *capitan*." He paused to let Creed look over his shoulder at the men he spoke of, but when Creed didn't bother to do so, he continued, saying, "Like I said, Miguel and his *muchachos* ride for General Cortina. I ride for *el presidente*, Benito Juárez. We fight for the same cause, but let us say that our methods are a bit different. Either way, I outrank Miguel, and he knows it. He doesn't like it, but he goes along because if he doesn't, General Cortina will have him shot. Isn't that right, Miguel?"

"*Sí-sí, Capitan!*" said Miguel, his voice filled with the meek subservience of a peon.

"Now, Mr. Creed, why don't you let Miguel go and give him back his gun? If he does anything besides get on his horse and ride out of here, I'll shoot him myself. Isn't that so, Miguel?"

"*Sí-sí, Capitan!*"

"I believe you would, too," said Creed. "But what about me? Do you intend to shoot me if I don't do the same?"

Hunter laughed and said, "Hell, no, Mr. Creed! I'm hoping to sit down and jaw with you for a while. It isn't often that I get the chance to talk with someone fresh from home.''

Creed released his stranglehold on Miguel and handed him his gun, barrel first and hammer down. The Mexican took the weapon, looked at Hunter, who was glaring at him, then rejoined his friends near Creed's bedding.

''And leave the man his weapons and his horse, Miguel,'' said Hunter. ''That Appaloosa looks like too much animal for the likes of you.''

Miguel and the others stormed off to their own mounts behind Creed and rode away.

''You were lucky we came along when we did, Mr. Creed,'' said Hunter.

''Oh, I don't know,'' said Creed. ''I thought I had things pretty well in hand.''

''In front of you, yes, but Miguel had two more men behind you. Fortunately, they saw me riding up with my troops.''

Creed looked at the rise behind him and saw three score of mounted Mexican soldiers, all dressed in a military fashion, although not all of them wore complete uniforms.

''All right, Mr. Hunter— Or should I address you as Captain Hunter?''

''Either one is fine by me,'' said Hunter. ''Call me John if you like. It makes no difference to me.''

''All right, John. So what do *you* intend to do with me?''

Hunter's bushy black eyebrows shot upward as he replied, ''Like I said, I just want to talk to someone fresh from home.'' He studied Creed for a moment, then added, ''You look like a man who could stand a cup of coffee and a hot meal. Maybe a shave, too. Why don't you get your gear and go down to the river and clean up, while I have my orderly get us up a pot of coffee and some tortillas and frijoles?''

Creed rubbed a hand over the bristles on his face and

said, "Sounds like a real neighborly idea, John."

A quarter of an hour later Hunter and Creed were seated on two large rocks by the campfire Hunter's orderly had started. Coffee was brewing and beans were cooking over the dancing flames. The aromas from the foods toyed sadistically with Creed's senses as he and Hunter talked.

"You say you're from Lavaca County, Mr. Creed?"

"That's right," said Creed, eyeing the food the Mexican was preparing over the open fire.

"Then maybe you heard of me and what I did up there last year?" said Hunter.

"Can't say that I have," said Creed, not really listening to Hunter too closely.

"Oh, you must have . . . if you were around. You were in Lavaca County last year, weren't you?"

"Last year?"

"Yes, last year when I was up in Lavaca County. If you were there, you must have heard about what I did. You were there, weren't you?"

"No, I was away from home last year."

"Fighting in the war?"

"Maybe."

"Which side? North or South?" asked Hunter.

"Does it make any difference . . . now?" retorted Creed. "Or down here?"

Hunter studied him for a second, then said, "I suppose it doesn't to some, but there are some it does make a huge difference to."

"Including you?" queried Creed.

"Ask me that last spring and I would've said yes."

"And now?"

"Now? Not a whole hell of a lot, I guess. You see, Mr. Creed, when the war was going on back in the States, I was down here because I'm a Texan who didn't think it was right for a state to leave the Union. At the same time, I didn't want to go up north and be forced to join the Union Army and have to fight my friends and neighbors from back home. So to avoid being forced to fight for either side, I left the country. Now that may sound like a coward's way out, but I don't look at it that way. I had to leave my family behind and come to a foreign country where Americans aren't exactly the most highly thought of people around. In fact, if it wasn't for the French and all those foreign mercenaries who are fighting for Maximilian, Americans would be fair game down here.

"Now I wasn't the only one who came down here to avoid the fight back home. There are lots of us. Most of us have joined up with Juárez and are helping him get his country back from the French. You see, Mr. Creed, we're not cowards. We just don't want to kill our own people."

The gist of what Hunter was telling him was slipping through Creed's brain for the moment because he was too hungry to think of much other than the tortillas, frijoles, and coffee Hunter's Mexican orderly was just about to serve up to them. The lecture would come back to Creed later, and he would study it once his innards were pacified. For the moment, he would let Hunter continue to talk while he surrounded a fork full of fried beans with a tortilla and ate it voraciously.

"Now that the war is over in the States we'd like to go home, but like I said a minute ago, we signed on to help Juárez and his people get their country back from Maximilian and the French. It's unfortunate, but we aren't the only Americans down here taking part in this fight. There are a lot of others, all of them former Confederates who are fighting for Maximilian. I would suppose that you know about General Joe Shelby and his brigade that's in Mexico City right now?"

Creed nodded, washed down a bit of tortilla with a swallow of coffee, and said, "I've heard of him, and I've heard how he and his men marched across Texas into Mexico. Haven't heard much about them since they entered this country though.''

"Well, allow me to fill you in," said Hunter.

6

General Joseph Shelby's "Iron Brigade" was a cavalry unit of the Confederate Army's Trans-Mississippi Department during the War Between the States. Its theatre of operations was Missouri and Arkansas. When Lee, Johnston, and the other Confederate field commanders surrendered in the spring of 1865, Joe Shelby rallied his troops and marched them across Texas to the Rio Grande.

When the Brigade started its trek to Mexico in early June, Shelby had the intention of joining Juárez, but his men had different ideas. They voted to join Maximilian and the French. Shelby had told them early on that they could be the deciding factor in the Mexican civil war and that they would receive rewards of land and gold for aiding one side in victory over the other. The men talked this over among themselves and came to the conclusion that the former arch-duke from Austria would be more inclined to pay them generously than would the Indian from Guelatao. Thus, they voted to volunteer their services to the emperor.

The Brigade crossed the Rio Grande on the old Spanish road at Eagle Pass. On the Mexican side of the river stood the town of Piedras Negras. Shelby notified the local Republican official that it was his intention to advance into Mexico, find the French, and offer his sword in the service of Maximilian. The local Liberal leader, Governor Andres Viesca, had no desire to fight Shelby's well-armed force, but he was willing to negotiate. The Brigade possessed a lot of unnecessary baggage, meaning arms and ammunition that had been removed from Confederate storehouses during the march through Texas. Shelby knew that his command of over a thousand men couldn't march into Mexico carrying enough equipment to outfit an army of five times their number, so he sold armaments to Viesca in exchange for a promise that the Mexicans would not use any of the weapons on his men.

Before the former elite unit of General Sterling Price's command headed south from Piedras Negras for Monterrey, a skirmish was fought in the streets of the Mexican border town. A handful of Shelby's men were surrounded by a squad of Mexican soldiers outside a cantina. The Mexicans had been led there by three Texans who claimed the horses Shelby's men were riding had been stolen from the Rosser ranch. One Texan ordered a cavalryman to dismount and surrender the horse he sat on. The veteran soldier replied by cutting off the man's arm with his sabre. A gunfight ensued that came close to turning into a full-fledged battle and would have had not the cooler heads of Governor Viesca and Shelby prevailed.

The road to Monterrey was fraught with danger. Juárez ordered his generals to attack the *norteamericanos* at every turn, to stop them from joining the French; and this they tried to do at every bend in the road. Or so it seemed.

Shelby approached the Rio Sabinas with great caution because he knew the ford of a river was an excellent place for an ambush. Juárez's Guerrilleros, over a thousand strong, waited for the new enemy. Shelby called for the charge, and his men responded with all the ferocity of a pack of crazed dogs on the scent of a wounded fox. Neither side asked for quarter, and none was given as the men of

the Iron Brigade slashed and hacked their attackers into
bloody pieces. Word quickly spread throughout Mexico of
the massacre on the Sabinas, and thereafter, fear struck the
hearts of Indians and Mexicans alike at the mention of
Shelby's name.

A few days later another band of Juáristas attacked Shelby's force, this time in the dark. Led by Fray Juan Anselmo
and a Cuban expatriot named Antonio Flores, the Mexican
force slipped into the Brigade's camp, thinking they could
kill most of Shelby's men while they slept. They opened
fire, arousing their intended victims, and a hand-to-hand
engagement was begun in which the priest and his coleader
were killed along with seventy-one of their followers.

At the same time Shelby was leading his men across the
Rio Grande, Colonel Pierre Jeanningros was capturing Monterrey for Maximilian and the Empire. The local population
celebrated the event with a fiesta, but Colonel Jeanningros
had little time for merrymaking. He had heard how Shelby
had sold cannons, rifles, powder, and shot to Viesca, and
this infuriated him. He would show this American *canaille*
how the French dealt with their lessers.

Shelby heard about Jeanningros's outburst against him,
so he sent a man ahead to Monterrey to spy out the town
and the French forces. The scout rejoined his commander
only four miles outside the city and reported that the French
were in firm control of all the countryside to the west and
south of Monterrey. Also, the city was crawling with ex-
Confederates, including Generals Walker, Smith, Preston,
Wilcox, Magruder, Price, and Hindman and two former
governors of Louisiana, Moore and Allen. A certain Captain
Frank Moore from Alabama led an American unit in a newly
formed regiment known as the Contre-Guerrillas.

Immediately after hearing the report, Shelby sent two men
to Jeanningros with the message that he had come to join
Maximilian's forces, but if he wasn't welcome in the city,

then he would attack it. Jeanningros knew an ally when he saw one, so he invited the Americans to enter Monterrey as friends.

Jeanningros accepted Shelby under his command and sent him west to Sonora, telling the American general that he could either occupy Guaymas or Mazatlán. The Brigade headed off in the direction of the Pacific Coast and had gotten as far as Parras when it was turned aside by the order of Marshal Bazaine, the supreme French military commander. Shelby was to lead his men to Mexico City, where he would have the opportunity of offering his services to the emperor in person. The general didn't understand why this was necessary, but he agreed to do it.

The Americans fought more skirmishes along the road to Mexico's capital city. They rescued an American woman from a brigand *ranchero*, then relieved the besieged French garrison at Matehuala. In another incident, two men in the command were taken prisoner by the Mexicans, but they later escaped and rejoined the Brigade.

At last, Shelby and his Iron Brigade arrived in Mexico City for his interview with the emperor.

7

"And that's where Shelby is now," said Hunter. "The last I heard he was still cooling his heels outside the palace, waiting for Maximilian to see him."

Creed wiped his mouth with the sleeve of his shirt and said, "That's all very interesting, John, but I could care less about Shelby and his Iron Brigade. They are in Mexico City, and I am here on business of my own."

"And what business is that?" asked Hunter.

"Personal," said Creed, looking Hunter straight in the eye without an eyelash quivering.

"Personal?" queried Hunter.

"That's right."

"I take that to mean that you're most likely running from the law, or . . ." Hunter intentionally let his voice trail off as he reconsidered his second deduction before voicing it. In another second, he had reassured himself and said, "Or you're chasing after someone else who is running from the law. Mind telling me which it is?"

"Yes, I do mind," said Creed, a bit belligerent about Hunter's ability to deduce his two reasons for being in Mexico.

"That tells me your answer would have been both," said Hunter. Then he laughed. "Mr. Creed, this is Mexico, not

Texas. Whatever you did up there is your business.'' Then turning more serious, he added, ''But what you do down here is mine as long as I'm a captain in the Army of the Republic. Now I don't want to exercise my authority over you, but I will if I have to. Rather, I'd be more inclined to help you—if I can—if I knew what it was you were about.''

The man spoke the truth. He could do just about anything he wanted to do with Creed, and he could do it legally because of the present state of affairs in Mexico. Creed knew this, but he was prepared to deal with it.

''Captain John Hunter, you say you sympathized with the Union during the recent conflict but that you had no desire to fight your friends and neighbors, so you came down here to avoid the trouble at home.''

''That is correct, sir,'' said Hunter.

''Then would you fight your friends and neighbors from back home in this country?''

Hunter was had, and he knew it. His insinuated threat rang quite hollow at the moment. Realizing this, he could do nothing except laugh and say, ''No, I suppose I couldn't do that down here either, Mr. Creed. Unless, of course, they were to take up arms against me and the cause that I'm fighting for.''

''Then you have no need to concern yourself with me, John, because I have no intention of getting myself involved in the war down here. I had enough war to fill my life three times over. I no longer have a taste for it.''

''I believe you, Mr. Creed,'' said Hunter thoughtfully. He studied Creed for a moment, then said, ''Yes, I believe you.''

The two men accepted the silence that suddenly separated them, each drinking from his own cup as if it would help him to think of what to say or do next. Creed took a second gulp of coffee, while Hunter held his away from him so he could speak.

"Where were you planning to go from here?" asked Hunter.

"Matamoras," said Creed, thinking it wouldn't hurt to tell Hunter this much.

"Why Matamoras?"

"Why not Matamoras?"

"Because the French have the town."

This was something Creed hadn't expected to hear. Caught off guard, he realized that he could have no more conversation with Hunter unless he played a few cards. Hunter was no fool, so it was senseless to continue trying to outwit him. Better to seek his help and hope for the best.

"I think the men I'm looking for went there," said Creed.

"Were they Unionists or Confederates during the war?"

"Cowards," said Creed bluntly.

"Then they probably went to Matamoras. How many men are you looking for?"

"Eleven."

"Eleven, you say?"

"That's right."

Hunter stroked his chin as he considered the number, then he said, "Our spies in Matamoras reported a group of eleven *norteamericanos* rode into town just last week and joined the Contre-Guerrillas."

Creed didn't understand the term and said so. "Joined the what?"

"The Contre-Guerrillas," said Hunter matter-of-factly. "Juárez calls his army Los Guerrilleros. The French call us Les Guerrillas. To fight us, the French have formed a regiment called the Contre-Guerrillas, which means 'counter-guerrillas.' They are led by a sadistic butcher named Dupin. If you go into Matamoras, you will no doubt meet him. The French took the town a few weeks ago."

"I sort of thought that's what you meant when you said a group of men joined the . . . uh . . . ."

"Contre-Guerrillas," said Hunter helpfully.

Creed smiled and said, "You know, John, I'm beginning to feel like I'm in a foreign country."

"You are, Mr. Creed. You are indeed. In fact, you might say that you are in two foreign countries. The one belonging to the Juáristas and the one belonging to the French. And the more you realize that fact, the better off you will be. As one Texan to another, Mr. Creed, let me give you this little piece of advice. Don't trust anyone you don't know, and even if you should meet someone you knew back home, be just a bit cautious with them, too. Remember that Texas has more than its share of snakes."

"I'll keep that in mind," said Creed.

Hunter stood up and said, "You do that, friend, and just maybe you'll get home in one piece."

Creed pushed himself erect and offered his hand in friendship, saying, "Thank you, John. For the breakfast, for your help with those . . . other men, and for the information and advice."

Accepting the grip, Hunter smiled and said, "There was a time when I would have said something like 'We gringos have to stick together.' But I don't think like that anymore, Mr. Creed. Now I'll just say, *vaya con Dios, mi amigo.*" He turned to his men and said, "*Vamanos, muchachos!*"

Creed watched Hunter and the Mexican soldiers mount their horses and ride away. As they disappeared in a cloud of dust, he couldn't help thinking that they might be wise to go to the nearest church and pray. If everything Hunter told him was true, then the Juáristas were in for some hard times, especially if Maximilian accepted Shelby's help. Shelby had a reputation in the South of being one of the finest cavalry generals in the Confederacy. The fact that he never surrendered to the Yankees would draw volunteers to him in Mexico from all the former Confederate states, and an army like that, with Shelby in command, could easily sweep across Mexico and eliminate all resistance to the Empire once and for all.

"*Vaya con Dios* to you, too, John Hunter," said Creed softly. And he thought, I hope we meet again.

8

Matamoras was in Mexico for sure, across the Rio Grande from Brownsville. But considering the amount of use the Confederacy got out of the town and its port of Bagdad during the War Between the States, a casual visitor could have thought it was all just another part of Texas.

When the Union Navy blockaded southern waters and effectively bottled up most of the South's commerce, Matamoras and Bagdad became the Confederacy's lifeline to the outside world. Wily Southerners shipped their cotton to Texas, then would swim it across the Rio Grande to Matamoras, where foreign merchants would buy it with real gold and silver coins. The Confederate government would trade the cotton it took in lieu of cash for taxes for the much needed arms and supplies that were hauled back across the Rio Grande to the Confederate armies.

But not everyone thought of the town as a commercial center. Other Americans used Matamoras as a refuge from the laws of the Confederacy, especially the conscription law.

When the French army invaded Mexico in order to collect the debts owed to their government and bankers by the Mexican government, Field Marshal Bazaine concentrated on taking Vera Cruz first, then Puebla, then Mexico City. After consolidating his hold on the heart of the country,

51

Bazaine began spreading his forces and expanding the area of French control. Bazaine sent his assurances to his emperor in France, Napoleon III, that the country was pacified sufficiently to be ruled by Maximilian, and in 1864, the Mexican Empire was born.

The American Civil War was drawing to a conclusion by then, while the conflict in Mexico was just beginning to heat up. When Lee and Grant were meeting at Appomattox, Juárez was retreating northward in front of Bazaine's armies. As peace was restored in the United States, the violence in Mexico increased daily.

Matamoras remained in the hands of the Republicans until late in the summer of 1865. As Shelby and the Iron Brigade were marching toward Mexico City, the Contre-Guerrillas were capturing one Juárista outpost after another and Colonel Jeanningros was driving Juárez from his own country, forcing the Mexican president to cross the Rio Grande and seek refuge in the United States.

Hunter had told Creed that the French had possession of the town, but he told him little else. Not much about the Contre-Guerrillas or the man who led them, Colonel François Achille Dupin. If Hunter had given him some details about Dupin, Creed might have thought twice about going to Matamoras and returned to American soil. But if—such a long, long word.

As Juárez was setting up his capital of exile in American El Paso, Creed was riding along the Rio Grande toward Matamoras. The sun was high and hot, but he paid it little mind as Nimbus carried him toward the town. The dusty two-track he traveled passed through flat cultivated fields of corn, beans, and cotton that were fenced in to keep out the cattle that wandered about the valley grazing on the lush, verdant wild grasses that grew there. This land appeared to be no different than that just across the river, but it was. Politics and people made it so.

Thoughts of the political situation were running through Creed's mind when he saw a body of armed horsemen approaching from straight ahead. All were dressed similarly, so he assumed they were wearing some sort of military uniform, although it was hardly like any he had ever seen before. Each of them wore baggy white trousers, black riding boots, a blue Zouave jacket, and either a flat-crown sombrero or a fez. Creed could see that they were heavily armed with cavalry sabres, rifles, and knives. He could only count seven men, but there had to be more because of the size of the dust cloud they raised behind them. As they came closer, he realized they numbered at least a squadron led by three officers. Creed reined in Nimbus and waited for the soldiers to pass him. But they didn't, halting several yards away from Creed. The commanding officer came forward alone and greeted Creed.

"Good day, sir," said the officer, saluting Creed in the French fashion. "I am Captain Frank Moore of His Imperial Majesty's Contre-Guerrillas."

Creed recognized the accent as being from somewhere south of the Mason-Dixon Line but not as far west as New Orleans. Georgia, South Carolina, or maybe Alabama. No matter. It sounded good, familiar, the same as Hunter's had.

"Good day, Captain Moore," said Creed. "I am Slate Creed, late of Lavaca County, Texas."

"Mr. Creed, would you mind stating what your business is here in Mexico?" The man was all business.

Creed didn't like Moore's tone. Too officious. Too stuffy and full of self-importance. He had met the like during the war. Southern gentlemen, they called themselves, the best of the breed, the aristocrats of the South. Certainly, they were chivalrous men, well mannered for the most part, and brave. But so many of them were also pompous and downright stupid when it came to fighting. They thought more of their uniform and their so-called crusade for freedom than they did of the lives of the men under their command. It took but a few bastards like that to lose a battle, and the South had been damned with more than its fair share of bastards.

"Nothing dangerous, I assure you, Captain Moore," said Creed with a smile that he hoped would convey his friendliness toward a fellow American.

"That doesn't answer my question, Mr. Creed. Therefore, I will have to take you into my custody and have you taken to Matamoras for further questioning by Colonel Dupin."

Creed had heard that name before, from Hunter who had pronounced it as if it were spelled "Doopin" with equal accent on both syllables. Moore pronounced it "Doopan," accenting the second syllable.

"Do you mean that I'm under arrest, Captain Moore?" asked Creed sarcastically.

"That is exactly what I mean, sir."

"Let me get this straight. You're arresting me because I won't tell you what my business is here in Mexico. Is that it?"

"Not exactly, Mr. Creed. I'm arresting you because you could be an enemy of the Mexican Empire."

"You think I'm a Juárista?"

"You could be," said Moore. "I know for a fact that several of you Texans have taken up arms against the Empire."

"Well, I'm not one of them, Captain. I could care less about your little war down here. I've got my own business to tend to."

"Even so, Mr. Creed, I must insist that you accompany me into Matamoras, where Colonel Dupin will determine whether you are telling the truth or not. Please hand over your weapons, Mr. Creed."

Creed shook his head and said, "I think not, Captain."

He looked past Moore at his squadron of men and added, "You have me grossly outnumbered, sir. I would be a fool to pull a gun on you."

Moore nodded in agreement, deciding not to argue the point any further. "At your convenience, sir," he said, then with a dashing wave of his hand he bid Creed to ride alongside him to the town.

The War Between the States had turned the sleepy little Mexican border town into a thriving city of strategic military importance. Before the war, Matamoras had consisted mostly of adobe houses with a few prominent structures of stone and brick. The need for warehouses and wharves brought in carpenters who in a short time threw up wooden buildings all along the waterfront. To keep stray cattle out of the town and the citrus groves that bordered the community, a strong fence had been constructed on the landward side of Matamoras. The barrier had only two gates: one for the road that went west to Monterrey and one for the road that went south to Tampico.

At the edge of the town, Creed noticed a rather large white house that had several other buildings behind it, including a horse barn. The grounds around the house were well groomed with evergreen hedges, palm trees, and flowering bushes of all kinds with blooms the colors of the rainbow. In the midst of all this beauty was a flower of a different variety. A swarthy señorita with almond eyes and raven hair watched him ride past the low-walled yard and into the presidio, the pseudo fortress that was the seat of the military government and the post for the occupying troops. Creed noted that she didn't turn away when their eyes met, and much to his surprise, he continued to look at her until he could no longer see her; she was that beautiful.

The center of Matamoras was dominated by the municipal building where the offices of the alcalde and the port revenue agent were located. Moore guided Creed toward the stone

steps that led up to the front doors of the local city hall. A
soldier took the reins of their horses while they dismounted,
and Creed followed Moore up the stairs. At the doors, two
soldiers in Maximilian's Mexican army snapped to attention, presenting their Enfield rifles in salute to Moore. He
ignored the courtesy and entered the building with Creed a
step behind.

Immediately inside was a spacious room that was divided
into working areas by slatted railings and a long aisle. Each
work square had a desk and two wooden chairs: one for the
French official and one for the Mexican he was attempting
to teach the ways of bureaucracy. The aisle that split the
room became a hall that had three doors: one on each side
and one on the end. Moore took Creed to the latter. Two
chasseurs, each brightly uniformed and heavily armed,
stood guard at the entrance. They saluted Moore, but he
ignored these as well. He knocked on the door, then waited
to be invited inside.

"*Entre!*"

One chasseur opened the door, then stood aside for Creed
and Moore to enter. The cavalryman closed the door behind
them. Moore stepped up to the desk, came to attention, and
offered a salute.

Inside the office were two more chasseurs, standing at
rigid attention at the rear of the room. Seated behind a desk
that dominated the space was a most unusual man. His hair
and beard, snowy white, contrasted strangely with a stern
set face that had been bronzed by the wind and sun of fifty
military campaigns from China to North Africa to Mexico.
He was beyond his middle years in age, but still he sat rapier
straight. He glanced up at Moore with cold, black shark's
eyes and returned the courtesy being extended to him. Then
he saw Creed, and his aspect changed from ice to fire.

"What have we here?" he asked Moore in impeccable
English.

"Colonel Dupin, this is Mr. Slate Creed," said Moore, "late of Lavaca County, Texas."

"Ah, a Texan," said Dupin without smiling. He stood up and towered over both Americans. "How do you do, Mr. Creed? I am Colonel François Achille Dupin, commander of His Imperial Majesty's Contre-Guerrillas." Creed noted that Dupin pronounced his name similarly to the way Moore did, the only difference being he barely enunciated the final letter.

Taken aback by Dupin's height, Creed hesitated to step forward and offer a handshake. Instead, he nodded and said, "I'm pleased to make your acquaintance, Colonel."

Turning to Moore, Dupin said, "And why have you brought Mr. Creed to me, Captain?"

"We caught him on the Monterrey road, Colonel."

"Caught him?" Turning to Creed, Dupin said, "Are you an enemy of the Empire, Mr. Creed?"

Creed glared at Moore for a second before answering Dupin. "I've already told Captain Moore that I could care less about your petty little war down here, Colonel."

"This is not a 'petty little war' we are fighting, Mr. Creed," said Dupin with a touch of storm in his voice. "We are fighting to bring stability to Mexico and to put the Empire on a firm foundation. We do not consider our battles to be petty."

"Bad choice of words, Colonel," said Creed. "The same as Captain Moore used when he said he 'caught' me on the Monterrey road. I was coming here anyway."

"I see," said Dupin. "And what brings you to Matamoras?"

"Personal business."

"Such as?"

Creed didn't want to answer him and said so. "Like I said, Colonel, it's personal business."

"Ah, I see," said Dupin. He sat down again and picked

up an official looking piece of paper, glanced at it, then set his eye on Creed again. "Do you know what this is, Mr. Creed?"

Creed shook his head and said, "Can't say that I do."

"This is the death warrant for all Juáristas," said Dupin. "In short, Mr. Creed, the emperor has decreed that all persons bearing arms against the Empire are now to be considered traitors to the Empire and may be shot on the order of an officer in the Imperial Army." He glanced down at the Colt's holstered on Creed's left side. "I see that you still have your weapon, Mr. Creed. I could easily consider you an enemy of the Empire and have you shot immediately."

"But you won't," said Creed confidently.

"And why not?"

"Because you won't kill me until you find out what I'm doing here in Mexico."

"Very clever, Mr. Creed," said Dupin with a mocking laugh, "and quite right, I might add. Yes, I would not wish to kill you until I've discovered your real reason for coming here."

Creed looked sideways at Moore, then said, "Like I told you before, Colonel, it's personal."

"Yes, that is exactly what you said." Then looking at Moore, he said, "Captain, would you excuse us please?"

"Certainly, Colonel," said Moore. He saluted, spun on a heel, and left the room.

"Now that we are alone, Mr. Creed, we can be a bit more open and honest with each other. Will you tell me about this personal business of yours now?"

Creed looked beyond Dupin at the chasseurs and said, "What about them?"

"They are my bodyguards. They never leave me. But if you are concerned about them repeating something you might wish to tell me, rest assured that you have nothing to worry about. They do not speak or understand English, especially your American variety of the language.''

After taking a moment to consider Dupin's words, Creed believed him and said, ''Colonel Dupin, I've come down here to Mexico to look for some fellow Texans.''

''Fellow Texans, you say?''

''Yes, sir.''

''I see. These men were your comrades-in-arms during the late conflict in your own country?''

''No, they weren't,'' said Creed.

''Then they were your enemies.''

''I didn't say that either.''

''I do not understand, Mr. Creed,'' said Dupin. ''I assumed from the cut of you that you had been a soldier or even an officer in the Confederate Army, but you say these men you seek were neither comrades-in-arms nor enemies. How can this be? Did you fight for the Union?''

''I didn't say that either.''

''Then what are you telling me?''

''I'm telling you that I came down here looking for some fellow Texans because we have some unfinished business that I'd like to get settled.''

''Personal business?''

''That's right, Colonel.''

''All right,'' said Dupin. ''Would you mind telling me who these men are?''

Creed was reluctant to give their names to Dupin. What if Dupin knew them? But how could he? But what if he did and had guessed his reason for wanting to find them? Would Dupin interfere or help him? There was only one way to find out.

''They're traveling in a group of eleven men,'' said Creed, ''and their leader is a man named Jim Kindred.''

''Kindred? I know this man.''

''You do?''

"Yes, of course," said Dupin. "He arrived here just last week, and I immediately enlisted him and his men in my regiment of Contre-Guerrillas. They seemed quite suited for the kind of work we do."

"I wouldn't know about that, Colonel," said Creed dryly.

"No, of course not, but I would be more than happy to tell you about my regiment."

"Some other time perhaps," said Creed.

"Yes, of course, you want to see your friends," said Dupin. "Unfortunately, they are not in Matamoras at this time. I assigned them to the squadron that patrols the Tampico Road. They left just this morning and will not be returning here for at least a week."

"A week?"

"Yes, that is correct," said Dupin. He studied Creed for a moment, then said, "Until they return, I would like you to remain in Matamoras as my guest."

"Your guest?"

"Yes, at the hacienda of Don Bernardo Abeytia, a most loyal servant of the Empire who has kindly permitted me to call his home my own while I am here in Matamoras."

"Well, that's very kind of you, Colonel," said Creed, "but I think I'll just stay at a hotel."

"You cannot do that, Mr. Creed. There are no rooms. Our French officials have them all. Therefore, I insist that you stay at Rancho Abeytia."

"You insist?"

"Quite so," said Dupin. "Let me put it this way, Mr. Creed. The only other sleeping space available in all of Matamoras is the jail."

Creed could take a hint. He offered a tired smile and said, "You're a hard man to say no to, Colonel."

9

Creed didn't know when he was riding into Matamoras that the big white house with all the outbuildings and corrals was Rancho Abeytia. He also didn't know that the beautiful girl he had seen in the yard was the daughter of the hacienda's owner.

Don Bernardo Abeytia could trace his paternal ancestors back to the time of El Cid, although the title of hidalgo was not bestowed on any of them until the days of Ferdinand and Isabella. His first forebear to settle in Mexico, Don Agusto, came to the Rio Grande at the same time the missions were being established in California. Don Agusto didn't like the climate of the river valley, so he built a house in Monterrey and only occasionally visited his hacienda along the Rio Bravo del Norte, as the Rio Grande was called by the people living south of it. At the time of the first Mexican Empire, Don Bernardo's father, Don Benito, who sided with the revolutionists against Don Bernardo's grandfather, took possession of the hacienda. When Don Benito died, he left it to his son.

Unlike his grandfather, who forbid Don Benito from marrying any woman who was not of pure Spanish blood, Don Bernardo's father encouraged him to marry a woman who had at least one Indian ancestor. His reasoning was quite

61

simple: Mexico was no longer a part of Spain, so having pure Spanish blood no longer meant what it once had. With such freedom to choose, Don Bernardo married the woman who put the most joy in his heart.

The year Mexico went to war with the United States, Don Bernardo's wife died giving birth to their only child, Silveria Maria Dolores Abeytia y Galvez. From that time, Don Bernardo devoted his energies to two goals: the happiness of Silveria and the accumulation of great wealth. To him, both went hand in hand.

During Mexico's first civil war, Don Bernardo wisely remained neutral, waging war against neither side, but when Benito Juárez and his Liberal forces triumphed over the Conservatives that were backed by the church, he quietly announced that he had been supporting Juárez all along. When the United States was divided by war, Don Bernardo saw the opportunity to increase his already considerable fortune tenfold and would have if his own country hadn't itself fallen into its second civil war. Once again, Don Bernardo declared his neutrality until the French captured Matamoras and the Rio Bravo valley. When Colonel Dupin and his regiment of Contre-Guerrillas marched into the town, Don Bernardo was among the first to greet him and throw open the doors of his hacienda to Dupin, and the colonel accepted the invitation with all the graciousness of a tiger being asked to dine with a flock of sheep.

The house at Rancho Abeytia, which Don Bernardo called Tres Palmes for the three imported Egyptian date palms that grew in the front yard, proved to be more luxurious than Dupin thought any domicile in Mexico could ever be. The carriage drive from the Monterrey road encircled the three palms and led up to a roofed patio that dominated half of the front of the house and that was separated from the yard by a hedge of thorny bushes. One entered the house here, stepping into a foyer that had two sets of sliding double doors and a hall leading from it. Through the portals to the right was the sitting room, and through the other pair of doors straight ahead was the dining room. The hallway led to the eight bedrooms. Beyond the dining room was the kitchen, and from the parlor, one could step into the library. Off the library and adjoining the dining room was the rear patio that was also covered but with hanging vines that extended over one of the two beautiful flower gardens. The other garden was located outside the four north bedrooms, while the four south sleeping rooms were protected from the sun by a row of magnolias overgrown with Spanish moss.

Creed and Dupin, followed by Dupin's four chosen chasseurs, rode onto the estate near sundown. It was almost supper time. A Mexican servant met them out front and took their horses. Without being told what to do, the quartet of cavalrymen went to their stations: two just inside the foyer and two in the dining room. Creed and Dupin stepped into the sitting room, where Don Bernardo and his daughter were chatting with two women. The master of the hacienda stood when the new arrivals entered.

"Good evening, everyone," said Dupin in Spanish. "We have a new guest. Allow me to present Mr. Slate Creed of Lavaca County, Texas."

Creed knew enough Spanish to understand what Dupin was saying, but he was hesitant to use the language to return the greetings he was now receiving in kind.

Seeing Creed's discomfiture, Dupin took charge and said, "Mr. Creed does not speak Spanish."

"Then we will converse in English, señor," said Don Bernardo in a heavy accent as he stepped forward to shake Creed's hand. "I have many friends who live on the other side of the Rio Bravo, in Brownsville, and it is from them that I learn your language."

"Mr. Creed," said Dupin, "this is Don Bernardo Abeytia, our host."

Creed accepted Don Bernardo's handshake and said, "I'm pleased to meet you, Don Bernardo."

Then in turn, Dupin introduced the three women.

The first woman Creed had seen earlier that day when he rode by the hacienda with Captain Moore. She was Don Bernardo's daughter, Silveria, a young lady of Spanish breeding and culture, although she was a mestizo, a mixed-blood of Spanish and Indian ancestry. Creed had to stop himself from staring, she was that appealing.

The second was Dupin's wife. Patrice Dupin was a good decade and a half younger than her husband, although appearing to be well past childbearing age. Her gray-streaked, dark brown hair was combed back and tied in two large loops that were bound together with light blue ribbons. The full-skirted, tight-collared dress she wore stated plainly that she was a quiet, conservative person, maybe even a bit on the stern and austere side. Yet her cerulean eyes and the delicately chiseled features of her face revealed her true gentle nature.

The third lady might have been dressed like one, but her purple eyes spoke volumes to the contrary. She was Claire Mounet, the strikingly beautiful younger sister of Patrice Dupin. The resemblance between them was remarkable. Claire was very much a younger version of Patrice in nearly every physical aspect from the color of her hair down to her finely boned hands. Age, of course, was a contributing difference between them; but the major factor was how Claire employed a touch of cosmetics in the French fashion to enhance her appearance, to present herself as a woman overflowing with a lust for life and all the living she could wrench from it. Creed saw her not as painted or jaded but as refined, complete in every detail that a master portrait artist could stroke on a breathing canvas. Even so, she was more. Exactly what, Creed wasn't allowed to discover just yet because there were introductions to finish and polite conversation in which he must partake.

"Ladies, it is my honor to make your acquaintance," said Creed, giving them a half bow that was stiff and forced but which showed them that he was not a man without manners or culture.

"Welcome to our home, Señor Creed," said Silveria. "I hope you find it to your liking."

"I'm sure I will, Miss Silveria," said Creed, his gaze concentrated on the swarthy beauty.

"And if you do not," said Silveria, "will you shoot us for its inadequacies?"

Creed was befuddled by the question until he saw that she was referring to the Colt's holstered to his gunbelt. He tapped its butt and said, "I have just spent a week in the wilds, Miss Silveria, and I have worn this gun every waking moment of that time. I have become so accustomed to having it at my side that I hardly know it's there until I need it." He turned to his host and added, "Please forgive me, Don Bernardo. I meant no discourtesy to you and your hospitality."

Don Bernardo was pleased by Creed's reply. He clapped his hands together, and another Mexican servant appeared in the room.

"Pepe, see that Señor Creed's belongings are brought into the house immediately and put in one of the guest rooms." Don Bernardo turned to Creed and said, "If you would like to refresh yourself before we dine, Señor Creed, Pepe will show you to your room now."

"Thank you, Don Bernardo. I would like to wash up a bit, and it will give me a chance to remove this hardware." He turned to the women and said, "It isn't easy to leave such lovely company, especially since we have just met. But I must. By your leave, ladies." Again, he gave a half bow, then he followed Pepe from the room.

As soon as he departed, Creed became the object of

interest among the conversers in the parlor.

"This man," said Don Bernardo in his native tongue, "he is a new officer in your regiment, Colonel?"

"No, but I think I would like to have him in my service," said Dupin. "Captain Moore met him riding toward Matamoras on the Monterrey road this afternoon and brought him to my office. He says he has come to Matamoras seeking some fellow Texans with whom he has some business to finish."

"I see," said Don Bernardo. "Do you think he is telling the truth? Or is he another one of these *norteamericano* adventurers that have come swarming into our country these days?"

"No, I think not," said Dupin. "I believe he is exactly what he says he is. From the look of him, I would have to say he is guileless." He turned to the women and said, "And what do you three charming ladies think of Señor Creed?"

"He certainly is handsome," said Patrice, "but he is so young. What sort of business could he have with anyone?"

"Especially here in Mexico," said Claire.

"I agree," said Silveria. "What sort of business would a man like that have in Mexico?"

"Maybe we should keep a close eye on this *Yanqui* from Texas," said Dupin, his view riveted on Claire.

"*Oui*," purred Claire, a catlike gleam in her eyes as she retreated to speaking French, "maybe someone should keep a close watch on Monsieur Creed. Who knows what sort of rogue he could be? Certainly, we must find out. Don't you think so, Sister?"

Patrice made no oral reply. The stark severity of the glaring look that she aimed at Claire said all that she wanted to say.

Claire was unperturbed by it, shrugging off Patrice's annoyance with the cunning smile of the vixen that she was.

She would get close to this man Creed, as close as she wished to get, and she would learn all that she could about him, using whatever means necessary. To fail to do so would be to fail as a Frenchwoman, and, of course, this could never be.

10

No sooner had he finished his dessert of diced guava fruit and peach slices covered with whipped cream, than Colonel Dupin had to leave the hacienda to tend to some military business in the presidio. Don Bernardo was then called away to the stables where a prize mare was in foal; Silveria accompanied him. Patrice then excused herself, saying she was tired.

Throughout the meal, Creed had had a difficult time keeping his eyes off Silveria, who sat across from him, and had had little chance to look at Claire, who was seated beside him. Not that he hadn't known that she was there. What his eyes had missed, his other senses had reaped. She had scented herself with a fragrance so pleasing to the olfactory that he had actually felt tantalizing, invisible fingers stroking him, caressing his chest, rippling over his rock-hard abdomen, and reaching deep to his loins. And more than once during the conversation, she had touched his hand to show her pleasure at some remark he had made or to emphasize some statement of her own. And, of course, there was her voice, so soft and soothing and possibly more; how much more was yet to be learned.

Claire was older than Creed by more than a few years. Even so, he caught himself thinking of her as being a most desirable woman. She was quite sensuous.

"Well, Monsieur Creed," said Claire, "it seems that we are alone."

Creed smiled and said, "Is that bad?"

"That all depends on you," said Claire.

Creed didn't have a lot of experience with women, but what he lacked in quantity he made up with quality. He knew a serious flirtation when he heard it.

"Well, I'm not one to spoil a party," said Creed.

"How much of a party can two people have?"

"That's a good question, ma'am. I don't really know the answer to that one."

"I do," she said coyly. "Would you like me to share it with you?"

Creed was already flushed with the heat of his body working on the food he had just consumed, and now Claire was adding fuel to that fire. It was a delicious warmth, but a little voice deep inside him said it spelled danger if left unchecked.

"Yes, I would," he heard himself say, "but do you think this is the right time and place?"

"The time, yes. The place? The moon is full tonight. Have you seen Monsieur Abeytia's hanging garden?"

"No, I haven't," said Creed.

"Then I must show it to you."

Creed helped her from her chair, then offered his arm to her. Claire directed him through the doorway that led to the rear patio, which was covered with trellises that were overgrown with bougainvillea vines in full bloom, the flowers an assortment of reds and pinks, the scent captivating in the cool night air. They talked as they left the patio to stroll through the garden.

"You and Mrs. Dupin were quite a surprise to me," said Creed. "I didn't expect to meet any French ladies down here."

"And why not? Mexico has many people from foreign lands living here. Mostly men, I will grant you, but also many women. Emperor Maximilian is an Austrian, and Empress Carlota is the daughter of the king of Belgium."

"I didn't know that," said Creed. "I thought the only foreigners down here were French."

"And what about you Americans? You are foreigners here, too."

"Yes, I guess we are. It's just that I didn't expect to meet any ladies here in Matamoras. Maybe if I traveled—"

Claire interrupted him, saying, "I have been living in Mexico for six years now. I came here with my late husband Antoine long before Napoleon decided to make Mexico his puppet."

"Six years ago? What brought you to Mexico then?"

"Antoine was a merchant. We lived in Mexico City at first, then came here when the war in your own country began. When Marshal Bazaine landed in this country in 1862, we sailed to Vera Cruz because Antoine thought our lives would be at risk here." Claire forced a snicker as she thought back to that time. "Poor Antoine! We went to Vera Cruz to save our lives, and that is where he contracted malaria and died."

"I'm sorry," said Creed sincerely.

"Thank you for that thought, Monsieur Creed. Antoine was a good man and a good merchant, but he was a terrible lover."

Creed blushed and could only stammer, "Oh?"

"Yes," said Claire quite matter-of-factly, as if she were speaking of the weather or a recipe for crepes. "He was much older than I. François's age."

"François?"

Claire smiled indulgently and explained, "Colonel Dupin. My brother-in-law. Antoine and François were just about the same age. Actually, Antoine was a few years older. Our marriage was arranged by my father. Patrice and I are but two of eleven daughters.'' She laughed gaily. ''Poor Papa! He wanted so badly to have a son, and when he had none, he married us off to men of means or position. Not one of us had a say in whom we wished to wed. Patrice is the oldest, but she was the next to last to be married. Papa thought it would be nice to have a war hero in the family, so he picked François for Patrice. She was already past her best years by then, but it was just as well. François has no interest in fathering any children. He says his soldiers are all the children he will ever need.''

''But what about you?'' asked Creed. ''Why did you stay in Mexico after your husband died?''

''I stayed for Patrice. She would not be able to bear the loneliness of this country.''

''Loneliness? But she's with her husband, isn't she?''

''François is a soldier first and a husband second. He is often away from her for weeks at a time. If I were not here, she would be bereft of all that is comforting to a woman.''

''I see,'' said Creed.

''Besides,'' said Claire with a touch of mischief in her tone, ''if I were to return to France, Papa would only try to marry me off again.'' She squeezed his arm and leaned against him. ''And that would spoil everything for me . . . again.''

Creed hadn't realized it as they walked, but Claire had maneuvered him to the darkest corner of the garden. She stopped, and he had no choice but to do the same.

''Now tell me about yourself, Monsieur Creed,'' she said.

''There's not much to tell, ma'am.''

''Please call me Claire. It is much more intimate. Do you not agree?''

''I guess it is,'' he said, beginning to fall under her spell.

''And I will call you . . . Slate? Or would you prefer something else . . . such as *mon cheri*?''

"Slate or Creed will do fine," he said.

"Now about you. I suppose you have a wife and children waiting for you in Texas."

"No, no wife and no children. Not yet anyway."

"Then you have a fiancée?"

"A what?"

"A betrothed."

Creed understood this term and said, "Well, not exactly."

"But there is a girl," said Claire. "A very pretty girl, I would guess."

For the first time that evening, Creed thought of Texada back in Hallettsville, and he longed for her, to feel her touch, to hear the gentle twang in her voice, to look into her eyes, and to tell her how much he loved her.

Instead, he was with another. A woman and not a girl such as Texada. Claire was a mature woman with life experience, and this fascinated and titillated him to the core of his desire. She was beautiful and sensuous, and he lusted for her.

Creed turned and faced Claire. "Pretty, yes," he said huskily, "but she's in Texas."

Claire put her hands on his arms and leaned into him, intentionally pressing her breasts against his chest. "And I am here," she said melodiously, her face merely inches from his.

He felt the hardness of her bosom against him, and he was aroused totally. "Yes, you are," said Creed, and a second later all resistance in him vanished. He encircled her with his arms and kissed her, mashing his slightly parted lips against her open mouth. Her tongue sought his, and he responded, increasing their passion to a feverish pitch. His hands began to slide down her back and would have had not the sound of several mounted horsemen riding by just beyond the garden wall refocused his attention. Creed broke off the kiss to listen.

The horses stopped, and their riders dismounted. Foot-steps—soldiers marching—approached. Four, maybe five men.

"Find the American," said Colonel Dupin in the darkness, employing his native tongue, "and bring him to me in the library."

Dupin and his chasseurs entered the garden through the rear gate, marched straight to the covered patio, then into the house.

Creed's sexual desire for Claire had abated, but not so hers for him. When he started to break their embrace, she held him all the tighter.

"There is no need to stop yet," she said. "They will not find us out here."

He saw the moonlight reflected in her eyes and was suddenly reminded of another night and another woman. Then he realized that Claire wasn't the one that he wanted. Texada was. But she wasn't there. She was back in Hallettsville—waiting—for him. He felt guilt.

"Maybe not," said Creed, "but I don't want to take that chance." He broke away from her and headed back to the patio.

Claire followed close behind him. When they reached the house, she stopped him from entering it through the library's French doors. "Not here," she whispered. "Through the dining room." When he hesitated, she added, "He will suspect something if you go directly into the library."

Creed understood and followed her to the dining room. Inside the house again, they parted: she going to the kitchen and he to the foyer where two chasseurs stood guard.

Upon seeing Creed, the cavalrymen remembered their orders and informed him that their colonel commanded his presence in the library. Of course, they spoke in French, so Creed didn't understand their words. But when one opened the door to the sitting room and the second pulled him by the arm with one hand and pointed with the other, he caught on that they wanted him to go into the parlor. Once inside, they made signs that he was to follow them to the library. Creed was compliant.

Dupin was pacing the room when Creed entered the library. He stopped as soon as he saw the Texan.

"Ah, Mr. Creed, how nice of you to join me."

"Not at all, Colonel," said Creed.

Dupin waved his hand, and the chasseurs left them.

"Mr. Creed, I will come straight to the point. These men you seek . . . Kindred and the others . . . they are your friends?"

"I thought we covered that ground already," said Creed.

"Yes, but I would like to go over it again," said Dupin. "Kindred and his men are your friends. Yes or no."

"Not exactly."

"Then they are your enemies?"

"That's not what I said."

"Maybe not your lips, but your eyes said they are your enemies. Very hated enemies, I might add. You seek revenge on them for some wrong they have done. In Corsica, they call this a vendetta."

"Where?" asked Creed, deliberately trying to distract Dupin from the purpose of the interview.

"Corsica," said Dupin.

"Where's that?"

"It's an island in the Mediterranean Sea south of France."

Creed knew this already but continued the charade. "What sea?"

Dupin glared at Creed and said, "You are trying my patience, Mr. Creed. I do not think you want to do that."

Creed flexed his eyebrows and said, "No, I guess not, Colonel. So what was your original question?"

"You have been warned, Mr. Creed."

Yes, he had. "All right, so what if Kindred and his gang are my enemies?"

Dupin stared directly into Creed's eyes and declared, "I will give them to you, so to speak."

"Give them to me?"

"That is correct. For a price, of course."

"A price?"

"Yes, a price."

Creed was curious. "How much?"

"Not money, Mr. Creed. I want you . . . in my service."

"I told you before, Colonel, I'm not interested in your little war down here. All I want is Kindred and the men who are riding with him."

"And I will give them to you. On a silver platter, if you wish, if only you will do a service for me."

"And what would that be?"

"I would like you to spy on the Juáristas."

"Spy on the Juáristas?"

Dupin was annoyed and showed it. "Why do you keep repeating me? Yes, I want you to spy on them. I want you to join them, then keep me informed about everything they are planning to do."

"What if I say no?"

"Then I will give *you* to Kindred. Obviously, he must be as anxious to finish with you as you with him."

Creed tilted his head at Dupin and said, "That's not much of a choice, Colonel."

"It is the best I can offer . . . for now. Think it over, Mr. Creed. Sleep on it, as you Americans say, and you can give me your answer in the morning."

Not if I get out of here tonight, thought Creed as he reached for the door.

"Oh, yes," said Dupin. "One more thing. Please do not try to leave the hacienda in the night. My men have orders to shoot anyone found beyond the house grounds."

"I'll keep that in mind," said Creed. Yep. I sure will, he thought.

11

Creed had thoughts of picking up where he and Claire had left off, but that's all there was to it. Just wishful thinking because Claire was nowhere to be found after his interview with Dupin. At least, she was nowhere that he could look without raising someone's suspicions. Just as well, he thought. How would he ever be able to look Texada in the eye again if he were to stray from the narrow line that he had promised—sort of—himself that he would tread while they were apart?

He went to bed early. Alone. His slumber was deep and dreamless. Until he heard a soft, urgent voice in the night.

"Señor Creed!"

He stirred.

"Señor Creed!"

Not a dream.

"Señor Creed!"

He rolled over and opened his eyes. Moonbeams stretched into the room through the window, casting a wide strip of light across the floor and over the foot of his bed. He propped himself on one elbow.

"Señor Creed!"

He thought he recognized the voice and answered, "Miss Silveria? Is that you?"

"Sh-sh-sh-h! Quietly, señor!" He repeated the question, and she answered in a whisper, "*Sí!* I mean, yes, it is I."

Creed drew back as he realized that he was naked beneath the cotton sheet and Silveria really was in the room. But where? No time to ask. He made certain that he had all the right parts totally covered, then whispered back, "Are you crazy or something, Miss Silveria? What in heaven's name are you doing in here in the middle of the night?"

"I must speak with you, Señor Creed," she said.

"Can't it wait until morning?"

She moved into the silvery light, closer to him, where he could distinguish her form from everything else in the room. Half of her face was illumined by the pale glow. In spite of the circumstance—or maybe because of it—Creed couldn't keep from thinking of how beautiful she looked, even more beautiful than in the soft light of the dining room. He was so captivated by her beauty that he failed to notice her attire, a low-cut satin chemise trimmed with lace, which hung only to the middle of her thighs while clinging tightly to her breasts.

"No, it cannot wait until morning," she said. "I must speak with you now." She sat down on the edge of the bed and leaned toward him. "You are in great danger, Señor Creed."

"I am?"

"Yes. Señora Mounet. You were with her tonight, yes?"

Creed was suspicious of the question and answered with a question. "Was I?"

"Señor Creed, this is no time to play games. I only wish to warn you about Señora Mounet. She is a very dangerous and sinful woman."

"Sinful I can go along with. But dangerous? What do you mean by that?"

"The señora," said Silveria hesitantly, "she . . . she sleeps . . . with Colonel Dupin."

"She sleeps with Colonel Dupin?" asked Creed. "What about Madame Dupin?"

"You do not understand, señor. Señora Mounet and Colonel Dupin are having a love affair."

"A love affair?" queried Creed. "Right under Madame Dupin's nose?"

"Yes, that is right. But that is not all. She is also having a love affair with one of Colonel Dupin's officers."

Creed was incredulous. "What . . . ? Why are you telling me all this? And in the middle of the night? I don't . . . What's going on here?"

"I am trying to tell you, señor," said Silveria urgently, "if you will only listen."

Creed sat up in bed, forgetting himself and exposing his bare chest as he did, and said, "All right, I'm listening."

Silveria stared at the thin, brown hairs that adorned his pectorals and sternum. She had never seen a man this way before, but the sight didn't affect her adversely. Actually, she thought his bit of hirsuteness to be attractive, and she wished to touch it to see if the short curls were soft like her pubescence.

When she didn't answer immediately, Creed repeated his statement. "I said, 'All right, I'm listening.' "

"Yes, of course," said Silveria, mildly embarrassed. She forced her eyes to look away from his chest, then said, "Señora Mounet is sleeping with Colonel Dupin and Captain Auber. Neither man knows that she is having an affair with the other." Her gaze drifted lower again.

"So what?"

Silveria barely heard him. She started to reach out to touch him but stayed her hand.

"I said, 'So what?' "

"So she is a sinful woman," said Silveria.

"I know that already," said Creed. "So what does that have to do with me?"

"The señora tried to seduce you tonight, did she not?"

Creed suddenly felt like an adolescent again. Like the time his grandfather caught him peeking at Cousin Lucille through the keyhole of the guest bedroom door at Glengarry. She was changing clothes, and he was curious about the female form, what made girls different from boys. He didn't see much, which was just as well because Cousin Lucille didn't have that much to look at.

"You need not answer," said Silveria. "I know she did. She is that kind of woman."

"Do you know everything that goes on around here?" asked Creed, trying to change the subject.

"I know enough. I know that Señora Mounet wanted more than love from you, Señor Creed."

"More of what?"

"Earlier in the evening, while you were in your room before supper, I overheard Colonel Dupin tell her to get you alone and ask you many questions about yourself and why you are in Mexico. She has done this sort of thing for him before with other *norteamericanos* who have come across the Rio Bravo. Some of them lived to return to Brownsville. Some did not."

"Now I see what you're getting at," said Creed. "But why are you telling me this? Aren't you and your father Imperialists?"

"Yes, we are."

"So why are you warning me about Claire?"

Silveria said nothing. She merely lowered her eyes.

Creed understood. Or at least he thought he did. He felt a stirring within himself. Not the heated passion he had felt for Claire Mounet, but something purer, deeper—from the heart, not the loins. The sort of feeling he had for—For Texada? Yes, the same emotion, he thought. Was it love? Or simply an infatuation? Was he substituting Silveria—

the raven-haired, almond-skinned, doe-eyed Mexican señorita—for Texada with her flaxen hair, lightly tanned complexion, and blue eyes? He wasn't sure, was undecided. He
did know that he wanted to take Silveria into his arms and
hold her close to him. Nothing more except a gentle kiss
or two and maybe a breathless three-word sentence: I love
you. And one more thing. Maybe he could pretend she was
Texada and that would make it all right with his conscience.
No! Yes! No! He was so undecided.

He said nothing, too.

Silveria rose gracefully, slowly, with elegance. She
looked down on him. At his eyes first. Then his chest again.
She heaved a sigh, then left him.

Creed sat there motionless for much of the next several
minutes, his mind in turmoil. By the time the last moonbeam
faded among the stars, he had come to a decision: he would
take each moment as it came because . . . because it could
very well be his last of this life.

12

The autumn dawn was calm, cool, and colorful. Creed missed it though because he slept late.

Soft fingers feeling the hair on his naked chest gave him a pleasant, last-second dream before he awakened. In his slumber, he saw Silveria in the room again, sitting on the bed, trying to arouse him. The dream was just beginning to manifest itself through his body when he opened his eyes to see Claire leaning over him. He didn't start; he was too tired for that. Instead, he let his head roll to one side and said, "Oh, it's you."

"You are disappointed?" asked Claire. She lifted the sheet and peeked beneath it. "No, I think not."

Creed turned his back to her and said, "Do you mind?"

She continued to hold the sheet up, giving an appreciative look to his posterior, and said, "No, not at all." She giggled like a mischievous schoolgirl and added, "In fact, I rather enjoy it."

Creed snatched the sheet from her hand and said, "There's a word for women like you."

Claire smiled and said, "Yes, I believe it is voyeur." Then she laughed. "You men. When you gaze upon a woman's nakedness, you think it is perfectly acceptable. But let a woman look at a man who is *au naturel*, and she is the whore. *N'est-ce pas?*"

The words were French, but Creed knew what she meant. She was right. He didn't like admitting it, but she *was* right.

"All right," he said, "you made your point."

"Have I?"

Creed threw back the sheet, totally exposing himself. "There! Seen enough now?"

Claire's lips parted for a second before she gently bit the lower one. Then she said, "Seeing is not everything, *mon cheri*. But there is no time for more now. Breakfast is being served, and François expects you to join him at the table immediately. Hurry. He is a very impatient man, and you would be unwise to keep him waiting."

Creed sat up and said, "I'll be along as soon as I can get dressed and . . ."

"Yes, of course, but be quick, *mon cheri*, and keep François happy. For the moment, anyway."

He sat there for a long moment, quite disturbed by Claire's casual attitude about nudity—his—and sex—hers. He had never known anyone to take such a serious subject so lightly—not even some of the raunchiest men he had known in the army, who around the campfire told of their multiple conquests in great detail; and definitely not any of the boys that had been his youthful chums back in Lavaca County. Even the girls at the bawdy house he had visited in Nashville during the war had imbued their brand of debauchery with a tad of sensitivity. Claire was so nonchalant about it all that he could only deduce she was driven by pure animalistic lust and nothing more. But when he considered that proposition, he had to ask himself if that was all that bad. It was a question he would have to answer at a later date because now he was expected to join his host and the others for the morning meal.

Creed was the last to arrive at the breakfast table that was set on the rear patio. The seating arrangement was different from the night before: Silveria beside him, Claire across from him, Don Bernardo to his right at the foot of the table, Patrice across from Silveria, and Dupin at the head of the table. The meal was eaten around bits of idle conversation: Did you sleep well? Yes, thank you. The night was cool, don't you think? Yes, it was. Do you think it will rain today? Not likely. Too soon for the rains. And so on.

The only excitement was caused by Claire, but only she and Creed knew about it. Under the table, beneath the white cloth, Claire used her bare foot to play with Creed's legs, stroking the insides of his thighs. He made no sign that anything was out of the ordinary, maintaining complete control of his desire much to Claire's displeasure.

At the end of their repast, Creed asked Dupin if he could accompany him into Matamoras that morning. The colonel politely said that he would be most happy to have him along—on most days, but today was not most days. Dupin urged him to remain at the hacienda all day, maybe have Don Bernardo show him the fine stable of horses, especially the new arrival of the night before. Much to Creed's surprise, Dupin left the house without asking him for a definite answer to his proposition of the previous eve.

Throughout the day, Creed successfully avoided being alone with Claire. He let Don Bernardo entertain him with a tour of the stables as Dupin had suggested, then ate lunch with everyone except Dupin in attendance. Again, Claire played her little game of footsie under the table with Creed, and again, he made no outward signs that anything was out of the ordinary. When siesta time arrived in the afternoon, he waited until he was certain Claire had retired before doing so himself. Even then, he sought out a hammock on the rear patio instead of the bed in his room. Upon rising again, he congratulated himself for being so clever, then prepared for supper.

Dupin was also absent from the evening meal. In his place was Captain Rene Auber, the French-Canadian mer-

cenary who commanded the First Regiment of the Contre-
Guerrillas. Creed could see why Claire—or any woman for
that matter—was attracted to him. Auber was handsome,
swarthy, wiry, and only a few years older than Creed. He
was charming, intelligent, personable, suave, and worldly
enough to prosper in better social circles. Creed liked him
and was grateful for his appearance at the table because he
kept Claire busy. Auber lingered through the evening, then
departed when the household was retiring for the night.
Creed felt safe at last and went to his room looking forward
to a good night's rest.

The moon was big and orange and barely over the horizon
when Creed slipped out of his clothes and into bed. He lay
there for the longest moment, thinking of his life, his future,
wondering if he had one.

Dupin wanted him to spy on the Juáristas and had made
him a proposition that would have been hard to turn down
a few weeks earlier in Texas when his hatred for Kindred
was almost as great as his love for Texada. Now? He wasn't
so sure that he hated Kindred and his gang all that much.
Certainly, they were responsible for his brother Dent's death
and their involvement with the Detchens made them share
at least a piece of the guilt for their murder of his best friend
Jess Tate. But that was in the past and already fifteen men
had paid with their lives for the two crimes. Maybe the dog
who had fired the bullet that had killed Dent was already
among the dead. Wasn't that enough revenge? Of course,
he knew the Detchens had murdered Tate, and they would
pay for that misdeed. But what of Kindred and the ten men
with him? Kindred should pay because he was the leader.
But the others? Were they worth the bother? He was beginning to think not.

So what would he tell Dupin? Yes? No? He still didn't
know. He wanted Kindred dead, but he didn't want to get
involved in the Mexican civil war. How to get one without

the other? That question plagued his thoughts as he drifted off to sleep.

Creed was close to deep slumber when suddenly the process was reversed and he became cognizant of a dream. He was being aroused by Claire again, and since it was only a nocturnal fantasy, he decided to let himself enjoy it. She was pressing her voluptuous form against him, and he turned to take her into his arms. The vision was beginning to be ecstatic when he became totally lucid and realized he wasn't dreaming. He started, then withdrew from her.

"Hello, *mon cheri*," she whispered huskily, casually.

"Claire! What the hell's wrong with you, woman? Are you crazy or something?"

"No, I am on fire . . . for you. I want you to make love to me." She reached for him, but he pushed her hand away. "Do not reject me, *mon cheri*. I need your love. Can you not see that?"

Creed could. He could see her form in the moonlight that was creeping through the bedroom window. She wore only a loose chemise that disguised nothing. Her nipples stood up against it like capstones on tiny mounds. Her chest and abdomen heaved alternately with each deep, hot breath she took. She had parted her legs, allowing the garment to fall between her thighs, accentuating the lay of her sex. Creed could see it all, and had he had no soul, he would have taken it all.

"Yes, I can see that," he stammered, his throat dry and unwilling to be used.

"Then make love to me."

"I can't."

Claire pulled the sheet back to take a full look at him and said, "Yes, you can."

"No, I can't," he stammered again. "There's another."

"There was no one else when we were in the garden last night," she countered. "Where did this other woman suddenly appear from?"

"She's back in Texas. We're promised . . . to each other."

"But as you said also last night, she is back in Texas."

"But she's not out of my heart."

"Maybe your heart belongs to this girl in Texas. I do not care. I am not interested in your heart."

Claire reached for him again, but instead of merely repelling her hand this time, Creed pushed her completely out of bed. Not expecting such a forceful rejection, she crashed on the floor and in the process knocked over the nightstand, sending the ceramic water ewer and drinking glass to a shattering end.

The noise was deafening in the bedroom. It must have been heard elsewhere in the house.

It was.

"You'd better get out of here quick," said Creed.

Claire scrambled to a sitting position and said, "No, I will stay and tell them how you tried to seduce me."

"Better tell them how I dragged you in here against your will, too."

That thought only sharpened her anger. "*Sanglant batard!*" she swore. "Bloody bastard! You will pay for this!" She was on her feet and gone an instant later, saying nothing more.

Creed leaned back on the bed, proud of himself for the control he had exhibited. Claire was a great temptation, but he knew that he couldn't bed a woman without feeling something for her in his heart. And he could never love a woman like Claire.

But he didn't know that he had made a new and extremely dangerous enemy.

13

Creed was up and already dressed when Silveria Abeytia tapped lightly on his bedroom door the next morning.

"Señor Creed?" she called to him.

He opened the door without answering, startling her. "Good morning, Miss Silveria," he said. Then seeing the mild fright in her eyes, he quickly added, "I'm sorry. I didn't mean to put a scare into you so early in the day."

"It is quite all right, señor," she said. "I have come to tell you breakfast will soon be served."

"Good! I'm starving." He closed the door, and the two of them started walking down the hall toward the foyer.

"You slept better last night," she said, making a statement instead of asking a question.

"As a matter of fact, I did," said Creed, "but I suppose you knew that already."

Silveria smiled and said, "This is my home, and I am the mistress here. It is my duty to know everything that goes on within these walls."

"Everything?"

"Everything."

Creed could tell by the width of her grin and the gleam in her eye that she knew about Claire's visit the night before. To his delight, he could tell that she also approved of the outcome.

A few steps farther Silveria asked, "What did she break?"

No sense trying to hide the fact, he thought. "The pitcher and glass," he confessed.

"Was it out of anger or by accident?"

"Accident."

She gave a short laugh and said, "Odd, but I would have wagered on the former."

"Why do you say that?" asked Creed.

Silveria stopped in the hall and turned to Creed, who also halted. Her aspect was quite serious now as she said, "Madame Mounet has displayed her ill-temper many times in the past. Usually when she cannot get what she wants. I have heard her berate a poor farmer in the market who did not have the kind of fruit she wished to eat that day, and I have seen her take a whip to her carriage driver when he did not drive the horses as fast as she wanted to go. Yes, Madame Mounet has a very bad temper, Señor Creed. You have deprived her of something she wanted, and I am much concerned that she will make you pay for it."

"Well, I appreciate your concern, Miss Silveria," said Creed, "but I wouldn't worry too much. I can handle Madame Mounet."

"But can you . . . as you say . . . handle Colonel Dupin as well?"

Creed's brow furrowed as he also became quite serious. "Why do you ask that?"

"As I said before, Señor Creed, this is my home, and I know everything that goes on inside these walls. I know that Colonel Dupin has asked you to join his army as a spy."

"Then you must know that I haven't said I'd do it."

"Yes, I know this as well."

"Do you think I should?"

Silveria turned away and said, "That is a decision that

only you must make, señor.'' Then she continued walking toward the breakfast table on the rear patio.

Creed followed a few steps behind her, wishing she had given him a more helpful answer. When he arrived at the table, Pepe, the servant, was seating Silveria. Don Bernardo, Claire, Patrice, and Dupin were already seated. They welcomed Creed with the usual pleasantries, then all ate while Dupin informed them of the latest news.

''Captain Moore's squadron captured a band of Juáristas yesterday and brought them back to Matamoras last night. Upon immediate questioning, we learned that Benito Juárez is now in San Antonio, Texas, trying to rally American support for his lost cause. Of course, this is an unconfirmed report.'' The last he directed at Creed. ''However, I expect confirmation one way or the other will be made posthaste.''

After the meal, Dupin requested Creed join him in the library.

''Mr. Creed, two nights ago I asked you to spy for me against the Juáristas,'' said Dupin, coming straight to the point as was his custom. ''I told you to sleep on the proposition I made you. I gave you all day yesterday and all of last night as well to think about it. I think I have given you more than enough time to reach a decision on this matter. Have you decided to accept or reject my offer?''

''Colonel, we Texans don't like being pushed into corners,'' said Creed. ''We have a bad habit of fighting back with everything we've got when our backs are to the wall.'' He paused for effect. ''But I don't believe you have me cornered just yet, Colonel.''

Dupin frowned and said, ''Are you saying that you will not do it?''

''No, I'm saying that you haven't made up my mind for me yet.''

''I haven't made up your mind for you yet?'' boomed Dupin. ''I haven't made up your mind for you yet? Is that what you said?''

Creed knew a reply was unnecessary and made none.

"Do you mean you want me to do something that will make you decide one way or the other? Is that what you mean, Mr. Creed?"

"That's about it, Colonel."

Dupin was livid. The veins in his forehead appeared ready to burst at any second. Had he had a weapon in his hand, no doubt he would have used it to kill Creed on the spot. Having none, he slammed the meaty part of his fist against the bookcase, then in a low growl said, "Then I will help you make up your mind once and for all, Mr. Creed."

14

Dupin's chasseurs handled Creed roughly when their colonel gave them the order to place him under arrest and throw him into the presidio jail.

Calling the place of detention a jail was being kind. It was more like a pen for humans, a circular area of open ground, five rods across, surrounded by a rough fence made of cottonwood limbs, and in the center was a well and a shady spot created by an awning of four poles and palm fronds. The prison was located behind the municipal building where Dupin had his office. To one side was the horse stable for the Contre-Guerrillas, and to the other was a cattle corral, holding only a few head at the moment. To the rear was an adobe wall beyond which were the crude houses of the town's peaceful population.

Most of the prisoners were congregated around the well when Creed was thrown into their midst. All of them turned and stared at this newcomer as he picked himself up from the dust and gravitated toward a vacant spot along the fence, where he squatted down with his back to the rough posts. He was there only a few minutes contemplating his plight before a large man came over to him and kicked dirt on his boots.

Creed looked down at his feet, then up at his antagonist.

"Aw, hell," he muttered. He let his head droop against his knees, thinking this was all he needed: another macho son of a bitch trying to pick a fight with him.

Looming over Creed was the biggest Mexican he had ever seen. This hombre had to stand at least six-and-a-half feet tall and had to have shoulders as wide as an ax handle is long. To make matters worse, he was ugly: face all pock-marked, skin red and appearing raw as if it had a bad rash; eyes set far apart and bloodshot, black mustaches cut un-evenly, wisps of whiskers in patches on his cheeks and chin. He smiled cruelly through broken, decaying teeth.

"Eh, gringo, *cómo se llama*?" he grunted. When Creed didn't reply immediately, the Mexican kicked him in the shin—lightly, of course—to get his attention. "*Cómo se llama*, gringo?"

Damn! thought Creed. Can't Mexicans talk to a man without using their feet?

Instead of kicking Creed when he didn't answer the sec-ond time he was asked his name, the Mexican stepped on the toe of Creed's left boot and placed all his weight on it. Creed countered by kicking him in the ankle. Hard. In-tending to cause him hurt. He succeeded.

"*Ai-ee-ee!*" screamed the Mexican as he danced back-ward from his assailant, hopping on one foot and holding the other for a moment before falling in a heap.

Creed leaped to his feet, ready to fight this mountain with his fists, feet, knees, and even his head if butting was called for. Out of the corners of his eyes he saw how the others had come closer in anticipation of just such an event, and he wondered if he would have to fight them as well.

The giant quit whining about his injury and regained his feet. He was thoroughly mad now, like a rabid dog. He went into a fighting stance, saying in Spanish, "Now you will pay, gringo." Then he started toward Creed, his fists revolving in little circles in front of him like someone who had seen a prizefighter but didn't really know the technique.

Creed, realizing this Mexican meant serious business, decided another tack might be wiser to take. Suddenly, he relaxed, stood straight as he could, put a pure look of innocence on his face, did a little half turn that put him in a dueling stance, then aimed his right index finger at his opponent and said, "Now look here, you." Seeing the Mexican hesitate, he went on, saying, "I'm the meanest son of a bitch north and east of the Nueces River. I've bitten off the ears of bigger bastards than you and then stuffed them down their throats, and when that didn't teach them nothing, I bit off their noses and stuffed them down their throats. And if they didn't have their fill of fighting by then, I scrambled their eggs for them with the toe of my boot and gouged out their eyes so they couldn't see that they no longer had a future that included women."

The Mexican stared down at Creed, wondering what in the hell he was saying. Then he looked aside for help from someone, anyone who could understand English and translate for him.

Off to one side, someone began laughing. By himself. Raucously. But only for a second.

Creed looked around to see who was laughing at him but couldn't find the man in the crowd. Then he noted that the big Mexican had his eyes fixed on a fellow about Creed's height, weight, and build who was dressed in the typical style of a Mexican peon but otherwise had little resemblance to one. His skin was tanned—by the sun, not by his ancestry; it wasn't the coppery shade of mestizos or *los Indios* but was more the color of good cow leather. His eyes were blue, hair—what could be seen beneath a large straw sombrero—sandy, eyebrows the same. His facial features were sharp, too, displaying none of the characteristics of those native to Mexico. If he wasn't an American, thought Creed, he was at least a European.

"Leave him be, Juanito," said this man in Spanish.

Juanito straightened up to his full height, appeared to be disappointed that he couldn't make taco meat out of Creed, and took a step backward.

"Now you're being sensible," said Creed, keeping up the charade of being a real frontier fighting man.

"Not quite, friend," said the pseudo peon in English, stepping out of the crowd. "He's just obeying orders like a good soldier." The man came closer to Creed, stopped a few feet away, and studied him for a second before saying, "You look familiar, friend, but I can't rightly place a name with your face. Mine's Newhouse. Frank Newhouse of Lavaca County, Texas. What's yours?"

This was a surprise, a shock, for Creed. A man from his own part of the country down here in Mexico? Creed's eyebrows shot up his forehead, widening his eyes with disbelief.

"You've heard of me?" queried Newhouse suspiciously.

"No. No, I haven't," said Creed. "My name is Creed. Slate Creed." Then, with intended deliberation, he added, "And I'm also from Lavaca County."

"Is that a fact?" Newhouse's face brightened. "Well, I'll be damned. Someone from back home. Creed, you say?"

"That's right."

"Hm-m. I don't rightly recollect anyone named Creed from around my part of the county. My pappy got himself a headright near Hackberry right after San Jacinto, and that's where I was raised. What part of the county are you from?"

"North," said Creed. "Up near Foley's plantation."

"Your family got land there?"

"No Creed land there now," he said, not lying. "Yankees got it all."

"Too bad," said Newhouse. "I suspect mine will be gone, too, if I ever get back there. Of course, I ain't so sure I want to go back."

"Why is that?" asked Creed, falling into a casual conversation with Newhouse.

Newhouse tilted his head sideways, squinted, and peered into Creed's eyes. "Hm-m. Well, I suppose it can't hurt telling now. Especially since the war's over back home." He moved even closer to Creed and lowered his voice to a conspiratorial level. "I deserted," he said.

"Deserted?"

"Yep. Back in '64. Came home on leave and saw how things was and where they was heading, and I decided the South was fighting a lost cause. I even wrote a little ditty about it. Want to hear it?"

Creed smiled indulgently and said, "Why not?"

Newhouse took the pose of an orator and began to recite:

> Am tired of Confederacy
>   Confound her may I say!
> By her I lost my property
>   For service got no pay
> So many Yankees now arrive
>   I see no chance to save my life
> But had to run away.

> It will not do to calculate
>   To save the country yet
> Tried our best until of late
>   Too many Yankees met
> The revolution is nearly past
>   Yankees got the most and best
> Soon have it all I bet.

"I heard that," said Creed jocularly. "You summed it up just about right, Mr. Newhouse."

Also smiling, Newhouse said, "Oh, I ain't a mister down

here. I'm Captain Francisco Newhouse of the Mexican Liberal Army.''

''A captain?''

''Down here. I was only a sergeant back home. President Juárez knows a good man when he sees one, so he made me a captain. In person. Himself, he did.''

''I gathered that already,'' said Creed. ''I met another captain in your army just a few days ago. His name was Hunter.''

''John Hunter?'' queried Newhouse, his voice dropping to a conspiratorial level.

''The same,'' said Creed.

''Good man, John Hunter. You say you met him a few days ago?''

''That's right.'' Creed gave a short laugh and added, ''Come to think of it, I met him under similar circumstances as these, Captain Newhouse.''

Newhouse fell into a deeper seriousness. ''Hunter was captured by the French?''

''No, he was saving me from a handful of Mexican bandits who were intent on taking everything I had, including my life, I think.''

''Sounds like some of Cortina's bunch.''

''That's who Hunter said they were.''

''Thought so. John did you a big favor. You get the chance, you ought to return it.''

''I will. First chance I get.''

''Good.'' Newhouse dropped his voice another level. ''You said you met Hunter a few days ago. What have you been up to since then?''

''I came into Matamoras looking for some men I knew back in Texas,'' said Creed.

''Did you find them?''

''No, they weren't here.''

''So what are you doing in this place?''

"I pissed off the French," said Creed.

"Is that a fact?" asked Newhouse with a smile.

"They wanted me to fight in their goddamned army, and I said I wasn't interested in fighting in anyone's army."

"Not in anyone's army?" asked Newhouse.

"Not in any army," said Creed. "I had my fill of fighting wars back home. The same as you, Captain."

"Now that ain't what I said, Mr. Creed. I said I was tired of fighting for the losing side, so I came down here to fight for President Juárez."

"But I thought the Liberals were losing this war down here?"

"Maybe we are today," said Newhouse with a wink, "but that might all change real soon."

"Oh, really?"

"Really," said Newhouse. "You just sit tight and see what happens before this day is through." He moved away from Creed, meandering back into the crowd.

Creed watched him for a moment and remembered Colonel Dupin saying that one of his companies had captured a bunch of Juáristas the night before. He figured Newhouse and this bunch must be them. Then another thought crossed his mind. If they were Juáristas, then possibly Dupin put him in jail with them as part of a plot to get him to spy on them. Or something like that. Whatever, he didn't trust Dupin's motives and wouldn't put himself in a place to betray anyone, especially a fellow Texan like Newhouse or Hunter.

Before Creed could give much more thought to the fix he was in and Dupin's scheming, the gate to the compound opened and two big French guards came inside while a dozen more guarded the entrance behind them. They grabbed one prisoner and started to drag him away, much against the man's will as he fought them as best as he could but to no avail. He was taken outside and into the municipal building.

When the doors to the city hall closed behind their fellow inmate, the other Mexican prisoners fell on their knees, made the sign of the cross on themselves, then said a prayer to the Holy Mother in behalf of their friend. Some of them wept as they prayed.

Creed didn't understand their profound compassion for their *compadre* until he heard the man's screams of incredible horror echoing up from the cellar of the municipal building. He sought out Newhouse and found him.

"My God, Newhouse," he said, "they're torturing him. Those dirty bastards!"

"You don't know the half of it, Mr. Creed," said Newhouse, suppressing his revulsion with a cold resolution that said someone would pay for this crime. "I'd hoped we could avoid this. It wasn't in the plan."

Creed stared at him curiously and said, "Plan?"

Newhouse ignored the question as he scanned the area, saw what he wanted to see—Mexican soldiers coming over the adobe wall—then leaned close to Creed and said, "Things are about to get real hot around here, Mr. Creed."

"How's that?"

Instead of answering Creed, Newhouse shouted out, "*Andale, muchachos! Su armas!*"

In an instant, the men in the prison were all in action, many digging in the dirt, others reaching down into the well, all suddenly producing weapons: knives, machetes, *pistolas*. A crack of gunfire sounded in the plaza in front of the municipal building. Another heartbeat and the thunder of several hundred horses' hooves rumbled up from the same direction.

"What's going on?" asked Creed. "Are you breaking out of here?"

"That's what we broke in here to do," said Newhouse. Then to his men, he yelled, "*Vamanos, muchachos!*" To Creed, he said, "Stick close to me, Mr. Creed, and we'll be out of here in no time at all.''

"That's all right," said Creed, not moving. "You go on without me."

Newhouse stopped, looked at him for a second, then said, "Suit yourself, friend. Stay here and get yourself shot in the morning, if you like, but we're getting the hell out of here now."

"Shot in the morning?"

"Either that or the French will cut off your legs or arms like they're doing to poor Paco right now.'' He paused to let that sink in before adding, "That's Colonel Dupin's way of dealing with captives. After they cut off a leg and an arm, they let you go so your friends will have to take care of you. You got many friends in these parts, Mr. Creed?'' The stark reality of what Newhouse was saying froze Creed's tongue. "I didn't think so. Myself, I'd rather be shot dead. But it's your choice. As for us, we're leaving now. Come or stay. It's up to you."

Creed swallowed hard, stimulating his entire speaking system into action. "Are you sure about that?"

"Sure about what?"

"The . . . amputations," said Creed.

"Yes, I'm sure. Did you see many men walking around outside when they brought you in here?"

"No."

"That's because they're either dead or laid up permanent because the French cut off their legs."

"I find that to be highly unbelievable, Captain Newhouse, but I don't think I'll stick around long enough to find out whether you're telling me true or not."

By now, a full scale firefight had begun with Mexican foot soldiers coming over the wall behind them and cavalry attacking from in front. The Imperialist defenders, members of the elite French Foreign Legion, were few in number because both regiments of Contre-Guerrillas had ridden out

that morning in search of more Juáristas to capture for Dupin's surgeons. The guards that remained behind sought out
defensive positions and opened up a steady fire on their
attackers.

The Mexicans inside the prison, led by Newhouse, rushed
the gate and forced it, breaking out and scattering in all
directions at once. Some ran for the corral and released the
cattle in order to add to the confusion. Others raced for the
stables and the horses. Newhouse and Creed were among
the latter. Creed saw Nimbus still saddled and tied to a
hitching rail, beat a Mexican to him, and leaped atop the
stallion. Newhouse and the others found mounts almost as
quickly, and in another few seconds, the Mexican unit was
formed up and ready to ride.

The remainder of the Imperialist garrison was now alerted
and joining the fray. They formed skirmish lines on each
side of the municipal building. Their officers would soon
have them ready for a counterattack that could be devastating
to the Mexicans.

Newhouse saw that he would soon be at a grave disadvantage. It was either escape now or be cut to pieces. He
gave the signal, then led the charge. The Mexicans kicked
their horses and rode like madmen toward a company of
Legionnaires that blocked their way to the plaza. Although
he was unarmed, Creed stayed close to Newhouse at the
vanguard.

A French officer raised his sword, called out the command
for the front line of two ranks to kneel, then ordered his
soldiers to fire in volleys at his command. He saw the
Mexicans bearing down on him and his men but waited until
they were almost at point-blank range before giving the order
for the kneeling rank to fire. He waited too long.

The Enfield rifles the French used flashed with gunfire,
then roared as a cloud of gun smoke instantly appeared
around the Legionnaires like a shroud. The bullets missed

nearly all of their targets, allowing the Mexicans to use their knives and machetes on the French foot soldiers as they rode into them. The well-disciplined Europeans held their ground, and some died bravely before the onslaught of cold steel wielded so deftly by the natives of the land. Those that lived were pushed aside by the Mexican horsemen and thrown into disarray.

A moment later Newhouse was leading his men from the presidio, through the plaza and then the town at a full gallop. Most of the prisoners had escaped alive and unharmed. Including Creed.

15

Once the escapees were in the open outside of Matamoras they formed up with their rescuers. Creed was surprised and delighted to see that this latter contingent was led by John Hunter. As a single unit now, they rode hard for an hour into the Mexican countryside without stopping or even slowing before Hunter signaled for the column to halt, dismount, and walk their horses.

Creed was unsure of what he should do at this point in time. Hunter and his company had broken him out of Dupin's jail, and for this, he was beholden to the Liberal army captain. Even so, he wasn't an enlistee in the Juárista cause and thus was under no obligation to follow any of Hunter's orders. On the other hand, he felt it would be rude of him to take his leave of Hunter and Newhouse at this time. So he dismounted with the rest of the men and walked Nimbus between the two captains at the fore of the column.

"Well, Mr. Creed," said Hunter, "you're the last man I expected to see during this raid. How do you come to be with Captain Newhouse and his men?"

"He was in prison with us," said Newhouse as if he and Hunter were the only ones there.

"I gathered that much, Frank," said Hunter, also bypassing Creed in the conversation. "What I'm curious about is how he got to be in there with you."

"Said he pissed off the French," said Newhouse.

"How was that?" asked Hunter.

"Said he wouldn't join their army," replied Newhouse.

"He said the same thing to me," said Hunter.

Newhouse finally looked at Creed and asked, "Is that what you meant when you said you weren't interested in joining any army?"

"That's exactly what I meant," said Creed. "Like I told you before—and I told that French colonel—"

Hunter broke in, saying, "You talked with Dupin?"

"I not only talked with him," said Creed, "I was also his house guest at Rancho Abeytia."

Hunter and Newhouse shifted their eyes at each other, both wondering the same thing but simultaneously hesitant to ask the question. They remained strangely silent for the next several paces, until Creed's curiosity got the best of him.

"Something wrong with that?" he asked.

"Wrong with what?" asked Hunter.

"My staying at Rancho Abeytia."

"I don't know," said Hunter. "What about you, Frank? You see something wrong with Mr. Creed here staying out to Rancho Abeytia as Dupin's guest?"

"That all depends," said Newhouse.

"On what?" asked Creed.

"On what you were doing there in the first place," said Newhouse, looking straight ahead.

Creed finally understood what they were getting at, and he knew how to reply. "I was a reluctant guest," he said. "One of Dupin's patrols led by a Captain Moore from Alabama caught up with me outside of Matamoras the other day right after we parted company, John. Moore took me straight to Dupin. After we talked a while, he invited me out to Rancho Abeytia. I said I could find accommodations elsewhere, but he insisted like I didn't have any other choice. Even while I was there, he gave me the impression that I was a prisoner instead of a guest.''

''What made him decide to change your residence for you?'' asked Hunter.

''Same thing I've already told you,'' said Creed. ''I told him I didn't want to serve in his goddamned army.''

''And you're not wanting to serve in ours either,'' said Newhouse. ''Is that it?''

''That's about as plain as I can get, Captain Newhouse.''

''You can call me Frank. After all, we're from the same county back home, ain't we?''

''What's this?'' asked Hunter.

''Didn't he tell you where he was from?'' asked Newhouse.

Hunter thought a second before answering, ''Sure he did. Said he was from Lavaca County, same as you. It's only that I didn't make the connection until just now.''

''John's a good man like I said,'' said Newhouse in an aside to Creed, ''but sometimes he lets the Yankee-lover in him come out, meaning he's a little slow to catch on now and then.''

''Now you listen here, Frank Newhouse—''

''Get's his dander up calling him a Yankee-lover,'' said Newhouse with a snicker.

''I think we've had enough of this conversation,'' said Hunter. ''We'd better be riding again. Mr. Creed, I'd be pleased if you would remain with us.''

Hunter's words sounded to Creed more like an order than an invite. Even so, he still felt it would be rude to leave them without being excused.

''It'd be my pleasure,'' said Creed cordially.

Hunter gave the command to mount up, and in another few seconds, the whole company was riding hard again toward a destination somewhere several miles distant from

Matamoras. At the first split in the trail they were following, Hunter halted the column again. Without dismounting, he told Newhouse to take his men by one path, while he took the other. Creed would ride with him. Newhouse nodded his understanding, then rode off with his contingent. Hunter explained to Creed that Dupin's Contre-Guerrillas would soon be looking for them and the only way to escape their pursuit was to divide up into several smaller units with each taking a separate route back to their base camp. Creed didn't say so, but he was familiar with the tactic, having ridden with Mosby during the War Between the States. He voiced his approval to Hunter, then they rode on.

Dusk came and went, and still they rode on into the night. They crossed a river, then a creek, then another river. Or was it the same river again? Creed couldn't be sure, but he had the very distinct feeling that Hunter didn't want him to be certain of where they were, where they had been, and where they were going. It was a game that Creed felt was unnecessary, but as long as Hunter was going to all the trouble, he might as well play along.

The sun was two hours down when Hunter halted his detachment for a much needed rest. Like a good military man, he ordered men to be picketed in every direction, then let the remainder relax. They could smoke but no campfires. Creed dismounted but didn't sit down on the ground and light up a *cigarillo*, the little brown cigars Mexican men were so fond of, like the Mexicans and Hunter.

"With all due respect, John," said Creed, intentionally looming over Hunter, "why are you going to all this trouble?"

"All what trouble?" asked Hunter, playing the innocent.

Creed knew the game was still on as far as Hunter was concerned, but he had different thoughts. He wanted to get everything out in the open and deal fair and square.

"John, we're both Texans, and as Texans, we like to

bullshit outsiders whenever we can. Now maybe I'm an outsider down here, and maybe that's the reason you and Frank are trying so hard to string me along. I don't know for sure. I'm only guessing. It makes no difference though. You can go ahead with this little charade of yours, if you want, but I'm tired of it, my friend. You can either tell me where I stand with you, or you can let me go my own way. You choose, John.''

After exhaling a stream of tobacco smoke, Hunter cocked his head and twisted his mouth as he gazed up at Creed for a few seconds before answering.

''All right,'' he said, ''I'll put my cards on the table, Mr. Creed. Frank and I have met others like you. Lone men come down from Texas. But you're a little different than most. Every one of them before you said right off that they'd fought for one side or the other in the war back home, and most of them said they wanted to join our army. Some— all of them Southern boys who had fought for the Confederacy—said they weren't sure what they wanted to do down here, said they wanted to have a look around first and get a feel for what was going on down here. We let those boys go, and most of them joined up with the Imperialists, mostly as Contre-Guerrillas serving under that bastard Frank Moore. The other boys—those who said they had fought for the Union—they said they had come down here to join our army and free Mexico from the French the same as they had freed the South of slavery. We let those boys join up with us, but we've had to shoot a lot of them because they lied to us.''

''Lied to you? That's all?'' queried Creed.

Hunter took a drag on his *cigarillo* and blew out the smoke slowly before answering. ''Not quite,'' he said. ''Those that we shot were some of those Southern boys who had gone on and joined up with the French and then came back to us, telling us they were Unionists back home and they wanted to join our army and fight the French. The truth was they came back to spy on us. Shooting spies is legal in any war, Mr. Creed.''

"How did you know they were spies?"

"Some of them," said Hunter, "had only met me or they had only met Frank. They didn't know that we were serving in the same outfit. Well, it seems that they'd tell Frank one thing when they were passing through the first time, then tell me something different when they came back. Or vicey-versey, depending on which one of us they met first and which one they met second.''

"Like how I met you first, then rode into Matamoras, and met Frank there.''

"In Dupin's jail," said Hunter. He inhaled the smoke of the *cigarillo*, then blew it out slowly as he let his last remark take its effect.

Creed understood now. "So you think I'm a spy like those others?"

"Let's just say the book is still open on you, Mr. Creed." He flicked the ash from his smoke. "So far, you seem to be on the straight and narrow with us, but that could only mean that you're smarter than the others were, is all. You might still be a spy.''

"I might be at that," said Creed, "but I'm not. I have no interest in your little war down here, John, and—''

Hunter cut him off, saying, "You've said that already. To me and to Frank.''

"And to Colonel Dupin," said Creed, reminding Hunter of that fact.

"So you say, Mr. Creed. We only have your word on that, and right now, your word ain't worth more than a paper peso." Hunter threw down his *cigarillo* and stood up. "Get my drift?"

Creed understood all too well. He nodded.

"Good," said Hunter as he stomped out the tobacco's

fire. ''We've got some more riding to do. You coming?''

Again, Creed took the man's words to be a command and not just a mere statement of fact followed by a question. He mounted Nimbus and rode off with Hunter into the night.

16

Hunter's detachment arrived at their camp well after dark and prepared to retire immediately. Hunter invited Creed to share his tent for the night; if he liked, Creed could bed down on the dirt floor, which wasn't much better than doing the same outside except that he would be out of the wind and cool night air. Surprised that an amenity such as a tent was available in this poverty-stricken army, Creed accepted the gracious offer.

The next morning Creed and Hunter were awakened by an orderly who informed them that General Cortina was waiting for them at his breakfast table.

"Cortina?" asked Hunter.

"*Sí, Capitan,*" said the orderly.

Hunter rubbed the sleep from his eyes, then said, "*Bueno.* You tell the general that we will be along shortly."

"*Sí, Capitan!*" The orderly saluted and left them.

"Damn!" swore Hunter.

"Something wrong, John?" asked Creed.

"I don't know yet. We'll have to talk with that son of a bitch Cortina first."

"I take it you don't like Cortina," said Creed.

"No more than I like rattlesnakes," said Hunter. "But he is on our side, so I have to be nice to him. Better hurry

109

and get yourself ready to meet *General* Cortina in person, Mr. Creed.''

Creed finished his morning ablutions in a nearby stream, then rejoined Hunter in the tent. Together, they walked the length of the camp to Cortina's breakfast table, which was under a canvas awning stretched between four cottonwood trees and propped up in the middle by a single pole. Standing at the table were three Mexican officers on one side and Frank Newhouse on the other. Next to Newhouse were two empty chairs, presumably intended for Hunter and Creed. Seated at the head of the table was their host, *el general*, Juan Nepomuceno Cortina, resplendent in his full dress uniform.

In Texas, Cortina was known as ''the Red Robber of the Rio Grande.'' He was a *huero*: a red-haired, red-complexioned man of stocky build with powerful muscles. The expression of his face was sinister, cruel, and sensual. A scion of one of the best border families of Spanish-Mexican days, he was born at his mother's ranch, the San José, along the Rio Grande only a few miles above Brownsville on the American side. His fellow patriots affectionately called him Cheno.

During the War Between the United States and Mexico over the Nueces Strip, the twenty-two-year-old Cortina served in the Mexican army as a spy and a guerrilla and was rewarded for his loyalty by being made a lieutenant. When he was detected in the unlawful act of selling horses belonging to the Mexican government, he was summarily dismissed from the army.

Cortina used his mother's rancho as a haven for his border *bandidos* when he began stealing horses and cattle after the war. He was indicted by a Cameron County, Texas, grand jury for theft and murder, but he eluded capture until the case was dropped.

In the spring of '59, Cortina was again indicted for a

different murder and theft, but this time he openly dared the local authorities—all Texans whose ancestors hailed from Europe by way of the United States—to arrest him, coming and going in Brownsville at will but always with an armed escort. On one such occasion, he saw a deputy sheriff abusing a Mexican that he was leading to jail. Cortina ordered the deputy to desist, and when the lawman refused to do so, Cortina shot him, put the prisoner on his horse behind him, and rode across the river to Matamoras, where he was acclaimed by the local citizens to be the defender of Mexican rights. A short time later Cortina led a raid on Brownsville in which five Americans were murdered. He took possession of Fort Brown, which had been abandoned by the army earlier in the year. Fearing reprisals, he left the fort for Rancho San José and began fortifying it against the day when the army or the Texas Rangers would come for him in force. That day wasn't far off. A combination of U.S. Cavalry and Texas Rangers chased Cortina and his men from American soil and even pursued him into Mexico. Although they failed to capture or kill Cortina, they put him on notice that his presence would no longer be tolerated in Texas.

When the French landed at Vera Cruz, Cortina declared himself to be a Mexican citizen and offered his services to President Juárez. When it became apparent that he would have to face the French without the aid of the United States, Juárez accepted Cortina and made him a general in command of the northeast sector of the country and governor of the Mexican state of Tamaulipas. Cortina took possession of Matamoras almost immediately, and with the town, he took control of the cotton trade then flourishing at the makeshift port of Bagdad. He grew richer every day until the war north of the Rio Bravo came to an end and the French began in earnest to clear Mexico of all elements opposed to the Empire. Late in the summer of '65, he was forced to retreat from Matamoras and seek refuge at Rancho San José, once again a safe house because most of those Texans who had opposed him before were either dead or out of power. He remained at home, licking his wounds, until he heard that his president had been driven from Mexico, crossing the Rio Grande to El Paso. Juárez ordered Cortina to meet him in San Antonio, where they would discuss strategy. Cortina obeyed, and that was the last anyone along the Rio Grande had heard of him—until now.

"Ah, *Capitan* Hunter," said Cortina, smiling gratuitously, "how good of you to join us! And this gentleman is Señor Slate Creed, I am told."

"That's correct, General," said Hunter, addressing Cortina by the title he preferred over his many others.

"*Por favor*, Señor Creed, sit down and have some breakfast," said Cortina cordially, waving a hand at the chair closest to him. "And you also, *Capitan* Hunter," he added, indicating the other empty seat.

"Thank you, General," said Hunter.

Creed stepped up to the chair Cortina had indicated was to be his, pulled it out, and at the same time said, "Thank you, General. I'd be honored." He sat down.

Hunter, Newhouse, and the three Mexican officers followed Creed's lead.

Cortina snapped his fingers, and platters of sliced hot roast beef, fried eggs, and melon wedges; bowls of red and green chili; and corn and wheat flour tortillas were brought to the table by three orderlies. The general and the three Mexican officers bowed their heads, muttered a prayer of thanksgiving, then crossed themselves. The Texans sat mutely, respectfully, until the general invited them to help themselves to the food. As each man filled his plate, Cortina opened the conversation.

"Señor Creed, *Capitan* Newhouse tells me that you and he come from the same county in *Tejas*," said Cortina, calling their state by its Mexican name, which was his way of insulting the Texans and at the same time exerting his authority over them.

"That's correct, General," said Creed as he spooned green chili over two eggs and four slices of beef. "Lavaca County. It's inland two counties from Matagorda Bay."

"Yes, I know it," said Cortina. "The Navidad and Lavaca rivers flow there. I have been there . . . when I was very young and *Tejas* was still a province of Mexico."

"That was before I was born," said Creed. "In fact, that was before my family ever stepped a foot in Texas."

"Then your people are not the ones who stole *Tejas* from my people, Señor Creed?"

"No, General, they weren't."

"But your people came from *los Estados Unidos*?"

"Yes, they did, but before there was a United States of America, my people were Choctaws and Cherokees." He looked Cortina directly in the eye and said, "Redmen, the same as yours, General."

"Redmen, yes," said Cortina as he dipped a tortilla in an egg yolk, "but that is where the similarity ends. Where your people lived in crude huts and hunted their food in the forests, my people were building empires of stone and—" He paused to take a bite of the tortilla.

Cortina was getting a little too snooty for Creed's tastes, and the Texan thought it was time to do something about it. He interjected, "And they were making human sacrifices to their pagan gods."

The Red Robber stopped in the middle of chewing the bread and glared at Creed.

Tension reigned over the other men at the table. They had stayed out of the conversation because they knew Cortina would want it that way. Each of the officers looked at their general with fearful anticipation.

Cortina smiled cruelly and said, "How do you know this?"

"I learned it in school," said Creed.

Cortina nodded and said, "It is true that my people once sacrificed their enemies to their pagan gods, and you might also say that we still do, Señor Creed." He swallowed the tortilla, then held up a finger for emphasis as he said, "But only our enemies. Now instead of cutting out their hearts on the altar, we are more civilized. We simply hang our enemies or stand them up in front of a firing squad. Either way, we rid ourselves of those who would deny us our right to our own land. Of course, since you are a Texan, you would not understand this."

"Oh, but I would, General Cortina," said Creed. "Besides having some ancestors who were Indians, I also have some ancestors who came from Europe, the same as you have. Mine came from Scotland because they were tired of serving their English masters who had taken their land from them."

"But this happened to your ancestors a long time ago," said Cortina, "did it not?"

"Yes, a long time ago."

"Then it is not the same. You Texans only recently took away our lands."

"As I said before, General Cortina, I was not a part of that and neither was anyone in my family. We came to Texas after the Revolution."

"From which part of *los Estados Unidos* did your people come?" asked Cortina.

"The South," said Creed.

"And they brought slaves with them when they came?"

"Yes, they did," said Creed honestly.

"They kept slaves instead of hiring hardworking *Mexicanos* to work in their fields and tend their livestock." Cortina made the statement sound like an accusation.

Creed didn't like it and said so. "General, I did not come here to have my family impugned by you or anyone else."

"Then why did you come here?" demanded Cortina.

Newhouse and Hunter started to answer that question, but Creed beat both of them, replying, "I thought I was to be a guest of two fellow Texans who gallantly broke me out of jail."

"A French jail," said Cortina.

"Yes, a French jail."

"And what were you doing in that French jail, Señor Creed?"

"Colonel Dupin put me there because I wouldn't join his army," said Creed.

"I don't believe you," said Cortina flatly. "I have reason to believe that you were purposely placed in the jail in order to spy on our men who were in there."

"I assure you, General—"

Cortina cut him short, saying, "You can keep your assurances, Señor Creed. My informant in Matamoras has already reported that you agreed to spy for the French in exchange for information concerning a group of Texans who have already joined Dupin's Contre-Guerrillas." Cortina took a bite of beef, then mumbled through his full mouth, "You may consider this to be your last meal, señor."

17

Newhouse and Hunter protested Cortina's treatment of Creed, both men expressing their belief in his innocence; but Cortina would have none of it. Creed was a French spy who would be shot summarily, and that was that.

Creed took Cortina's decree calmly, continuing to eat his meal without haste. His casual attitude disturbed everyone else at the table, especially Cortina.

"Señor Creed, you do not believe that you will be shot within the hour?" asked Cortina.

"Oh, yes, General," said Creed. "I believe that you fully intend to have me shot within the hour."

"I intend to do it, but you think I will not do it?"

"Oh, sure, you'll do it all right, and I'll be dead, and that will be that . . . as you say."

Cortina's brow furrowed with curiosity. "I sense that you think there will be something more after you are dead."

"Don't let it bother you, General. You're only doing what you think is right."

The general laughed out loud and said, "You play games with me, Señor Creed. You think you are the gambler who can bluff me into sparing your life by hinting at some terrible disaster that will befall me if I have you shot. Is that not so?"

Creed smiled and said, "I wouldn't think of doing such a thing, General. You are much too clever a man for me to try to outsmart."

Cortina couldn't accept this statement of denial. He tilted his head and studied Creed as he said, "Yes, I believe you mean that, but there is more to what you say than you are willing to admit. Is that not so?"

"Now that you mention it, General, there is."

"And what is this extra bit of thought you have, señor?"

Creed put down his knife and fork, folded his hands in front of him in a most reverent manner, and said, "General, I'm not an overly religious man, but I do know that the Lord moves in mysterious ways, just like the Bible says."

Bringing God into the conversation further unnerved Cortina. In his mind's eye, he saw his saintly mother kneeling at the altar in the family chapel at Rancho San José as the priest spoke the communion mass. The vision shook him as he recalled the strength of her faith and how she often proved to him that God directed their lives in so many little ways, with such near-invisible discretion that they could not see it happening at the time but would only recognize His hand touching them long after the event. This was the mystery of God, she would say, and Cortina would cringe at the knowledge that there was a power so much greater than he.

Not wishing to show his fear of God, Cortina thought to mock Creed, saying, "So you think the hand of Providence will reach down from the sky and stop the bullets from my soldiers' guns?"

"I didn't say that, General. I was going to say that the Lord has ways of righting all wrongs."

"Wrongs? I do not understand."

"If you shoot me, General, you will be committing a grave error because you will be murdering an innocent man."

"And for this, God will punish me?"

Creed bore his stare into Cortina's cold dark eyes and said, "One way or another, General."

Cortina did not laugh, did not show any emotion. He sat motionless, showing neither fear nor anger, hiding his thoughts as he stared back at Creed, studying him intently, trying to break through Creed's own diamond-hard facade but not succeeding. At last, he leaned back and let a smile creep over his face.

"It will not work, Señor Creed," said Cortina. "I will still have you shot."

Cortina ordered the entire company to assemble to witness the execution that he was making into a spectacle. Against the advice of his officers, he even went so far as to include all sentries, pickets, and scouts, leaving the entire camp literally unguarded. By the time everyone was in place, the sun was almost directly overhead.

Saying it would be too cruel of him to force either Newhouse or Hunter to lead the firing squad that would be executing a fellow Texan, Cortina gave the detail to one of his Mexican officers. Of course, he wasn't all that concerned about the feelings of the *norteamericanos*. Rather, he thought it would be more appropriate—and just—for his own people to do the job of ridding their land of one more foreign son of a bitch. After all, they would enjoy doing it, whereas Newhouse and Hunter would have one more complaint against him with *el presidente*.

As Creed was being led to the place of execution on the banks of the Rio Grande, the Mexicans were taking bets on which way he would fall. The firing squad was in place as he approached the spot, which was something of a natural amphitheater carved out of the earth by the roily river over countless decades. Every man in Cortina's army as well as the men of Hunter's and Newhouse's units was perched on the semicircular slope, eagerly awaiting Creed's final minute.

Creed marched toward the river between two pairs of uniformed Mexicans. He was unfettered. At the very least, he thought, Cortina was giving him a proper military send-off. He didn't want to die; who did? He had a full life ahead of him—or he would have as soon as he could prove his innocence of the crime for which he was convicted and sentenced to hang back in Texas. Even so, he wasn't about to leave this world looking like a coward. His two grand-fathers would never approve of any tears or whining. He would face death as they would want him to: like a brave warrior in both the Scots and Indian ways. He would show his enemy no fear.

Cortina was impressed by Creed's demeanor. He enter-tained thoughts of allowing Creed to speak a few last words but quickly discarded the notion, thinking how Creed was only another Texas bastard. His men would stand Creed near the Rio Bravo del Norte, then he would rise and make a brief speech about justice being done to another enemy of Mexico. At the conclusion of his remarks, the condemned would be shot; his men would give a rousing cheer; and they would all go back to their business of recovering their country from the foreign invaders—first the Europeans and, when Maximilian was gone, then the Americans.

Death with dignity was all right when there was absolutely no hope of surviving, but Creed figured that was all a lot of horse dung as long as he was conscious and capable of thinking and using his body. He had other plans.

As he neared the river's edge, he suddenly stopped, took a single step backward, and slammed his elbows, one each, into the midsections of the two surprised guards behind him, effectively knocking the wind from them. Then he spun around and grabbed a rifle from one of them. Using the Enfield like a staff, he banged the butt into one's head, knocking him unconscious. Then he jabbed the other in his solar plexus with the muzzle, again forcing the wind from the man and doubling him into a position where Creed could use the butt on him as well.

The sudden movement of the condemned man brought a roar from the already excited crowd and also brought those who were sitting to their feet. The noise was the first indication for the two guards in front of Creed that something was amiss behind them. They turned in time to receive from Creed treatment similar to that which he had given their comrades in the rear.

With his escort effectively out of action, Creed dropped to one knee, rifle still in hand, and took quick aim at the officer in charge of killing him. The Mexican already had his sword raised in preparation to giving the order to the firing squad to shoot Creed. He was a little slow. Creed shot first and accurately. The officer stumbled backward a few paces from the bullet's impact to his chest, then fell dead. Creed flung the Enfield at the firing squad, then broke for the river.

18

Watching the scene along the Rio Grande was Colonel Dupin. His scouts had discovered the Mexican encampment, then reported back to him, telling him that there were no pickets in place and that the Juáristas were gathering for some sort of military exercise along the river. Thinking that the Liberals were planning to cross into Texas immediately, Dupin made a quick plan of attack whereby his Contre-Guerrillas would come at the enemy from three different directions: two along the river and his own unit from the low hills behind the Juáristas.

While Dupin waited for the other two companies to arrive at their points of assault, he looked down on the Mexicans through a pair of binoculars. He was astounded at the sight. Here were not only the birds who had flown their cage in Matamoras but also a very much greater prize in the person of *el general* himself, Juan Cortina. Dupin was quite delighted.

Then he saw Creed being led down to the river by four armed men. What was this all about? he wondered. Cortina was having the Texan executed? Yes, of course. But why? He must ask one or the other—if either should live through the forthcoming battle.

Having a taste for the dramatic, Dupin decided to wait

before ordering the attack until Creed was in place to be shot. Then just as the firing squad officer raised his sword, he would give the command for the assault to begin. But much to his surprise—and perverted sense of pleasure— Creed rewrote Dupin's script by making a break for freedom.

"Valor such as this," said Dupin to his aide, "should not go unrewarded. Bugler, sound the charge!"

The soldier did as ordered, and all three Imperialist units began their convergence on the Liberal position.

Hearing the bugle call and recognizing its meaning, Cortina forgot about Creed and ordered his men into action. An orderly brought his horse, and the general mounted up. He drew his sword and called out several commands, the gist of which was that he and his personal bodyguard would retreat across the river and everyone else was to stand and fight.

As much as they despised him, Newhouse and Hunter knew that Cortina was important to the Republican cause. His safety was utmost in their minds as they led their own men in a rearguard action against the attacking Imperialists.

Creed also heard the trumpeting as he splashed into the water but thought it was coming from a Mexican horn. This only hastened his freestyle strokes in the swift, shallow river. Feeling his best chance was to get as far downstream as possible as quickly as possible, he swam with the current, slowly working his way toward the far shore. As he moved downriver, the sounds of hundreds of gunshots broke through the swash of his arms and legs. Several moments passed before he realized that none of the flying bullets were zinging into the water near him. Was he so far away already that the Mexicans couldn't hit him? No, of course not! With all those men shooting at him, at least a few had to come close to the target. But they weren't. Why?

Creed turned on his side to take a look back over his right

shoulder. He couldn't believe his eyes. The Mexicans were running everywhere, some on foot, some on horseback. Why all the confusion? he wondered. Then he saw Dupin's Contre-Guerrillas bearing down on the Juáristas. What great luck! he thought. No one was paying any attention to him. All he had to do was swim across the river to safety. How easy!

Not quite. He had Nimbus to consider. He wouldn't let a Yankee officer keep him when they were captured at Shiloh, so he would be damned if he would allow either a Mexican or a Frenchman to have the stallion now.

Creed swam for the right bank of the Rio Grande.

Although the Contres had scattered the Liberals' remuda, many of the Mexicans had gotten to their horses and mounted up. Even so, the Liberals were being completely routed.

Cortina and his bodyguard had fled across the Rio Grande, and once they were on the American side of the river they rode as fast they could for even safer territory because they feared Dupin would follow them.

Some of the Mexicans had dashed into the river after Cortina in order to escape the onslaught of their attackers, only to be cut down by the sharpshooting Imperialist Legionnaires who could keep a steady bead on a target a hundred yards away although atop a shying horse. Those Liberal soldiers who attempted to escape on their own soil, whether afoot or on horseback, were being ridden down and hacked to death by sabre-wielding Contres.

Only two groups of defenders held their ground: Newhouse's company and Hunter's. But as soon as they saw that Cortina was safely away, Hunter and Newhouse ordered their men to mount up for a counterattack. They would attempt to break through Dupin's line of reserves and ride for the interior with all haste, hoping Dupin would follow them instead of Cortina. Hunter gave the command, and both companies surged forward, firing their *pistolas* and swinging their machetes at the Contres. They fought with all the ferocity of cornered animals because they knew the Contres would give them no quarter. Theirs was truly a case of kill or be killed.

Dupin, having watched Cortina escape his clutches, shifted his attention to Creed. He had spied the American pulling himself out of the water, then followed his every movement as he stealthily worked his way through the combatants toward . . . ? The colonel was unsure of what until he saw Creed pick up a rifle and aim at a Mexican heading for the river on a gray Appaloosa. Creed fired, and the Liberal soldier toppled to the ground. Dupin was pleased— but only for a moment. In the next instant, he saw Creed unhorse a Contre who tried to cut him down with a swipe of his sword. Then when the Frenchman came at Creed on foot, the American clubbed him to death with the rifle. Dupin couldn't help admiring Creed's fighting ability and reasoned that his score was even: a Mexican for a Contre.

Creed called out to Nimbus, and the stallion came to him. Master leaped into the saddle, and the beast sped away downriver, which seemed to be the safest direction to take.

Seeing Creed escaping, Dupin sent two of his chasseurs to intercept the now unarmed American, ordering them to bring Creed back alive.

Most of the battle was over, and what was left of it was behind Creed now. Then he saw two Contres pursuing him. He kicked Nimbus in the ribs and at the same time told the horse that they were in a race for his life. His master's words seemed to inspire Nimbus to greater speed. It availed him naught because in the trail ahead were Dupin's chasseurs.

Creed thought to evade the fancy French soldiers, but when he realized that they had no weapons in their hands, he figured they meant to take him alive. When a bullet from a Contre behind him whizzed past his ear, he decided that surrendering to the chasseurs wasn't all that bad an idea. He reined in Nimbus as soon as he was close enough to Dupin's bodyguards, and they waved off the pursuing Contres, shouting at them in French that Creed was their prisoner.

The chasseurs took charge of Creed and led him to Dupin, who was still watching the fight on the hillock above the Mexican encampment.

Below them Creed saw Hunter and Newhouse leading a counterattack against the Contres. Unlike their flight from the presidio at Matamoras, where the French defenders were fewer and less able, the Liberals struggled to break through the Contres' lines, fighting desperately for every foot of ground that separated them from freedom. In more than a few minutes, Hunter and Newhouse had broken through the French ranks and were escaping north along the river with less than half of their men. Creed was happy that they had made it, but he felt sorry for the Mexicans who failed to get away because the Contres were methodically killing each and every one of the wounded and those who refused to surrender.

Assured that his force had carried the day, Dupin turned his attention to Creed.

"Ah, Mr. Creed," said Dupin. "How nice to see you again."

"I wish I could say the same about you, Colonel," said Creed with a touch of bitterness.

"You are not pleased that my men have rescued you from the grasp of this Mexican bandit?"

"As a matter of fact, I am rather grateful that you and your men came along when you did."

"Then what is it, if I may ask?"

"The last time we saw each other, Colonel, you had me thrown into your jail."

"And you did not like it. Yes, I can see your point. And now you fear that I will return you to that very same jail. Yes?"

"Oh, it's not your jail that bothers me, Colonel."

"Then what is it, may I ask?"

"Let's say it's your medical practices that disturb me just a tad."

Dupin laughed sadistically and said, "Then you have heard of how we take care of this Mexican rabble that opposes the emperor?"

"I've heard a few stories about what you do to prisoners."

"Some of them exaggerated, no doubt," said Dupin. "Quite simply, Mr. Creed, my physicians amputate a leg and an arm or both legs of prisoners, and then we set them free to be cared for by their friends and relatives. If a Mexican is busy raising corn for his family, then he cannot make war against the emperor. And it takes two whole Mexicans to feed and care for one . . . shall we say, handicapped Mexican." He laughed his perverted laugh again, then said, "I cut off the legs of one, and I effectively remove three Mexicans from the rebellion against the emperor. Subtract one and you get three. Quite simple, yes?" He laughed all the more.

"Quite simple, Colonel," said Creed.

"But you do not think that I would do this to you, do you?"

"The thought had crossed my mind."

"Do not concern yourself about losing a limb or two, Mr. Creed. I have other plans for you."

Yeah, I'll bet you do, thought Creed.

19

The few prisoners that the Contres rounded up after the battle were summarily shot on Dupin's order. Considering the other method of dealing with Juáristas that Dupin employed, Creed thought shooting them was an act of humanity—for the French colonel.

On the ride back to Matamoras, Dupin questioned Creed about his presence in the Mexican camp.

"I was a prisoner," said Creed.

"A prisoner?"

"Just the same as I was prisoner in your jail, Colonel."

"But you escaped with the Juáristas I had in my jail. Why did you run away with them if you were not one of them?"

"I met a fellow American in your jail," said Creed. "His name is Newhouse."

"Yes, I know of him. A Texan, like you, yes?"

"Yes, he's a Texan, but he's not like me. I'm not fighting for Juárez, but he is."

"So you say."

"What do I have to do to convince you, Colonel, that I am not a Juárista?"

Dupin didn't answer Creed's question, allowing dead air to fill the gap between them until he finally said, "Go on."

"Go on?"

"With your story of how you came to be in the Mexican camp," said Dupin simply.

Creed shook his head, not sure of what exactly to make of this foreign officer who would rather maim his enemies than kill them. Was he insane? A morbid ghoul? A fiend in military clothing? Or was he merely being pragmatic in dealing with a problem that had no kind solution? It was hard to tell.

"Newhouse convinced me to escape with him and his men," said Creed. "He said I could either stay there in the jail and be shot . . . or worse, or I could go with him. Of course, I chose to escape. Outside of town, we joined up with another American and his Mexican company."

"This would be Captain Hunter, yes?"

Creed stared at Dupin and wondered how he knew so much. And since he did know so much, why was he making him tell him this story? Either this man was smarter than he looked or he had a lot of people in all the right places gathering information for him. Or maybe it was both. Whichever, Creed decided then and there to be on his constant guard in Dupin's presence.

"That's the name he gave me," said Creed.

"Another Texan, yes?"

"Yes, another Texan."

"It seems that there are many Texans down here now," said Dupin. "You, this man Newhouse, and this man Hunter, and of course, this man Kindred that you seek and his men, they are also Texans. Who knows how many more Texans there are here in Mexico these days? You may even know some of them, Mr. Creed."

"What does that mean?" asked Creed.

"Nothing. Please continue with your tale."

"After we met up with Hunter," said Creed slowly as he studied Dupin, hoping the colonel would make some movement or give him some sign that would reveal his inner thoughts, "we rode for some distance and then split up into smaller groups. I stayed with Hunter all the way to their camp. We got in late that night, and this morning we woke up to find out that General Cortina was in camp. He sent an orderly to fetch us to breakfast with him, and at breakfast, he accused me of being a French spy. Of course, I denied it, but he didn't believe me. I think he wanted to shoot me just because I'm a Texan. Cortina hates Texans, you know."

"Yes, I do know," said Dupin. "Your people took his land from him."

"Not my people," said Creed. "My family didn't come to Texas until after the Revolution of '36. We didn't take anyone's land."

"No, but your people came from the United States, did they not?"

"That's right, they did."

"Cortina considers all Americans to be his enemies since they took so much of his country from his people in the recent war between Mexico and the United States."

"Colonel, Juan Cortina was born on the north side of the Rio Grande. He's as much an American as I am."

"Is he really, Mr. Creed?"

Creed thought about Dupin's question for a moment, then said, "No, I guess he isn't. He's a Mexican, and I guess that's what he'll always be."

"Yes," said Dupin, "that is what he will always be because your people . . . you Texans will not let him be anything else."

Creed knew exactly what Dupin was saying, and he knew Dupin was right. As long as Texans remembered the Alamo, Mexicans would be less than equal to them.

"But we are digressing here, Mr. Creed. Please continue your tale."

"There isn't much else to tell, Colonel. Cortina ordered

me to be shot, and he brought in the whole camp to watch. I made a break for it and jumped in the river, and that's when you came along.''

"Yes, I know," said Dupin. "I watched your escape from the firing squad from the top of that hill behind Cortina's camp."

"Then you believe me?" queried Creed.

"A story like that has to be believed, Mr. Creed."

"Then you know that I'm not a Juárista."

"I have known that for some time now. Of course, you are no Juárista. You are not a fool, Mr. Creed."

With this last, Dupin fell silent for the next mile of their trip back to town. Then he ordered the column to halt, dismount, and walk their horses for a while. Once they were afoot Dupin picked up the conversation again.

"Mr. Creed, I have given it some thought, and I have decided that I have been a rude host. Please except my apologies for the way you were treated on your first visit to Matamoras."

In some men, Creed would have thought an apology to be a sign of weakness. But not Dupin. When he apologized, it was for a reason, one that said he had something up his sleeve. Creed wasn't certain that he wanted to find out what it was, but he played along just the same.

"Your apology is noted and accepted, Colonel," said Creed.

"Excellent! Excellent! Then you will honor me by being my guest at the Rancho Abeytia again, yes?"

At the mention of the hacienda on the edge of Matamoras, a vision of Silveria Abeytia flashed into Creed's head. He saw all her loveliness, and more so, he saw her in his arms. He flinched and shook her beautiful face from his mind.

"Yes, I'd be honored," said Creed. "The other available accommodations in Matamoras fail to measure up to Don Bernardo's stable, not to mention his home."

Dupin laughed at Creed's joke and said, "Good! Good! You have not lost your sense of humor. Excellent! Maybe now you will see the advantages of being in my service, yes?" Dupin watched Creed out of the corner of his left eye, waiting for the right answer.

So that's it, thought Creed. The son of a bitch won't give up, will he? Won't take no for an answer. Damn! I hate repeating myself!

"Colonel, you aren't going to start that again, are you?"

"Start what again?" asked Dupin.

"This business about me spying for you," said Creed. "I would think that after today that you would see that it's no longer possible for me to spy for you. So why bother to even ask?"

"I saw you fight today, Mr. Creed," said Dupin. "I saw your courage in the face of death. You have obviously faced such situations before."

"Yes, Colonel," said Creed, "I have been in a tight spot or two in my life."

"During the recent war, yes?"

"Yes," said Creed, lost in thought.

Dupin was so right. Creed had faced several such situations before this one. One in particular—the incident in the Shenandoah Valley—came to mind. He was dressed in civilian clothing while on a scout. He was doing just fine getting through Union lines until a Yankee picket noticed the butt of his Colt's sticking out of his trousers under his coat. The sentry stopped him and called the corporal of the guard, who searched Creed and discovered the revolver was a Confederate weapon. Creed tried to lie his way out of the predicament, but the corporal wasn't buying his story about taking it off a dead Reb. The Federals decided Creed was a Confederate in civilian clothing—which was exactly what he was—and that made him a spy. Spies were to be shot on sight, and the corporal ordered the private to shoot Creed right there and then. To Creed's good fortune, the private was young and hadn't ever killed a man or even shot at one at close range before. He raised his rifle, took aim, then hesitated to pull the trigger, taking his attention off Creed to argue with the corporal about shooting a man in cold blood. Creed saw his opening, ducked, and barreled into the private, knocking him into the corporal and sprawling both of them on the ground. He took the rifle and crushed the corporal's face with the butt, then put the muzzle up to the private's nose and said, "We're fighting a war here, Yank, and there's no place in it for squeamish yellow bellies. I ought to kill you, but I don't think I will. I'm letting you live in the hopes that some day you'll give another man a fighting chance like I'm giving you now." Creed picked up his weapon and vanished in the brush. He often wondered if that Yank ever returned the favor.

"And you fought for the Confederacy, yes?" asked Dupin.

Creed groaned and said, "Maybe so. Maybe not. What difference does it make down here?"

After saying the words, he realized that he had said them before. He was growing weary of these mental games that Dupin—and almost everyone else he'd met in Mexico so far—insisted on playing. Suddenly, all he wanted to do was to go home, back to Texas, and be free again and to hell with these people. This wasn't possible yet, and he knew that, too. He'd come down below the Rio Grande to avenge his brother's death, taking an oath on Dent's grave that he would, and he still had that pledge to fulfill.

"I think maybe so," said Dupin, "and that is why I would like you to join my Contre-Guerrillas, Mr. Creed. You fought for the losing side in one war, and now you have the chance to fight for a winning side. Maybe you do not realize it, but our forces have complete control of the country now. The standard of the emperor flies boldly over every city and village in Mexico. Juárez has forsaken his people by leaving the country, so the emperor has made him an outlaw. All that we have left to do is eliminate these other outlaws who call themselves patriots, and Mexico will finally find the peace and prosperity she has so much desired all these years.''

''That's a pretty speech, Colonel,'' said Creed, ''but I don't think those men you fought today would buy a single word of it. As far as they're concerned, you're an invader of their land and they won't rest until they've driven you into the ocean or laid you in your grave.''

''Or until they are dead, yes?''

''That's the way I see it, Colonel.''

''And I also. We must exterminate this pestilence before peace and prosperity can be bestowed on Mexico.''

''You're talking about killing a lot of men,'' said Creed, ''and frankly, Colonel, I've had enough of that sort of killing.''

''Then you will not join my service, no?''

Creed heaved a frustrated sigh, then said, ''Colonel, what's to prevent me from riding off for good or from joining the Juáristas once I'm away from you and your men? Nothing, right? So why would you even want to trust me to spy for you?''

Dupin smiled and said, ''You have made a very good point, Mr. Creed. Why would I even want to trust you to work for me? Let me answer this way. Do the names Flewellyn, Simons, and Reeves mean anything to you?''

Creed was stunned but tried not to show it.

''You know them, yes?'' queried Dupin, studying Creed's face for any sign that said he did know these names and the men who went by them.

Although he had enough control of his emotions to prevent his facial muscles from making any noticeable involuntary contortions, Creed couldn't control the flow of his blood and thus, couldn't stop his face from blanching.

"Yes, just as I thought," said Dupin smugly. "You know them." He looked closer at Creed. "You know them quite well, too. I have four men in my jail who have these names. I believe they are friends of yours, Mr. Creed, and I also believe that you would not want any harm to come to them." Dupin let that soak in before continuing. "So I will ask you again, Mr. Creed. Will you join my service and fight the Juáristas with me?"

Creed was suspicious. Was Dupin playing another one of his mental games? Maybe he had learned the names of his friends from Kindred and was only bluffing about having them in jail. This was a distinct possibility that he shouldn't let go without challenging.

"How do I know you really have them in your jail, Colonel?" demanded Creed. "I told you about the men I came down here looking for, and you told me that you had them in your service. How do I know you didn't talk to them and find out about my friends back in Texas?"

"Again, you make a very good point, Mr. Creed. Of course, you should not take my word for this. You should see for yourself that I have them in jail." Dupin stopped and told his aide to give the order to mount up, then he climbed into his own saddle with all the grace of a young expert equestrian. "Mount up, Mr. Creed. We will ride directly for Matamoras so you may see for yourself that I have your four friends in my jail."

20

"What in the hell are you boys doing here?" demanded Creed when he saw his four friends in the Matamoras jail. He stood outside and talked with them through the gate. "Haven't you got the sense that God gave a piss ant?" He was angry on the one hand and so very glad to see them on the other. Until this exact moment, he hadn't realized how much he missed Texas and everyone who meant anything to him back home.

"Hey, we were only looking out for you," said Jake Flewellyn in their defense.

"Looking out for me? What in the hell does that mean?"

"It means," said Flewellyn, "that Miss Texada would've come down here herself if we hadn't done it."

This caught Creed off his guard. "Texada? Is something wrong with her?"

"Nothing no one ain't noticed before," said Clark Reeves as he jostled his brother Kent in the ribs with an elbow.

"That'll do, Kent," said Bill Simons as if it were his duty to ride herd on the twins.

"I'm Clark."

"No matter which dumb Reeves son of a bitch you are, that'll do," said Flewellyn firmly. "We got more important

135

catfish to fry here, so shut up and let me tell Clete what's going on.''

Clete. It sounded so good to Creed. It rang of freedom and better days, but it also reminded him that he was a man who had been convicted of a crime that he hadn't committed and for which he was now being hunted.

"Jake, down here I'm known as Creed," he said in a more conspiratorial tone, "so I'd appreciate you calling me that for the time being."

"Creed? What kind of name is that?" asked Flewellyn with his nose slightly turned up as if something malodorous had just then attacked his olfactory.

"It's a good enough name for now," said Creed, not feeling any necessity to explain why he had chosen the moniker. "But never mind all that. Tell me what you boys are doing down here."

"Well, sir," said Flewellyn, suddenly taking on the same tone as Creed but acting a bit uppity as he did, "we came down here to save your ass from Crit and Charlie Golihar and that bunch from Somer's Thicket."

Creed's brow furrowed for a moment, then he realized the implications of Flewellyn's words. "You mean the Golihars and their gang are coming down here after me for killing Champ?"

"That's it exactly," said Flewellyn.

Creed shook his head as a wry smile came over his face, then he said, "I'll be damned. That little son of a bitch tried to kill me first, and besides that, he was with Kindred over in Louisiana when Dent was killed."

"We know all that, Clete, er . . . uh, Mr. Creed," said Flewellyn, "but Crit and Charlie ain't seeing it that way. All they know is you killed their brother—shot him in the back even—and they plan on making you pay for it."

"That figures," said Creed. "Dumb sons of bitches!

Don't they know they got a regular shooting war going on down here and neither side is taking any prisoners right now?'' He stared at Flewellyn and the others and repeated the point. ''Matter of fact, why don't the four of you know that?''

''We do,'' said Flewellyn, ''but if we didn't come down here to warn you, Miss Texada would have. She was that bound and determined to do it.''

''Knowing Texada,'' said Creed, ''I can truly believe that.'' Then, as if he were seeing them for the first time, he looked at the wooden bars that separated them and said, ''But how in the hell did you boys wind up in here?''

''That's simple,'' said Flewellyn. ''Who do you think runs this jail?''

''The French,'' said Creed.

''Maybe they're the top dogs around here,'' said Flewellyn, ''but they got some real mean curs working underneath them in this place.''

''Meaning?''

''Meaning Kindred and his boys are the jailers here.''

''Kindred?''

''That's right.''

Creed looked beyond his friends at the jailyard behind them and asked, ''Are they here now?''

''Nope,'' said Flewellyn. ''They were here this morning, but I guess they changed the guard this evening. Ain't seen hide nor hair of them since sundown.''

Creed turned away and looked at the two chasseurs standing several yards away. Dupin had sent them along to make sure that Creed made it back to the hacienda that night.

''That dirty son of a bitch!'' swore Creed.

''Who's that you're talking about now?'' asked Flewellyn. ''One of them fancy French soldiers over there?''

''No, their commanding officer,'' said Creed, turning

back to his friends. "He's been after me to join his outfit
ever since I got here, and now he's using the four of you
to get me signed on."

"How's that?" asked Simons.

"You boys aren't just prisoners here," said Creed.
"You're hostages. Insurance that I'll fight for the Imperialists and won't betray them."

"Is that a fact?" asked Simons.

"You can take that to market, Bill," said Creed. "His
name is Colonel Dupin, and he's the bloodiest son of a bitch
I've ever met."

"Worse than Bill Anderson or Quantrill?" queried Flewellyn.

"Worse. Dupin doesn't kill his enemies. He cuts off their
arms and legs so their friends and family have to take care
of them and can't make war against the emperor any more."

Instinctively, the four Texans felt the joints of their arms,
and Simons said, "Now we know what all that screaming
was we heard earlier today."

"That's right," said Clark Reeves. "I thought it was
coming from a hospital or something like that."

"It was," said Creed. "Dupin has his doctors cut off a
man's arm and a leg, and they don't give him anything for
the pain before they go to cutting on him."

"I think I'm going to be sick," said Kent Reeves.

"Me, too," said Clark.

The twins turned away and wretched, heaving up what
little there was in their stomachs.

"So you think he's planning on doing that to us?" asked
Flewellyn as calmly as how he would ask for an opinion
on the weather over the cracker barrel at John Kelly's store
back in Hallettsville.

"No, he won't let anything happen to you boys as long
as he wants me to fight for him," said Creed.

"Are you planning to do that, Clete?" asked Simons.

"I told you, Bill, call me Creed." He looked down at the ground and said, "Yes, I suppose I'll have to join his army. With you boys in here, I don't see that there's anything else I can do for now."

"What about Kindred and his bunch?" asked Flewellyn. "We had words with them this morning, but they acted as if they didn't know you were around."

"I haven't been," said Creed. "I was staying out to this hacienda on the edge of town when I first got here, and then Dupin threw me in here because I wouldn't join up with him."

"How'd you get out of here?" asked Simons.

"Broke out with a bunch of Juáristas who didn't want their legs and arms cut off. I rode with them back to their camp, but I got the same sort of treatment there that I got here, only there I was getting it from a Mexican general named Juan Cortina."

"That ain't the Juan Cortina who terrorized Brownsville back before the war, is it?" asked Simons.

"The same man," said Creed.

Flewellyn spit on the ground in disgust, then said, "That filthy greaser has been killing Texans for over twenty years, and now you tell me he's a general."

"He's a general in the Liberal Army of the Republic of Mexico," said Creed, mocking the title.

"The truth is he's still a cattle-thieving, greasy Mexican," said Simons. "Am I right, Clete?"

"Bill, call me Creed, will you?"

"Ain't I right though?" said Simons, ignoring Creed.

"Yes, you're right. That's exactly what he is, only now he's got a whole army to help him do his killing and rustling, which means he's no one to be fooling with."

"He can't be any worse than this Dupin fellow you've

been telling us about,'' said Flewellyn.

"Maybe yes and maybe no," said Creed, "but I'd rather
not come as close again to finding out for sure as I did this
morning. Cortina was going to put me up in front of a firing
squad and would have, too, if I hadn't made a break for it
and if the French hadn't come along when they did."

"Is that how you come to be back here in Matamoras?"
asked Simons. "The French catch you again?"

"That's about it, Bill. But you boys still haven't answered
my question about how you landed in here."

"French caught us almost as soon as we crossed the Rio
Grande at Brownsville," said Flewellyn. "They brought us
straight here last night and locked us up quicker than you
can call the hogs in for evening slops. They didn't give us
no reason. Just said we were trespassing in their country
without permission, and that was that. Some old geezer
asked us a bunch of questions about who we are and what
we're doing down here, and we told him straight that we
were looking for a friend of ours who had come down here
just a few days ahead of us looking for some other fellows
we knew from back home."

"We tried not to give away anything," said Simons.
"You know, like who you are and all. Miss Texada warned
us you'd be traveling under an assumed name, and we were
to be careful about saying how we were looking for you."

"Then you didn't tell Dupin that you knew me?"

"Hell, no, we didn't," said Flewellyn. "Matter of fact,
we haven't even met this Dupin."

"Are you sure?" asked Creed. "Tall man, leathery looking, white hair?"

"That's the old geezer who questioned us," said Flewellyn. "You mean to tell me he's a colonel in Maximilian's
army? Old as he is?"

"Don't let the old bastard's age fool you, boys," said

Creed. "He can ride as hard as any one of us. Maybe two. He's one tough old buzzard."

"If you say so," said Simons.

"I know so," said Creed. "I rode back here today with him. He never even broke a sweat, and we rode all afternoon and evening to get back here. And that was after he rode most of the night and the morning tracking us down." Creed scratched his head as it suddenly struck him that something didn't add up here. "Wait a minute, Jake. When did you say you talked with Dupin?"

"I didn't," said Flewellyn, "but it was last night."

"How late last night?"

"Must have been an hour or two after sundown. Why?"

"Why? Because we broke out of here yesterday around noon, and we rode all the rest of the day and most of the night before we reached Cortina's camp. We must have ridden sixty or seventy hard miles before we got there. I know we were doing a lot of track covering and doubling back and all, but even so, that camp has to be a good thirty-five straight miles from here. I know because that's how much ground we covered riding back here this afternoon and evening, and it took us nearly nine hours to do it. How could Dupin track us all night and morning and cover all the ground we did getting away from here yesterday? I mean, how could he track us in the dark that fast?"

"He couldn't have," said Flewellyn.

"That's what I'm thinking, too, Jake," said Creed.

"But what's all this got to do with us?" asked Simons.

"It might have everything," said Creed. "Or it might have nothing. I don't know yet, but I do know this, boys. Dupin wants me in his army real bad. I don't know why, but I'm sure as hell going to find out why. And until I do, you boys will just have to sit tight."

"You won't leave us in here too long, will you, Clete?" asked Simons.

"Bill, my name is Creed now. Slate Creed. Will you get it right? Just once?"

"If you say so, Creed," said Simons. "But you ain't going to leave us in here too long, are you?"

"I'll get you out of here just as fast as I can, Bill. Even if it's the last thing I ever do."

21

Dupin's chasseurs escorted Creed back to Rancho Abeytia, where the Texan found the French colonel waiting for him in Don Bernardo's library.

"Ah, Mr. Creed," said Dupin as if he were seeing Creed for the first time in several days, "how were your friends? In good health and good spirits, I trust."

"Good health, yes," said Creed, seething with anger, "but not in good spirits. Why in hell did you make Kindred and his men their jailers? Don't you know Kindred can't be trusted?"

"Mr. Kindred obeys my orders," said Dupin flatly, "like every other soldier in my regiment. If he does not obey, he faces punishment, and in my regiment, that can be most severe. In his case . . . death. Mr. Kindred and his men have been warned that if any harm should come to your friends, they will be placed before a firing squad and summarily executed." Dupin paused to smile wryly. "That is, of course, as long as you cooperate with me."

"That's what I thought," said Creed. "My friends are your hostages."

"Precisely, Mr. Creed."

Creed shook his head slowly and said, "Colonel, I don't want any part of your war down here, and from what I saw today, you don't need me to help you defeat the Juáristas.''

"Ah, there you are mistaken," said Dupin, raising a forefinger to accentuate his point. "I do need you. I need you because you are a Texan."

"Because I'm a Texan?"

"Yes, because you are a Texan. You can move among the Juáristas much easier than any of my other operatives could because they were not Texans. Also, you have gained the trust of your fellow Texans: Captains Newhouse and Hunter. The proof of that lies in the fact that they took you to their camp, which means they must have confided in you.''

"Not quite, Colonel. They took me to Cortina's camp, and they didn't tell me a thing about what their plans are.''

"Mr. Creed, I will forgive your ignorance of these matters and explain things to you. Captains Newhouse and Hunter have only recently come into this part of Mexico with their companies. Captain Hunter was in Matamoras before the town was secured for His Imperial Majesty, but he left to join Juárez in Monterrey. Since that time, he has been fighting in the vicinity of El Paso in rearguard actions. Captain Newhouse is a deserter from the late Confederate Army who was given command of a company by General Escobedo, who also had been fighting in the El Paso area until Juárez was driven from the country. Shortly after our victory at El Paso, Newhouse and Hunter brought their companies into this sector. There were a few skirmishes but no battles until two days before your arrival here, when my men captured Newhouse and his company during the attack on Bagdad. I would have executed them, but as you know already, they escaped. And when they did, they took you with them to *their* camp, not Cortina's camp.''

Dupin's rather extensive knowledge of Newhouse and Hunter bothered Creed. How did he know so much about them?

"All right, it wasn't Cortina's camp," said Creed. "I

don't see the big difference.''

"The difference lies in the fact that Hunter and Newhouse trust you.''

"Or they did until you attacked them.''

"They will still trust you, Mr. Creed, because you are a Texan as they are. They will accept your explanation of how you came to be captured and how you escaped again.''

"They might, but Cortina won't,'' said Creed. "They're only captains, and Cortina is a general, and he thinks I work for you already and wants to shoot me.''

"Mr. Creed, I have studied you quite closely, and I am of the opinion that you are quite intelligent and very clever. You will find a way to endear yourself to Cortina, and he will no longer want to kill you.''

"I don't think you know too much about General Juan Cortina,'' said Creed. "He hates Texans because we stole his land from him.''

"Stole his land?''

"We took Texas away from Mexico.''

"Oh, yes. I see. But you Texans hate Mexicans for what they did during your war for independence, do you not?''

"Texans who were in Texas then hate Mexicans for what they did at the Alamo and at Goliad. Most of us who came to Texas after the war have no complaint against them. I know my family certainly has none.''

"And I would suppose that the families of Newhouse and Hunter also harbor no ill will toward Mexicans or they would not be fighting alongside them against the emperor.''

"You could say that,'' said Creed.

"All the more reason for you to be able to endear yourself to Cortina.''

"Colonel, you're missing the point here,'' said Creed. "I don't have anything against Mexicans, but Cortina hates Texans. All Texans. Not just the ones who gave Santa Anna the boot. He hates every Texan who lives in the Nueces Strip because he considers that to be part of Mexico. To this day, he thinks that way. As far he's concerned, every Texan living in the Nueces Strip is fair game for his *bandidos*. They can kill any Texan found in the Strip, and they can steal any horse or cow belonging to a Texan living in the Strip, and they can do this with Cortina's blessing and his protection.''

''I see,'' said Dupin. ''But I do not see how he can cross the Rio Bravo and seek sanctuary in Texas whenever he chooses. Does not your government wish to stop his depredations in Texas?''

''The Federals run things in Texas now,'' said Creed, ''and they're on Juárez's side in this fight. They aren't going to stop Cortina for you or make him stay on this side of the Rio Grande. If anything, they're probably helping him, supplying him with guns and ammunition and money.''

''Which is precisely the reason I need you for this covert operation, Mr. Creed. If I can prove the Americans are doing this, then the emperor can call their action an act of war and declare the United States to be an aggressor. This will cause many European nations to come to the aid of Mexico with either their armies or their diplomats or both, if necessary. Whichever way, the United States will be forced to withdraw its support for Juárez, and the Liberal cause will become a paragraph in the history books of Mexico.''

''I don't care much about that one way or the other,'' said Creed. ''You're still asking me to spy for you, and I'm telling you again that I won't spy for you. That's not the way we do things in Texas.''

''And how are things done in Texas?'' asked Dupin dryly.

''Most Texans shoot first and ask questions later,'' said Creed in a mild attempt to put a little jocularity into the conversation. Then looking much more serious, he added, ''But more so, we don't believe in an eye for an eye and a tooth for a tooth. We believe in a head for an eye and an arm for a tooth. For every Texan Cortina's *bandidos* kill, Texans usually kill twenty-five Mexicans, whether they were responsible for killing that Texan or not. It's the same with Indians."

"And with cattle rustlers, Mr. Creed?"

Creed's focus narrowed as he said slowly, "And with murdering cattle rustlers, too."

Dupin studied Creed for a moment, then said with equal slowness, "My offer still stands, Mr. Creed. Work for me, and I will give you Mr. Kindred and his men."

"And if I refuse again," said Creed, "you will kill my friends and me."

"Not all at once," said Dupin with an evil grin that twisted his face eerily.

"Look, Colonel, I can't spy for you. That won't work for two reasons. First, Cortina already suspects me of being a spy, and second, because I won't be a Judas."

"Then—"

Creed held up his hand to stop Dupin from speaking and said, "Let me finish, Colonel. I won't spy for you, but I will scout for you. On either side of the Rio Grande. You want Cortina, and quite frankly, I'd like to give the son of a bitch to you on a silver platter."

Dupin took his lower lip between two fingers and worked it nervously as he mulled over Creed's counteroffer. At last, he released the flap of flesh and said, "Yes, now I see your point. All right, Mr. Creed, I welcome you into my service as a scout. But let me warn you that I will deal very harshly with you and your friends if I detect one bit of treachery on your part."

The clarity of Creed's eyes faded to the cold, dull hue of death as he said, "And let me warn you, Colonel, that if any harm comes to my friends, whether it's by your order or not, those four fancy soldiers of yours won't—" He cut himself short, then added, "Let's just say you'd better keep in mind what I said about how things are done in Texas."

22

After spending a restless night tumbling with his conscience, Creed was up with the cocks and walking in the garden at Rancho Abeytia. The faintest pale glow of dawn delineated the eastern horizon, making him appear to be but a silhouette in the early glimmer. He continued his mental wrestling as he wandered along the wide sandy path that wound between gaily colored arrays of flowers and deep green shrubs. He was so absorbed in thought that he failed to notice Silveria Abeytia sitting on the garden wall bench seat.

Silveria had been watching Creed from the first moment that he entered the garden. As he meandered about, she neither spoke to him nor made any movements that would reveal her presence. Then he was directly in front of her.

"Good morning, Señor Creed," she said. This was a gross impropriety on her part; no single young lady of Spanish heritage spoke to a man without the presence of an older woman, such as an aunt or a governess.

Of course, Creed wasn't all that well informed on Spanish customs, so he saw nothing wrong with the greeting other than that it startled him and stopped him only inches from her. "Señorita Abeytia," he said awkwardly, "you're up early, aren't you?"

"I could say the same of you, Señor Creed." She smiled

ever so slightly, her teeth so white that they seemed luminescent in the dim light. Faint shadows recast her natural loveliness with a provocative veneer that gave her the aspect of a woman of desire. The scent of jasmine permeated the air, mingling with Silveria's body fragrance, concocting a perfume that stirred the heart as well as the loins.

Creed was defenseless against this sensual assault; a crimson tide washed over his face as he lost control of his emotions for the moment. Here he was again with this beautiful young woman in a romantic setting, and his first thoughts were of taking her into his arms and kissing her with all the seething passion he kept cached deep within his being. Feeling the blush in his skin embarrassed him and increased the disorder within him; he looked away from Silveria toward the distant river.

"Well, I guess you could," he stammered, trying to regain full control of his feelings, "but back home, I was always up early. Chores to do before breakfast and all."

"Chores?" she queried.

"Work around the ranch," he explained.

"Oh, yes, of course."

"Even before the war, when we still had slaves, I had to get up early. My grandfather insisted on it. He warned us that the day would come when slavery would be abolished, and he said we should be prepared to do our own work then. That's why he made us— Us, meaning my brother and me. That's why he made us take care of our own horses and the cattle on our place. He said that was where our future lay. In horses and cattle. Not cotton. Not in our part of Texas. Horses and cattle would be the way we would earn our money." Creed peered wistfully in the distance and added, "He was so right." More relaxed and under control now, he looked down at Silveria and said, "I see your father grows cotton as well as corn and hay. Does he ship much of it?"

"We have only two small fields of cotton," she said as if she were Don Bernardo's partner instead of his daughter. "Our workers take it to their wives, and they make their clothes from it. We do not sell any of it outside of this area."

"That's wise," said Creed. "My grandfather always said it was smart not to be too dependent on cotton for a living. He said he'd seen too many men ruined because of it. Of course, he also said he'd seen quite a few men grow rich off cotton. I suppose he meant growing cotton could be a kind of two-edged sword or something."

Silveria studied him for a second before saying, "Yes, a two-edged sword." Then almost as an afterthought, she added, "You speak of cotton this way, but I think you have other matters pressing on your mind this morning that make you think of a two-edged sword more than cotton."

Creed looked directly into her almond eyes and saw not morbid curiosity but warmth and understanding. She had recognized how troubled he was, and he was actually glad of it because he could see that she was willing to share his burden, if need be. In but a few rapid heartbeats, he debated within himself whether he could trust this seemingly innocent Mexican girl, and equally as fast, he made his decision.

"I think you're right," he said. "And I think you already know what's bothering me."

Silveria didn't look away, instead pinpointing the most vulnerable spot of his soul with a hard stare as she said with all honesty, "Yes, I do. It is this business with Colonel Dupin that worries you so this morning."

Creed heaved a mental sigh of relief and said, "Yes, it is. He has me trapped, and I can't figure any way out of it."

"Trapped?"

"Miss Silveria—"

"*Por favor*, Señor Creed," she said, halting him before he could start, "you must not be so formal with me, not when we are alone. Please, address me only as Silveria."

"I will if you'll drop this señor business."

Silveria reached out and took his hand. "I will call you Creed," she said, tugging gently on him, "because it seems to fit you." Then she tilted her head and added, "But I do not know why." She pulled stronger on him and said in almost a maternal way, "Please sit beside me and tell me how Colonel Dupin has you trapped."

Creed hesitated to move—but only for a second. Then he let instinct take command of him. His fingers surrounded Silveria's, and he sat down beside her, still holding her hand. Her touch comforted him in one sense and sparked a lusty hunger in another. The turmoil within him bubbled and boiled all the faster as he couldn't decide which he wanted more: to kneel at her feet and worship her or sweep her into his arms and ravish her. For the moment, he would choose neither as he forbade his eyes the pleasure of gazing at her loveliness and stared off at the horizon.

"You must know that he has some friends of mine locked up in his jail in town," said Creed matter-of-factly.

"Yes, I have heard this."

He released her hand, leaned forward placing his elbows on his knees, then looked sideways at Silveria and said, "Well, he's holding them as hostages so I'll work for him. I don't want to work for him . . . or anyone down here. I don't want any part of this war you folks are fighting. All I want is the men who killed my brother."

"The men who killed your brother?" queried Silveria.

"Yes. That's why I came down here in the first place. Some of the men who killed my brother came here to hide from me, and I came looking for them."

"To kill them?"

Creed looked away from her and said coldly, "Yes."

"And you found them?"

"Yes. In Dupin's army. He said they were away when I first got here, but now they're the guards at the jail. Dupin says he has ordered them not to harm my friends as long as I do as I'm told. We made a deal that I would scout for him and find the Juárista camp of General Cortina, and once I've done that Dupin said he would release my friends and turn over the men I came here to kill. When I first came here, I didn't want to get involved in this war, but I've been sucked into it anyway. I don't really want to scout for Dupin because a man who befriended me and saved my life is on the other side.''

"And you feel you would be betraying him if you scouted for Colonel Dupin?''

"That's about the size of it.''

"So you are torn between loyalty to your friends in the jail and your honor to repay this man who saved your life,'' said Silveria, summing up his feelings for him.

"Yes, I suppose you could put it that way.'' Then he thought for a moment before saying, ''Yes, that's exactly what it is. In order to save my friends, I have to betray the man who saved my life. I'm not sure I can do that, but I almost have to. I can't see any other way out of it. Not now anyway.''

Silveria squeezed his hand and said, ''You are a strong man, Creed, and strong men find solutions to their problems. You will find a way. Of this, I am certain.''

Their eyes met, and suddenly, the rest of the universe vanished. Nothing existed except the two of them, so nothing else mattered. Their lips joined them as one, and their tongues touched, kindling the smoldering passion that each kept suppressed deep inside. They embraced, pulling at each other as if he desired to become a part of her and she a part of him, forever entwined in body and soul.

Creed felt the fire in his loins, welcomed it, encouraged it by sending his hands exploring over Silveria's back, one of them caressing down to her waist over her hip and onto her thigh.

The same burning lust began to consume Silveria. She

returned his touch with the fingers of one hand kneading the nape of his neck while the other dug their nails into his back and shoulder. When she felt his hand on her thigh, she took it in hers and pulled it to her bosom, forcing its palm against her hardening breast. Then she wrenched her mouth from his, kissing his cheek along an invisible line until her lips reached his ear. She nipped the lobe, then whispered hoarsely, breathlessly, "Creed, we must not do this. Not here. Not now." She heard herself speak and hated the reason of her plea, her heart and body knowing the mind that forced the syllables to come forth was right, was only being logical and sensible; this was neither the time nor the place for young lovers.

The sound of her voice jerked Creed back to the reality of the moment and the situation. She was right, and he knew it. More than the fact that they were in the wrong place at the wrong time was one more item in Creed's conscience: As beautiful and desirable as Silveria was, she was the wrong woman. In the few seconds of their embrace, he had imagined he was holding Texada, had wanted Silveria to be Texada; but the accent of Silveria's words said she wasn't the girl he had left back in Texas. Guilt mocked him for straying, and he felt shame for having succumbed to the weakness, if only for such a short time. He disengaged himself from her and said resolutely, "Yes, this is wrong."

He could have slapped her face and called her a whore and gotten the same result as he did achieve. Silveria was hurt; the pain glistened in her eyes. Wrong? she heard herself scream inside her head. How can this be wrong? I love you, and I know you love me. This is not wrong! This is love!

Although the words formed in her brain, they never escaped her lips. Instead, Silveria also withdrew from him and took on the appearance of suffering from contrition, her hands folded primly on her lap, her head bowed. She would play the role of the sinful, wayward woman who only wished to be loved and would give up her virtue to satisfy that exigent craving. She would play the role—but only for the moment.

The sun peeked over the eastern skyline as Creed stood and moved a few feet away from Silveria. He turned and looked back at her. More guilt attacked him. He had almost led this innocent girl to sin, or so his conscience, branded by the unbending teachings of an unforgiving religious upbringing, wished him to believe. Logic said different. It said there had been no seduction, no coercion, no cajoling or coaxing on either one's part. It said that they had been two people drawn to each other, both physically and emotionally, and that they had allowed their desire to make the connection of their mutual attraction. Nothing more, nothing less. Who would be hurt by their actions? Certainly not Silveria and not he. But what about Texada? No, she wouldn't be hurt because she would probably never find out. Probably never. Only Silveria and he would ever know. He was almost sure of that. Yes, almost sure, and therein lay the reason for him not to make love with Silveria. There would always be that possibility, no matter how thin, that Texada would some day learn about his tryst with Silveria and would be hurt by it. Therefore, he refused to take any such risk of hurting her, no matter how minute the chance.

"I better be leaving now," he said.

Silveria said nothing, didn't even look up at him.

Creed mistook her silence for repentance and said nothing more. He nodded, then turned and departed.

A rising anger within Silveria had hypnotized her into a temporary catatonia with the monotonous repetition of his words, "Yes, this is wrong." The tattoo of Creed's boot heels on the walkway broke the spell. Slowly, she allowed her eyes to wander after him, finding him before he entered the house, and in that instant, the seed of hate was sown.

23

As he rode out of Tres Palmes that autumn morning, Creed noted that the number of Imperialist troops in Matamoras had increased substantially over the last few days. However, he thought little of this fact until he had ridden a mile into the countryside, where he passed a column of soldiers marching toward the border community. Riding at the head of these reinforcements was a Mexican officer who sat his white horse with all the pride of a European field marshal. From the size of the epaulets on the shoulders of his uniform, Creed supposed him to be a general. That was curious. Someone who outranked Colonel Dupin. And a Mexican at that.

Some major strategy was in the works, surmised Creed, and he wondered what his part in it would be. The possibilities seemed endless, and he considered as many of them as he could while riding toward the last place he had seen any Juáristas: the camp along the Rio Grande. It was as good a place as any to start looking for the Liberal general and his ragtag army of peones and border ruffians.

Several hours later, at the river's edge, Creed attempted to recollect the events of the day Cortina ordered his execution. He recalled his flight for freedom, swimming with the current, then looking back to see the battle; but no images

of Cortina escaping appeared in his mind's eye. He quickly
deduced that the Red Robber had fled across the river,
probably to his mother's Rancho San José. With this thought
in mind, he urged Nimbus into the water and returned to
his native soil.

The Texas side of the Rio Grande was much the same as
the Mexico side: flat, lots of grass and shrubs, chaparral,
and tall palms and cottonwoods, but not much in the way
of civilization. Good country for hiding.

Creed had no idea where Rancho San José was located,
but on the north bank he came across the tracks of several
horses headed northeast. He guessed that this was Cortina's
trail because he recalled how Hunter and Newhouse had led
their men into the interior of Mexico to escape Dupin's
soldiers. He squeezed his legs against Nimbus, and the
stallion moved off at a walk along the trail.

A mile into Cameron County the trail turned eastward,
and a mile more it twisted due south and ran that direction
for several hundred yards to a thicket of scrub oaks. At this
point, it split; most of the horses of the original trace heading
eastward again, while three sets of tracks continued south-
ward.

Creed thought this curious and wondered which he should
follow. He opted for the larger contingent, although he had
a hunch that the smaller group would prove to be more
interesting.

Shortly before nightfall, Creed saw several columns of
smoke rising straight up against the deep blue eastern sky.
A large camp of some sort, he thought. A mile, maybe a
mile and a half ahead. Cortina's? Not likely. Too many
fires for that few men. Federals? Probably. He'd seen
enough of them when he was riding south a few weeks
earlier. But maybe they weren't Federals. The fact that the
trail he was following led directly toward the smoke said
bluntly that the Mexicans had gone that way, and possibly

they had met up with another band of Cortina's so-called soldiers. Better proceed with caution either way, especially with so much open ground to be covered before he could get close enough to ascertain positively who they were.

Creed guided Nimbus through the brush as silently as he could until he was as close as he dared go on horseback. He dismounted and tied the Appaloosa to a thorny bush, then moved nearer to the camp on foot. He had only crept a few feet when he saw something of a familiar sight: a blue-coated Union cavalryman standing picket duty. The only difference this time was that the man in uniform was of African ancestry. Creed had fought Negro infrantrymen during the war but never any mounted blacks. As foot soldiers, they had been among the best he'd ever faced. He wondered how good they would be as cavalry. Probably just as good as they had been as infantry, he figured, if not better, especially those former slaves who had worked with horses and knew them better than most other men.

Finished with that chain of thought, Creed turned his attention to the camp itself. Beyond the sentry, he saw the peaks of several tents rising above the scrub oak. He didn't bother to count how many they were, noting only that they had to house at least two companies, maybe three. Either way, that was a lot of soldiers to be bivouacked this close to Mexico. So what were they doing here? He just had to find out.

Creed crawled past the guard in the dusky light and was able to get within a few feet of a row of tents. At this proximity, he could hear men talking in the camp. Most of them were speaking geechie, the lingo of slaves, and some were conversing in eastern American English. Creed also heard strains of Spanish- and Mexican-accented English, and this piqued his interest. What were Mexicans doing in an American army camp? He had to learn this, too.

Night was now in full, and Creed used it to his advantage,

creeping unobserved around the perimeter of the camp in order to get the lay of everything.

The tents of the enlisted men were pitched in two rows, each facing a sort of street, while the officers' tents stood at the head of the lane. At the opposite end were an ambulance and several heavily guarded covered supply wagons. Too many supply wagons for a unit of this size, with too many men guarding them. Hm-m. Beyond these, the Mexicans had made camp in the open. Creed recognized them as Cortina's men, but the general was nowhere in sight.

Cortina wasn't so much on Creed's mind right now as were those supply wagons. Why so many? Did this unit expect to be in the field for a very long time? If so, what enemy would they expect to encounter? Indians? Not here. Border bandits? All those Mexicans in camp dispelled that notion. Imperial Mexican troops or French Foreign Legionnaires? Quite possibly.

Yes, that had to be it! That would explain the increase of Imperial troops in Matamoras. The French expected to be attacked by the American army.

No, that couldn't be. Those Yankees weren't too bright, but they weren't that stupid either. They'd never attack Maximilian's men. That would bring half of Europe down on them; maybe all of it. No, an American army wasn't about to attack Matamoras.

Someone was. But who?

A new thought struck Creed. Cortina had been camped just a few miles from here. Why? To rendezvous with this American unit? Possibly. But why? He looked at the wagons a little closer and noticed that many of them sat heavily, their wheels buried a few inches into the soil. What were they carrying that was so weighty?

Creed crept in among the wagons without being detected by the guards. He carefully lifted a canvas cover on one wagon and saw that the wagon was loaded down with boxes of Enfield rifles, estimating them to be twenty in number. Another wagon was loaded with kegs of black powder, and a third contained kegs of lead balls, boxes of firing caps, bags of wadding, and a few cases of Colt's .44-caliber pistols.

This was too much extra firepower for a cavalry unit of this size. So why did they have it all? To sell to Cortina? Possibly but not likely. The Red Robber didn't have that kind of money at his disposal. Was the army planning to trade the weapons and ammunition to him? What did Cortina have to exchange? Stolen cattle and horses? There were none in sight, so what was left? His word that he wouldn't raid any more ranches on the Texas side of the Rio Grande? No one who knew anything about Cortina would take his word on that. So maybe the Federals were simply giving the weapons and ammunition to Cortina. This was the most likely answer. The Americans couldn't fight Imperial Mexico, but they could supply the Liberal army of Benito Juárez and let it fight for them.

Creed's thoughts were suddenly in a turmoil. He was delighted that the Mexicans were getting help with their war against the Imperialists, but he was concerned that the arms were going to Cortina, who would probably use them on Texans after he was finished with the French Foreign Legion in Matamoras. And that was another problem. What of his friends in Dupin's jail? What might happen to them if Cortina attacked the town in force? Would Dupin let them go? Not likely. More probably, he would execute them. And what if they survived? What would Cortina do with them? Execute them, no doubt. To further confuse him, Creed was obligated to report this discovery to Dupin in order to save his friends. He would just as soon see the Mexicans attack Matamoras and drive the French into the sea. What to do? He would decide that later. Now he had to get out of the

Federal camp and back to his horse without being caught.

Retreat was only a matter of retracing his steps—or so Creed thought. It was the supper hour in camp and time to relieve the sentries so they could eat. This meant Creed had to slip past twice as many guards or wait until they had finished exchanging places. He decided to sit tight for the moment, but then he noticed that not all the guards were going to eat at the same time. This meant another delay, and the night seemed to be getting darker by the minute. He chose to risk discovery and continued to follow the same route that he had used to get into the camp.

Just as Creed feared, a big sentry blocked his path. The man had his back to Creed and appeared oblivious to any possible danger. Creed considered what he should do now. Sneak up on the man and cut his throat? He had done this a few times during the war when it was a matter of his life and the lives of his friends and compatriots as opposed to the life of one Yankee he didn't know or care about. But this wasn't the war in his own country, and to kill this soldier would be murder instead of a minor increase in the casualty list. No, cutting the man's throat was out. Knock him unconscious with a rock or the butt of his Colt's? Maybe. Creed had seen men whose skulls had been crushed by a well-aimed rock or pistol grip, and he had seen some that took the blow and turned and killed their assailants. He might accidentally kill the sentry or he might only give him a headache and the guard would turn and do him in. What was left? Jump him and tie him up? With what? Damn! What else? Not much. Just keep sneaking along, he guessed.

Thwack! A twig snapped under Creed's foot. Dammit to hell!

"Who goes there?" demanded the guard as he turned and aimed his rifle in the direction of the sound. He took two quick steps closer to Creed and repeated the question. "Who goes there?" He thumbed back the hammer of the Springfield.

Creed had run out of alternatives. He crouched a little
lower, then sprung at the man, who was only fifteen or so
feet away now. He kept as low as he could in order to avoid
a bullet, knowing that the soldier would fire his piece at
chest level. Two quick steps and more twigs broke, making
what Creed thought was a hell of a racket.

Bang! And the soldier's rifle belched a lead ball and a
tongue of flame in Creed's direction but above his head.
The fire cast a thunderbolt flash of light over Creed and the
guard, but neither man had the time to really discern the
other.

In the next heartbeat, Creed was beneath the barrel of the
gun, driving his shoulder into the sentry's rock-hard mid-
section.

"Oof!" the guard grunted as he took the full force of the
blow. He was more stunned and scared than he was hurt.
Only part of his wind escaped his lungs as he was driven
backward. He dropped the rifle, then went down on his butt
with Creed still holding on to him. He rolled instinctively
to one side, taking his attacker with him. They struggled to
get the upper hand on each other, but only the guard succeeded. He grabbed Creed by the right wrist and pinned it
to the ground, while his right hand made a fist and prepared
to smash Creed's face.

The other guards heard the explosion of the Springfield
and came on the run, shouting and demanding to know what
was wrong. The whole camp was now alerted, and everyone
steeled for action.

Creed looked up into a deep chocolate face and saw two
hundred years of hate. It frightened the hell out of him.

The guard looked down at Creed and saw a white man.
Although he had killed other white men during the war, he
had never fought one hand-to-hand. He hesitated to strike
the blow as his whole life experience of fearing white folks
stayed his hand. He reconsidered hitting Creed, then decided

against it when he realized that he was bigger and stronger and could hold him there until help arrived. The guard pinned Creed's other hand to the ground, then waited.

Creed didn't wish to wait. He continued the struggle as best as he could, but it wasn't good enough to remove the bigger man from atop him. He finally heaved a sigh and resigned himself to his fate. He was captured. Again.

"Bailey!" shouted another sentry who was coming near.

"Over here!" said the man on Creed.

"You all right, Bailey?"

"Caught me a . . ." His voice trailed off as he peered down at Creed rather quizzically. Then he laughed and said, "Hell, I don't know what I done caught here."

Bailey and Creed were suddenly surrounded by more soldiers, each pointing a weapon at Creed.

"You can get up now, Bailey," said a white officer who joined the circle of men.

"Yes, sir," drawled Bailey. He relaxed his grip on Creed's arms, moved aside, then stood up to his full height of six feet four inches. From Creed's vantage point, Bailey looked like a mountain.

"On your feet, mister," said the officer.

Creed lay still for a moment, scanning the area. He was trapped; no way out. Better to follow orders. He rolled onto his hands and knees, picked up his hat, then stood up.

"All right," said the officer. "Who are you and what are you doing here?"

Before Creed could reply, more men arrived on the scene. They were mostly officers, but a few were Mexicans come to see what the ruckus was all about. Creed knew one of the latter in particular.

"I know this man," said the Mexican.

Creed squinted at the man and recognized him as Miguel, the bandit that had awakened him rather rudely that first morning below the Rio Grande.

"You do?" asked the officer.

"*Sí, Capitan* Becker," said Miguel. "His name is Creed. He is an enemy of the Republic of Mexico. General Cortina ordered him to be shot, but his French *amigos* saved him from the firing squad."

That wasn't quite the truth, and Miguel knew it, but he hated Creed for the one simple reason that Creed had bested him on the first occasion of their meeting. Miguel's machismo had been seriously injured that morning, and now he gloated inside because the opportunity to regain his *virilidad* over this *norteamericano* had finally come.

"So this is the man?" queried Becker.

"*Sí, Capitan.*"

Becker smiled and said, "Well, we'll just have to turn him over to you then, won't we?"

Miguel grinned like the Cheshire cat who was about to devour an unsuspecting mouse and said, "*Muy bueno, Capitan.*"

24

Two things made Creed grateful that night: he had been captured on American soil by Americans, and no one in the camp recognized him as Clete Slater, escapee from a Federal noose. If Miguel and his bunch had caught him, he would have been a dead man before morning; and if anyone had realized that he was a fugitive of so-called military justice, then Captain Becker wouldn't have held him for Cortina but would have shipped him north to be hung. Even with so much to be thankful for, Creed didn't sleep all that well that night.

The next morning the camp was all astir with anticipation. Someone important was due any minute.

Creed observed all the hubbub from the base of a palm tree to which he had been chained hand and foot the night before, to be kept there under guard by Becker's orders. He asked the soldiers guarding him who was coming, but they either didn't know anything or simply refused to tell him. He couldn't be sure of which, but by midmorning it made no difference.

Riding up the lane between the two rows of enlisted men's tents and coming from the Mexican encampment toward the officers' quarters was none other than Juan Nepomuceno Cortina. He was attired in the full uniform of a Mexican general. Flanking him on each side were two lesser officers who were also dressed in complete uniform. The trio made quite an impressive show, but when only a handful of soldiers turned out to salute them, Creed got the notion that Cortina and his aides weren't the reason for all the hustle and bustle in camp.

Becker greeted Cortina with much of the courtesy a junior military officer would normally extend to a senior but not quite as much as he would have given an American general. He saluted the Mexican general when he dismounted his horse, then offered Cortina the comfort of a chair beneath the awning attached to his tent. Becker's words and actions were right, but the tone behind them was downright dull and unresponsive. Plainly, Becker considered Cortina to be his inferior although a superior in rank.

Cortina didn't seem to mind Becker's curt behavior as he accepted the feigned hospitality and seated himself. After more casual courtesies were extended and accepted, he directed his attention to Creed.

"I see you have captured the spy I was about to shoot the other day," said Cortina with an ingratiating smile.

"Yes, we did," said Becker proudly. "He was sneaking around our camp last night, and one of my boys latched on to him in the dark. That wasn't all that hard though. Black as Bailey is he could sneak up on anything in the dark." Becker laughed.

Cortina's response to the racial slur was a glare of disdain. Slavery had been a banned institution in Mexico for several decades, and he, like most Mexicans, did not judge a man by the hue of his skin but by the iron in his heart.

Becker stopped laughing and cleared his throat. "Ahem, uh, yes. Well, anyway we got him for you, General."

"Captain Becker, I would like to execute this man as soon as possible," said Cortina.

This was a real surprise to Becker. His bushy eyebrows

shot up his forehead, his brown eyes bugged out, and his sunburned face took on an unhealthy pink glow. He pushed back his campaign hat, exposing a balding pate, and wiped his forearm over his eyes as if he had been perspiring copiously in a hot sun when actually he was just beginning to sweat. Finding himself suddenly short of air, he sucked in a deep breath and let it out rapidly before speaking.

"General Cortina, I know this Creed was spying on your people when you were all in Mexico," said Becker nervously, "but this is Texas, and I'm not so sure I can let you do that here."

Cortina shrugged and said, "I see no problem with it, but if it concerns you that much, Captain, then I will take him across the Rio Bravo and shoot him in Mexico. I was just thinking that it would be so much simpler to shoot him here. My men would find it so reassuring that our brave allies to the north felt the same way about our enemies as we do."

"I meant no disrespect, General," stammered Becker. "It's just that I'm not so sure that I can allow you to do that here. I mean, we do have our laws and all."

"Captain, he was caught spying in Mexico and we were about to execute him when his French friends attacked our camp. He is an escaped prisoner under sentence of death. Please, humor me. Allow me this one request."

Becker was still unsure of where he stood legally, and for a career officer, knowing on which side of the fence to stand was of paramount importance to a successful career. Politics was everything, and one mistake could put him in Arizona fighting Apaches instead of in Washington, where he could curry the favor of generals, senators, and other government officials. He gave Cortina's request another few seconds of thought, then said, "All right, General. I guess it'll be all right. He is a condemned man, so I guess it won't make any difference where he's executed."

Cortina smiled evilly and said, "No, Captain Becker. No difference at all." He turned to his aides and said in Spanish, "Get our best men for a firing squad. I don't want that son of a bitch to get away this time."

The aides saluted, then ran off to comply with their general's wishes.

Creed was close enough to hear the entire conversation. It didn't surprise him all that much, but it did annoy him. Here he was back in Texas, chained to a palm tree, a prisoner of a Yankee cavalry unit, and about to be shot by a Mexican bandit who called himself a general. And why? Because he had gone after some of the men who were responsible for the deaths of his brother and his best friend and he wanted to exact revenge on the cowards. Just maybe, he reasoned, he had exacted too much revenge. Maybe enough men had died for Dent and Jess. Maybe the Bible was right when it said that stuff about an eye for an eye and a tooth for a tooth and vengeance belonged to the Lord. Maybe he had no right to be the avenger and this was God's way of setting him straight. He wasn't sure what the answers were, but he did know that Cortina was about to have him shot, which concerned him greatly for the moment.

Word that Creed was to be stood up against the palm tree and shot spread rapidly through the camp. Two Yankee lieutenants spoke briefly about it to Becker, each expressing their doubts as to the legality of allowing a Mexican firing squad to shoot an American citizen. Becker argued that Creed had forfeited his rights as an American when he signed up with the French against the real government of Mexico. He also reminded them that their initial reason for being there wasn't exactly legal either. This argument silenced their objections.

With his execution being quite imminent, Creed began thinking of ways to extricate himself from this predicament. He couldn't run, that was for sure, not with chains on and a couple of guards who looked like they could catch a deer even after they'd eaten a seven-course meal. Trying to convince Becker that he shouldn't let Cortina shoot him on American soil was out because his own officers had failed in that debate. The only reasonable alternative seemed to be a confession; if he told Becker that he was Clete Slater, escaped prisoner from a Federal noose up in Hallettsville, he might be saved—for the moment. Sort of like going from the frying pan into the fire. But, of course, anything might happen when you jump out of a red-hot skillet.

Creed was giving the latter proposition a lot of thought when a blue-coated rider atop a big chestnut suddenly raced down the lane to Becker's tent, reined in his horse, jumped down, saluted the captain, and made a breathless report.

"He's coming, sir," said the scout. "About a mile back, I seen him. He's riding in a coach and wearing a big silk hat like Mr. Lincoln did. Got him two companies of cavalry with him, too. Led by white officers just like us."

"Very good, Private," said Becker. He turned to a sergeant standing near and said, "Sound the assembly, Hooks."

Hooks called for the bugler, and the call was blown for the men to form ranks.

Cortina angrily called for his aides and said to them in Spanish, "Take Creed and hide him. And hurry before they get here."

The two aides approached Creed's guards, and one said, "We will take charge of the prisoner now."

The two soldiers shifted their eyes in each other's direction, each silently questioning the other as to what they should do.

Creed saw his chance and took it. "That's right," he said. "I should go with them now." He stood up, his chains rattling as he did. He held out his hands to one guard and said, "You'd better remove these first."

"You sit down, white trash," said the guard angrily, taking the opportunity to vent a little pent-up hatred by insulting Creed with the worst possible slur he could hurl at him. Then turning to the other soldier, he said, "You best get Top and find out what we supposed to do here."

"I ain't leaving my post," said the second man. "You wants Top, then you goes and get him."

"I's in charge here, boy," said the first, "and I says for you to go. Now get!"

"You ain't in charge," said the second.

The first guard knew his partner was right, so he backed off. He turned to the Mexican officers and said, "I ain't letting no one take this prisoner less Top say so or one of our own officers say so."

The Mexicans took their turn at exchanging questioning looks, as neither of them knew what to do now.

Creed saw another chance to pour oil on the fire and said, "You hombres better not go back to *el general* without me or you'll be in big trouble."

Just then, the first guard hit Creed in the stomach with the butt of his Springfield, knocking the wind out of him, doubling him up, and landing him on his behind at the base of the palm tree. "I told you to sit down!" growled the guard.

His gut hurt like it had a knife stuck in it, but Creed was happy otherwise. He wasn't going to be shot as soon as Cortina wanted to shoot him, and for that good news he could take a little pain. He leaned back against the trunk of the palm and casually became the obedient prisoner again.

"Now you gentlemens can go get the Top or one of our officers to release this man if you want," said the first guard, "but we ain't releasing him to no one until you do."

The two officers stalked off, angry with the guards on the one hand and on the other fearful of what Cortina would say and do when they returned without Creed.

Coming up the lane now was a regular procession. To Creed's surprise, Captain John Hunter rode at the forefront of what was left of his company in the Mexican Republican Army. Following them was a black Baker brougham with an armed guard riding beside the driver. Creed couldn't see who was inside the carriage but didn't care right then because bringing up the rear was Captain Frank Newhouse and the remainder of his company. This was a real wonderment. What were they doing there? And—now—who was in that carriage?

Hunter led his men to a spot just to the left of Becker's tent, halted them, then ordered them to wheel right. Smartly, they obeyed the command. The carriage drove up to Becker's tent, turned to the left, and came to a halt with the passenger door facing the awning on Becker's tent. Newhouse did the same thing with his company as Hunter had but on the right side.

Becker led his officers to the edge of the awning and waited at attention for whoever it was to alight from the carriage.

Cortina and his two aides did likewise.

The guard atop the brougham leaped down from his perch, opened the door of the Baker, then announced, "*Presentando el presidente de la Republica de Mejico, Su Excelencia, El Señor* Benito Juárez."

And President Benito Juárez emerged from the carriage, silk top hat in hand, cape over his shoulders. He stood at the door of the brougham for a moment and surveyed the scene. His head bobbed ever so slightly in a sign of approval until his gaze fell on Creed. Recognition, as if he knew Creed, was in his eyes, which was strange because Creed had never seen Juárez before, and as far as he knew Juárez had never seen him before; but, of course, Hunter and Newhouse—or somebody—must have told Juárez about him. Then the small smile that had curled the president's lips upward drooped to a stern frown. Almost as if in a huff, he turned toward his waiting host and marched up to him.

"Mr. President," said Becker, starting his welcoming speech, "on behalf of the United States government, I wish—"

Juárez cut him short, saying, "Never mind that, Captain. Why is that man in chains?" He nodded toward Creed.

Becker turned to look, having forgotten for the moment about the prisoner. Then he addressed his attention to Juárez again.

Cortina jumped into the conversation, saying in Spanish, "Mr. President, that man is an Imperialist spy."

"The man is a spy, Mr. President," said Becker, reiterating Cortina's statement in English.

Juárez called over his shoulder, "Captain Hunter, come here." He waited for Hunter to dismount and present himself in the proper military fashion. "Captain Hunter, is that man a spy for the Imperialists?"

"No, sir," said Hunter.

"We have it on good authority that this man is not a spy for the Imperialists," said Juárez.

Becker was flustered and acted like it when he said, "But he was caught sneaking around our camp last night, Mr. President."

"I do not doubt this," said Juárez, "but he is not a spy. He is a victim of this unfortunate conflict much the same as many of my people are victims of it. I wish for you to release this man immediately."

"Let him go, Excellency?" queried Cortina anxiously. "But he is a spy!"

Juárez turned to Cortina for the first time and said to him in Spanish, "General Cortina, I am astutely informed that this man is not our enemy."

Cortina was livid but able to keep his voice low enough to continue showing respect for his country's leader. "Excellency, these other men who told you this are Texans just like the man Creed. They are lying to save him from execution.''

"General, I know how you feel about Texans," said Juárez calmly, "but I do not share this feeling with you. I know this man to be innocent of your charges and I wish him released this very moment. Do you understand, General?" Then he turned to Becker and said in English, "Captain, I realize we are in your country as your guests, and I know this man is your prisoner, but could I ask you to grant me this one request and release him from those chains and place him in my custody?"

Becker hadn't understood a single word of the conversation between Cortina and Juárez, but he knew the tone. Cortina was upset that Juárez wanted Creed released and that he was powerless to stop it. And Juárez was exerting his authority over Cortina by releasing Creed. Exactly why, he didn't know, figuring it was some sort of Mexican power game between the general and the president, and presidents outranked generals where he came from.

"Certainly, Mr. President," Becker said. He turned and gave the order for Creed to be released from his chains, while Juárez told Hunter to take charge of Creed and bring him to his quarters for a private audience after he was finished with all of Becker's formalities.

25

When Hunter freed him, Creed asked one simple question. "What the hell's going on here, John?"

Hunter explained that the United States was clandestinely supplying munitions to Juárez and that they had come there from San Antonio to receive the first shipment. Cortina's presence, and Creed's as well, was unexpected; they had thought the general had retreated to his mother's ranch and wouldn't come out of hiding until he was called out by Juárez. The president was glad to see his general and to see Creed.

"But how did he know me?" asked Creed.

"That's the thing about President Juárez," said Hunter. "He's spooky, sort of. He seems to know things before they happen or, like in your case, he knows who people are without being introduced or being told who they are. I'll tell you this much. He must think you're pretty important to the cause or he wouldn't have lifted a finger to help you. He would have let Cortina stand you up against a wall and never given you another thought. But he didn't, so thank the Lord and don't ask me why. Just go see him and see what he wants from you."

As he entered Becker's tent, Creed was asking himself how he suddenly became so important that the president of Mexico wanted to speak to him alone.

"Ah, Mr. Creed," said Juárez as he shook Creed's hand, "I am so happy to see that you are alive and well."

"So am I, Mr. President," said Creed with intended irony.

Juárez laughed a little laugh and said, "I see you have not lost your sense of humor through all this. That is good. A man must retain a proper balance in himself if he is to survive times such as these. Do you not agree?"

"Yes, sir," said Creed.

"Very good, very good." He waved to a chair opposite his and said, "Please sit down, Mr. Creed. We have much to discuss."

"We do?" queried Creed as he seated himself.

"Why, of course," said Juárez as he also sat down. In a much more serious tone, he said, "Mr. Creed, I have heard that you have no desire to be involved in our business here in Mexico, but whether you like it or not, my young friend, you are very much involved in it now. General Cortina has stated that you are a spy for this Colonel Dupin of the French Foreign Legion in Matamoras." He raised his hand to keep Creed from arguing the point with him, then said, "His informer in Colonel Dupin's camp has told him this. But Captain Hunter and Captain Newhouse have both assured me that you are no spy. I also know that you were caught in this camp, and that is certainly damning evidence that you are a spy or at least a scout for the French. However, I happen to know that you have a very honorable reason for serving this French butcher."

Creed's mind was suddenly flooded with questions, theories, suppositions, and chaos. Juárez seemed to know more about what he'd been doing and why he'd been doing it than he did. How? Who told him? And what about Cortina? How did he know so much? Why was he so vehement about Creed's guilt? Creed felt himself being pulled in several different directions at one time as if he were a fly caught in a spider's web; the more he tried to free himself, the stronger the hold on him.

"Mr. President, I am no spy. You know this obviously, but I do confess that I am a scout for Dupin. I agreed to scout for him because he has friends of mine in his jail and he will kill them if I don't work for him."

"Yes, I know this, too. Your four friends are his hostages, but they are in no danger for the moment." Juárez leaned a little closer to Creed, conspiratorially, to confide in him. "Mr. Creed, Mexico is fighting for her very freedom. Just the same as your Southern states did so recently. I know that you fought in that war, but I do not know nor do I care on which side you fought. There are many men from both the North and the South now fighting in our army, so you see, it makes no difference to me. But as I have said already, I know that you have no desire to involve yourself in our war for freedom, and in spite of this, you have become involved.

"Mr. Creed, I trust the judgment of very few people, but I do have some advisers and confidants in whom I place complete faith. Among these is Captain Hunter. He has told me that you are an honorable man who has come to Mexico to avenge the murders of your brother and your best friend. I can sympathize with you in this desire. However, you have become a reluctant participant in our war. On the wrong side, of course, but now that you have, I would like to ask you to join our side and once again strike a blow for freedom and democracy."

Creed knew that was coming, and he thought of giving Juárez his stock answer but just as quickly realized he couldn't because, as *el presidente* had pointed out, he was already involved in their war. So Creed simply sat there and let Juárez continue speaking.

"I would like you to return to Matamoras and report to Colonel Dupin that you have accomplished your mission to locate General Cortina's camp.''

Creed reacted to this tack, saying, ''I'm supposed to tell Dupin that General Cortina's camp is on the American side of the Rio Grande?''

''No, tell him it is on the Mexican side,'' said Juárez.

''But where? He'll want to know exactly where it is, so what do I tell him?''

''Tell him it is in the same place that Colonel Dupin attacked the other day.''

''And you think he'll believe that?''

Juárez smiled mischievously and said, ''When he attacks it again, he'll believe it.''

''I can't lead him into a trap, Mr. President. He'll have my friends executed if I do that.''

''Do not worry about your friends in Matamoras,'' said Juárez confidently. ''They will be safe, I assure you.''

Creed studied this little Indian lawyer for a moment, and while he did, he heard Grandfather Hawk saying, ''Look into a man's heart and see the truth of him. It is there, through his eyes, the tunnel to his soul.'' Creed's Cherokee and Choctaw heritage came to the fore as he looked deep into Juárez's heart and saw that sincerity, honesty, and compassion held prominence over all his other attributes. He felt good about the Mexican president.

Slowly, Creed said, ''Mr. President, I believe you.''

26

Surprisingly, Cortina made no objections when Juárez released Creed; surprisingly because he wasn't apprised of the president's reason for setting his prisoner free. This small fact made Creed quite wary on the trail back to Matamoras, but the long ride passed without incident.

The supper hour was past and the stars glittered in the clear evening sky when Creed rode through the main gate of Tres Palmes. Instead of going to see his friends in jail in Matamoras, which had now become a well-armed Imperial fortress, he decided to stop at the hacienda to report to Dupin. He reined in Nimbus at the walkway leading to the front door, dismounted, then tied the Appaloosa to the hitching post. He was too tired to notice—or even care—that he was being watched.

Silveria was alone, wearing a combless mantilla against the chill night air and sitting on the veranda chaise, when she heard the steady clippity-clop of a horse's hooves beating a rhythmic staccato on the carriage drive. She peered into the darkness and recognized Creed's form atop the Appaloosa. Without hesitation, she rose and went to meet him, moving silently over the cobbled patio until she stood before him at the post. "I trust your mission was successful," she said coolly, hiding the jubilation she was feeling.

Although weary from the long ride, Creed wasn't too tired to be startled. He was still leery from the trail. With the reflexes of a cougar, he stepped back and aside, bent into a semicrouch, and reached for the Colt's on his belt, his left hand steadying the holster while his right grabbed the butt of the pistol, thumb and index finger on the hammer and trigger respectively, ready to deal death—if necessary. He had the gun half out before he realized that the person addressing him was Silveria.

"Why do you do that?" he demanded with a bit of exasperation in his voice. He replaced the revolver, straightened up, and moved closer to her. "Do you like scaring people or something?"

"I did not mean to frighten you," she said apologetically.

"Well, you did."

"I am sorry."

Creed felt a little silly for chastising her over something so minor, but he wasn't about to apologize for it. Instead, he took a deep breath, let it all out, and said, "Forget it."

"I am glad you have returned safely," she said, moving a half-step nearer to him, her eyes reflecting the starlight as she gazed up at him.

"So am I," said Creed. Try as he might, he couldn't ignore the implication of her words. He saw love and desire in her face, and those two emotions swept over him, too, in a wave. Even so, he was able to control himself—for the moment.

"I worried that you would be hurt," she said a bit huskily. She pulled the black scarf from her head, letting it drape over her bare shoulders; then she touched his left bicep. "I am glad no harm came to you."

Creed smelled no perfume on her, but a subtle scent did permeate the air around them, which he failed to consciously recognize, although some primordial instinct deep within his soul did sense it. Suddenly, he was aroused with lust for this woman of dusky beauty. The puckish voice of passion whispered lascivious suggestions in his head, raising haunting, phantasmal visions of Silveria and him in the throes of lovemaking. He slipped his left arm around her waist and pulled her hard against him, then tilted her head to one side with his right hand as he savagely kissed her, his lips wrenching at her lips and his tongue jabbing and probing deep into her mouth.

Silveria returned every bit of his aggression. She threw one arm around his neck and the other around his back and pressed her hardening breasts against him. Her tongue fenced visciously with his, meeting his every parry and thrust with equal force and fire. His chin stubble and mustache scratched at her face, but she didn't care, actually reveling in the burning sensation it inflicted on her skin. Then for want of air, she ripped her mouth away and offered up her cheek and throat and earlobe to his deliciously consuming kisses.

"Come," she rasped. "Over here. Away from the door."

Creed heard her speak but was slow to react. When what she was trying to tell him finally penetrated his conscious mind, he pulled away from her, taking his hand from behind her head but not his arm from around her, then kissed her again, fully but with tenderness, before guiding her into the shadows of the patio. He embraced her again. His free hand started to wander over her back, moving up and down and then coming to the side; but when he touched her upper arm, she raised the limb as if to invite his fingers forward to caress her breast. He eagerly began to accede to her wishes when—

The front door of the hacienda creaked open.

—the lovers parted instantly as if they had been naughty children caught in the middle of exploring their blossoming sensuality—together.

A tall, thin silhouette of a man was framed by the light

from the foyer behind him. Creed didn't recognize him, but
his guilt made him think that the man was Don Bernardo
and that he had been discovered manhandling the *haciendado*'s daughter. Silveria knew who was interrupting them
but said nothing.

"Ah, Mr. Creed, you have returned," said Dupin.

The first thought that struck Creed was a question: Why
do educated people always sound like they are having their
throats examined by a doctor when they begin a conversation? It sounded so insincere.

"Good evening, Colonel," said Creed cordially, almost
relieved that it was the colonel and not Don Bernardo.

"I trust you had a successful mission," said Dupin.

"Yes, I did," said Creed. "I was just telling Miss Silveria
all about it."

"So I see," said Dupin sardonically.

"If you will excuse me, Señor Creed, Colonel Dupin,"
said Silveria, "it is late and I wish to retire." The latter
she said directly to Creed, pleading with her eyes.

Creed understood and awkwardly said, "Yes, I'm ready
to turn in myself, but I suppose I'd better do my duty to
the colonel first."

"Good night, gentlemen."

Dupin stepped aside, allowing Silveria to enter the house.
Then he motioned for Creed to follow, saying, "Come, let
us remove ourselves to the library where we can discuss
your mission in privacy."

Creed led the way to the library, noting that Dupin's
chasseurs were close at hand—as always—two in the foyer
and two at the library door, which one of them closed after
Creed and Dupin were inside. Dupin opened a humidor on
the desk and removed a cigar. He offered one to Creed.

"No, thank you, Colonel. I never acquired the taste for
tobacco. I don't smoke it or chew it."

"Cigars are not a regular vice of mine," said Dupin,

"but I do enjoy one now and then. The smoke gives me a sort of heady feeling. Something similar to the exhilaration and excitement of going into battle against a foe who is just as capable of defeating me as I am of defeating him." He took a lucifer from a wooden box beside the glass tobacco container, struck it on the rough side of the box, and lit the cigar, puffing and drawing on it until the end of the rolled weed glowed red, and blue smoke began to fill the air. Satisfied that the tobacco was afire, he took it from between his lips and gave it an appreciative look. "The Cubans make the best," he said. "The Turks make them, too, but their tobacco is too harsh. The smoke burns the throat. I do not like that." He sat down behind the desk and motioned for Creed to sit in the chair in front of it. When both were seated, he said, "Now tell me of your mission," then he drew on the cigar once again as he settled back to listen.

"If it was up to me, Colonel, I wouldn't tell you a thing about what I found."

Dupin smiled like the hungry tiger that he was and said, "Then you must have discovered more than I had hoped. Tell me, did you find Cortina's camp?"

"I found it all right. Right where it was the day you attacked it."

The colonel snorted a small laugh and said, "The audacity of the man! I must respect that. He has the cunning to deceive me by returning to the very same spot. I would never have thought he would do such a thing." Dupin inhaled on the cigar, blew out a cloud of gray smoke, and nodded grimly. "Yes, this proves he is nothing but an animal. Just like all these other oily Mexicans." He nearly spat the words.

Creed wasn't sure of whom Dupin was referring, but he figured the colonel was bitter about something that involved someone on his side of the fence.

Dupin studied Creed for a moment, then said, "But you

have other information as well, do you not?''

"As a matter of fact, I do," said Creed steadily. "Cortina has just received a shipment of guns and ammunition."

"Guns and ammunition? From whom?"

"Hold on to your pants, Colonel. He got them from the United States Army."

Dupin's head bobbed up and down and his lower lip protruded from his face a bit as he considered Creed's answer. "Yes, I can believe that," he said. "I have been wondering how long it would be before the American government finally involved itself in this war."

"I don't think the Yanks are ready to make an announcement to that effect, Colonel. They delivered the guns to Cortina on the Texas side of the Rio Grande, and from what I saw, they didn't want anyone else to find out they were doing it."

"Yes, of course," said Dupin, exhaling another cloud of tobacco smoke. "The Americans would not wish for us to know about such activities. That would be an act of war, and I do not think your nation is ready to do battle with half of Europe over a few million dirty, ignorant peasants."

"Colonel, those dirty, ignorant peasants as you call them are ready to march into hell to get you people out of their country. Their freedom means that much to them."

"Their freedom?" said Dupin, spitting the words. "What do they know of freedom? All of their previous rulers gave them the freedom to starve and live in abject poverty. Under Maximilian, they will know peace and prosperity. How much of Mexico have you seen, Mr. Creed?"

"Not much," he admitted. "Just this area around here."

"I have seen very much of it," said Dupin, stubbing out the cigar in a sandstone bowl, "and I can tell you that Mexico is a rich land with great mineral and agricultural wealth. But it has a poor people. And why? Because the government in the past has been very weak and, worse, it has been run by thieves who have stolen nearly everything these poor peasants can produce.''

''And you think this will change under Maximilian's rule?''

''Yes, I do,'' said Dupin. ''It will change because we will teach these peasants to be like our citizens in Europe.''

''What if they don't want that? What if they want to stay the way they are now?''

Dupin suddenly realized that he had been drawn into a philosophical discussion for which he had very little desire. He had more important business on his agenda.

''Mr. Creed, I have no more time to discuss these matters with you. I have to send someone to verify your story, and you are keeping me from it. You are excused, but do not leave the hacienda.''

''I'm a prisoner again?'' queried Creed.

''Of course,'' said Dupin. Then he saw the look of anger on Creed's face, smiled consolingly, and said, ''But only as a precaution. If what you have told me is the truth, then I will keep my bargain with you. You will be set free with your friends, and I will hand over Kindred and the men with him.''

Creed nodded and said, ''Good enough. I believe you, but there's something I . . . uh, forgot to tell you.''

''Yes, and what was that?''

''Benito Juárez is with Cortina.''

''Juárez? Are you certain of this?''

Dupin was both excited and apprehensive. If Creed was telling him the truth, then the prize that had eluded him at El Paso was once again within his grasp. But if Creed was lying . . .

''It was Juárez all right,'' said Creed. ''I've heard enough about him to recognize him when I see him.''

''What did he look like?''

''Short. Dark like an Indian. He wore a black suit and a

black silk hat. I know it was Juárez, Colonel. Who else would the American army throw out the red carpet for?''

''You saw him in the American camp? On their side of the river?''

Creed had slipped up, but he was always quick to cover his tracks. ''Last night before he crossed over the river with Cortina this morning. They took delivery of the guns and ammunition last night, then crossed the river this morning. They were still setting up camp when I left to come back here and report to you.''

''You were not discovered?''

''I'm here, ain't I?'' said Creed to keep from lying.

''Yes, you are,'' said Dupin suspiciously. ''And here you shall remain until I am able to confirm your report. You may sleep in the same room you occupied on your previous stays with us, Mr. Creed. Good night.'' Not waiting for Creed to return the valediction, Dupin called out to his chasseurs to assemble his officers, and then he began the business of planning a battle.

Creed pushed himself from the chair and left the room without bidding Dupin adieu. He walked wearily through the parlor, the foyer, and down the hall to the room that had been his each night he had slept at the hacienda. He opened the door expecting to enter a dark space but found just the opposite. Someone—Silveria, he presumed—had lit the candle on the nightstand and turned back the covers for him. He was grateful for that much as he sat down on the edge of the bed with his thoughts centered on Silveria and the hinted invitation to come to her room that night. The idea was appealing, he had to admit, but not before cleaning up a bit. That could wait a minute or two. The bed was so soft and comforting; he would lean back and relax for just a few minutes and then see about Silveria.

In seconds, Creed was fast asleep.

27

A blaring French bugle sounding assembly invaded Creed's sleep the next morning shortly after dawn. In his last dream, he was once again in battle, only this time he was fighting an unknown enemy. He was about to discover the identity of the villain when his conscious mind interfered and stirred him to awaken.

In his haste to report to Dupin the night before, Creed hadn't noticed that the Contre-Guerrillas were now bivouacked next to the grounds of Tres Palmes. Upon recognizing the shrill notes of the military musical instrument, he rose and went to the window but didn't see anything. Still hearing the bugle call, he entered the hall but was stopped by one of Dupin's chasseurs.

"*Non, monsieur!*" growled the guard blocking his path.

Creed wasn't about to argue with a man who stood over six feet tall, who was at least two feet wide at the shoulders, and who had a face that could stop a mad bull in full charge. Instead, he bowed politely, backed away, and said, "Sorry, I didn't know you were planted there." He backed off another step.

The chasseur relaxed and blinked his eyes.

Creed hit him. Square on the jaw with everything he had. A solid right cross.

The guard's head snapped to one side but only for an instant. He turned back to face Creed, who was holding a painful fist.

Creed looked up at the chasseur's face, saw the hate and anger, and wished he'd never been born.

Then the Frenchman's eyes rolled up into his head, and he collapsed in a heap at Creed's feet.

"Next time, stay out of my way," said Creed as he stepped over the brute. He was still holding his painful hand as he headed down the hall. The mitt hurt but wasn't broken.

Before he could reach the foyer, another of Dupin's bodyguards blocked his way.

Creed stopped and muttered, "Dammit all to hell! I should have remembered that you boys always travel in pairs. Now what?"

The soldier looked past Creed at his compatriot on the floor, then glared at Creed for a second. Just as quickly, he began to smile a cruel grin that said Creed was in bigger trouble than he had been before. He moved toward Creed, one giant step at a time, his fists ready to pummel the Texan for hurting his friend.

Creed's hand hurt too much to hit anyone with it again— at least not for a while. But it didn't pain him so badly that he couldn't handle a gun with it. He drew his Colt's, cocked the hammer, and pointed it at the advancing chasseur's nose.

"You just hold your ground, son," he said as if the Frenchman understood every syllable.

Of course, the soldier didn't know the words, but he was right familiar with the tune. He backed away into the foyer with Creed still holding the six-gun on him.

"Very good," said Creed as he followed the man into the anteroom. "Now just stand aside," he said, motioning with the pistol for the guard to move to the left. When the chasseur did as he was bade to do, Creed reached for the front door with his free hand, opened it, and stepped outside.

"Ah, Mister Creed," said Dupin behind him. "You are awake."

Creed spun around to face the colonel, thinking they were alone. He was incorrect in his assumption. Dupin's other two chasseurs were with him, both aiming their cocked muskets at Creed. The Texan quickly realized his disadvantage and lowered his weapon.

"Just getting a little exercise, Colonel," said Creed.

"So am I," said Dupin, ignoring Creed's meager effort at humor. "I am about to lead my men to victory once again. Would you care to join us?"

"Colonel," said Creed more seriously now, "our deal was for me to scout for you, and I've done that. There was nothing in the bargain that said I had to fight for you, too."

"I was only asking," said Dupin.

Creed looked beyond Dupin to the carriage drive and saw several mounted Contres waiting for the command to move out. "I guess all this means my report checked out true," said Creed.

"Yes, it did. Cortina is camped exactly where he was the other day. I will attack him again, only this time I will not let him escape."

"And Juárez? Is he with Cortina yet?"

"As far as we can tell, yes," said Dupin.

Creed smiled and said, "Then I guess this means I can go into Matamoras and get my friends out of your jail, right?"

"Not exactly," said Dupin.

"Why not?" demanded Creed. "We had a deal, Colonel."

"And I will keep my end of the bargain," said Dupin with as much fire as Creed had used.

"When?"

"As soon as I have finished with Cortina and captured Juárez."

"What if you lose?" asked Creed. "Then what happens to my friends and me?"

"The only way I can lose this battle is if I am riding into a trap. If you are telling me the truth, then there is no reason for you to fear for your friends and for yourself. But if you are lying and I am riding into a trap, then you and your friends will pay for it with your lives. I have given Captain Auber orders to that effect. He will be in charge here until I return from the battle."

Creed didn't understand this because Captain Rene Auber commanded a company of the Contre-Guerrillas. Why would Dupin leave him behind when there was an important battle to be fought? Obviously, Claire Mounet had something to do with the handsome French-Canadian mercenary remaining at the hacienda. Either that or Dupin wanted a capable man to hold down the fort while he was away. It made no difference to Creed because he thought himself to be once again caught on the horns of a dilemma.

28

Dupin's chasseurs rode off with their colonel but not before they disarmed Creed and turned his weapon over to Captain Auber, who then took charge of the prisoner.

"Come with me, Mr. Creed," said Auber.

And Creed did so, following the captain back into the house, through the foyer, and down the hall to his own room. This didn't make sense to Creed, and the expression on his face told Auber so.

The French-Canadian answered Creed's unspoken question, saying, "You appear to be a man who would like to wash and shave before having breakfast with ladies. Also, you could stand a change of clothing. I will have hot water brought to you immediately, *mon ami*, and as soon as you are presentable, please join the ladies and Don Bernardo and me at the breakfast table on the garden patio." He started to leave, then realized he still had Creed's Colt's. "Oh, yes. And please put this away someplace," he said, handing the revolver to Creed. "It is impolite to be armed at the breakfast table."

Creed accepted the return of his gun, not really believing Auber was giving it back to him. He wanted to ask why, but the words refused to form in his throat and pass through his mouth. He was totally perplexed by this turn of events.

"Ask me no questions, *mon ami*," said Auber, "and I will tell you no lies." He winked at Creed, patted him on the shoulder, and added, "Now hurry. We must not keep the ladies and Don Bernardo waiting too long." And with that, he left.

Creed was still incredulous but decided against trying to solve the riddle of Auber's actions. He would simply chalk it up to the man's friendly nature and leave it go at that. For the moment. Because now a serious hunger pang twisted his gut, reminding him that he hadn't eaten since lunch the day before, and that breakfast was waiting.

As soon as the hot water arrived, Creed hurried through his ablutions and donned a clean shirt. He was about to leave his room when someone knocked at the door. "I'm coming right now," he said, not knowing who was knocking but suspecting it was one of the servants. He opened the door to find Silveria standing resolutely in the hall. One look into her eyes and he forgot about food.

"You did not come to my room last night," she said flatly, making the statement sound like an accusation.

"I wanted to," said Creed, feeling somewhat like a schoolboy caught playing hooky, "but I fell asleep. I guess I was too tired from riding most of the day. I'm sorry."

"There is no need to apologize to me. I should have realized how weary you were and come to your room." She wrapped her arms around his neck and added, "Tonight, perhaps, if all goes well." She kissed him. Lightly at first. Then with open mouth and darting tongue.

Creed returned her embrace and responded to her kiss in kind, all the time wondering what she meant by "if all goes well." He figured he'd find out soon enough.

Silveria broke off their kiss and said, "Come. We must join the others now." And she led him to the garden patio.

Before sitting down at the breakfast table, Don Bernardo informed Creed that he had ordered his stableman to feed, water, brush, and currycomb Nimbus. Creed thanked him, and they joined the others for the meal.

Captain Auber and Claire sat across from Creed and Silveria, respectively; Patrice Dupin was seated at the foot of the table; and Don Bernardo at the head. Auber dominated the conversation by giving everyone a rather detailed report on the military situation in Mexico in general, around Matamoras in particular.

For the most part, the Juáristas had been subdued throughout the country, although there were some pockets of sporadic resistance. These were few, however, and very scattered. With Juárez now out of the country, the Mexican peones were without effective leadership and therefore no longer offered a serious threat to the government in Mexico City. Of course, there were still men like Juan Cortina to deal with, but not one of these petty regional dictators presented a real problem. They would be eliminated or neutralized in due time.

If this were so, argued Don Bernardo, then why had General Mejia come to Matamoras with so many Imperialist troops?

Auber quickly explained that the government of Maximilian was facing a possible new enemy in the form of the United States. Already, thousands of Federal soldiers were being posted along the Rio Bravo as if preparing to invade Mexico. He turned to Creed and asked him to verify this fact. Creed demurred, saying he could only vouch for what he had actually seen and that was only one small cavalry detachment that was delivering arms to Cortina. "Precisely," said Auber. The United States was merely taking the first steps toward hostilities by giving weapons to the Juáristas. The next phase would be an outright declaration of war.

During the lecture, Creed noted that Don Bernardo appeared to be nervous about something. In fact, Claire, Silveria, and Auber also seemed preoccupied. Only the colonel's wife ate with indifference to everything except the food. Odd, he thought, but why? What was on their minds?

Before Creed could conceive any possible answers, the boom of a single cannon silenced the chirping birds and put them all to flight.

"What was that?" asked Claire with excited innocence.

"Cannon fire, I would say," said Auber calmly. "Wouldn't you agree, Mr. Creed?"

"That's what it sounds like to me," said Creed.

"Artillery practice for General Mejía's troops," said Auber nonchalantly.

"Why would they be practicing with only one cannon?" asked Don Bernardo.

Creed wondered the same thing. Why only one cannon?

"To shoot them all at once might disturb the populace," explained Auber. He looked at Creed and added, "The people might think the town is under attack, and we all know what a foolish thought that is, don't we, *mon ami*?"

"I'm not so sure about that, Captain," said Creed. "That round didn't sound like it—"

Another explosion in the distance interrupted Creed but only for a moment.

"There," said Creed. "That's what I thought. That shot and the first one didn't come from anywhere near the town." He stood up and looked over the garden wall toward Matamoras. "I'd say it came from south of the town instead of from it."

"You seem to know a great deal about cannon fire, *mon ami*. Were you in an artillery unit in your late war?"

"Cavalry," said Creed without thinking and still studying the horizon.

Before anyone else could speak, the thunder of several hundred horses' hooves began rumbling toward them.

"What is this now?" asked Don Bernardo.

Creed looked hard at the *haciendado* and saw feigned

innocence. Don Bernardo was acting, lying. He knew what was happening, but he was trying to hide the fact from everyone else. Why?

Pepe, the house servant, ran onto the patio from the kitchen. He was plainly agitated as he cried, "Don Bernardo, Don Bernardo! *Los bandidos estan viniendo! Andele, mi patron! Los bandidos estan viniendo!*" He pointed toward the front of the hacienda.

Don Bernardo rose from his chair and threw down his napkin on the table. In Spanish, he said, "Calm down, Pepe. It is all right. Come. We will see about these bandits."

"Yes, I think we should," said Auber as he also left his seat and followed Don Bernardo toward the kitchen.

Creed turned to the women and said, "Ladies, I think it would be wise if you went into the house now."

"Yes, I agree," said Patrice Dupin. "Come, Claire. We must retire."

"I think not," said Claire. "I wish to see these bandits, too." She looked at Silveria and said, "What about you? Do you fear these bandits as my sister does?"

"Certainly not," said Silveria. "I would like to see them, too."

"I don't think your father would like that," said Creed.

"This is my house, Señor Creed," said Silveria, "and only my father has the right to tell me what I can do and I cannot do." She turned to Claire and said, "Madame Mounet, shall we go?"

Claire smiled evilly at Creed, then followed Silveria toward the kitchen the same as Auber had followed Don Bernardo.

Creed helped Patrice Dupin from her chair and said, "I'll be glad to escort you to your room, ma'am."

"No, I think not," she said. "Please go after my sister and Mademoiselle Silveria. They may need you more than I at this moment."

The cannon boomed in the distance again.

Creed nodded and said, "Yes, I think you're right."

Instead of following Claire and Silveria out the front door, Creed went to his room and retrieved his Colt's, strapping on the gunbelt as quickly as he could. Then he rushed outside to join Don Bernardo, Auber, and the two women as they stood waiting at the circular carriage drive for the bandits to ride up.

Pepe's so-called *bandidos* turned out to be Mexican cavalry led by John Hunter and Frank Newhouse. The two Americans rode up to the small group at the door, dismounted, and stepped forward to address them.

"Don Bernardo, I am Captain John Hunter of the Army of the Republic of Mexico," said Hunter in Spanish. "I declare you and your entire household to be my prisoners." Then to Auber, he added, "I see that you are an officer in the Imperial army, sir. Are you in command here?"

"Yes, I am," said Auber. "I am Captain Rene Auber of His Majesty's Imperial Contre-Guerrillas." He bowed like a European, then straightened up, saluted, and clicked his heels. "At your service, sir."

"Captain Auber, do you wish to surrender?" asked Hunter.

Auber looked beyond Hunter and Newhouse at what had to be two hundred or more armed men. Then to Hunter, he said, "I would be a fool to resist you with only the token force I have at my command. Yes, Captain, I do wish to surrender."

"Your sword then," said Hunter.

"Pepe," said Auber, "go to my room and fetch back my sword."

Pepe bowed and said, "*Sí, Capitan.*" Then he ran off to do Auber's bidding.

The cannon boomed again, but this time it was followed by small-arms fire.

"I didn't expect to see you again," said Hunter, looking at Creed. "I thought you and your friends would be long gone by now."

"No such luck," said Creed. "They're still in the jail in town."

"They won't be for long," said Newhouse. "General Escobedo should be taking that part of the town right about now."

"General Escobedo?" queried Auber. "He is here?"

"Don't you worry your head about that, Frenchman," said Newhouse. "By sundown, the war will be over for you permanent."

"Easy, Frank," said Hunter. "Captain Auber's guilt has yet to be determined. We'll give him a fair trial first, then shoot him."

Auber smiled wryly and said, "Ah, yes. American justice. I have heard of it. A man is innocent until proven guilty, *n'est-ce pas*?"

"Exactly, Captain," said Hunter. Then to Creed, he said, "I assume you are eager to see about your friends, Mr. Creed. You are free to leave at any time you wish. If you would like an escort, Captain Newhouse would be glad to accompany you into the town and help you locate them."

"I'd like nothing better," said Creed. He turned to Don Bernardo and said, "Don Bernardo, your hospitality has been quite gracious, and I thank you for sharing your home with me. Captain Auber, it's been a pleasure. I wish you luck in staying alive."

"Do not worry about me, *mon ami*."

"Madame Mounet," said Creed, offering her a half bow. Then he turned to the one person for whom he wished he had more time. "Miss Silveria, I wish . . . that I could have gotten to . . . know you better. I think we could have been . . . good friends . . . under different circumstances."

"Yes, I think so, too," she said bravely, outwardly, while

inside her heart was breaking.

"Captain Newhouse, I'll get my things and meet you in the stables," said Creed.

Pepe returned with Auber's sword and gave it to him.

"Pepe, go tell Miguel to saddle Señor Creed's horse," said Don Bernardo in Spanish.

"*Sí, mi patron.*"

"Thank you, Don Bernardo," said Creed. Then he disappeared into the house.

While Creed was in his room gathering his things, Madame Dupin entered silently and stood at the door waiting for him to turn around. When he did, he was startled but didn't show it. "What is happening, Mr. Creed?" she asked.

"The Juáristas have captured this place and are now attacking Matamoras," he quickly explained.

"I see," she said. "And what of you? Are you leaving?"

"Yes, I am. Two Americans command the bunch that captured this place, and one of them is going to take me into town to help me get my friends out of jail there. Then we're riding straight for Texas."

"I see. Mr. Creed, allow me to give you a small piece of advice. When you cross the Rio Grande, do not look back. No matter what, do not look back here. Never come back here as long as this war continues. There is only danger here . . . for you and . . . for those you care for."

Her voice and words were so ominous that they sent a chill down Creed's spine. Like the time Grandfather Hawk foretold his father's death at the hands of the Comanche. He had dreamed a nightmare that night and had cried. But when the prophesy came true, he didn't cry; he simply learned to respect his grandfather's prophesies.

Now he was getting that same feeling again, and it frightened him.

29

Matamoras was under attack.

President Juárez had sent General Escobedo to relieve Cortina of command of the Liberal army in northern Tamaulipas. Escobedo was immediately informed that Imperialist General Mejia had recently arrived in Matamoras with several hundred fresh troops and was presently constructing defenses at strategic points throughout the town. Although his army lacked cohesion, Escobedo had determined that the best time to strike was before Mejia could complete building his forts.

While personally directing two thousand foot soldiers armed with the Enfield rifles that Juárez had acquired from the American army, Escobedo sent the Liberal cavalry under Hunter and Newhouse to secure Rancho Abeytia as a base of operations. *El general* divided his force for a three-pronged attack on the town: two units feinting and drawing fire from the Imperialists, while the third attacked in earnest at the southwest quadrant. Cortina and his border *bandidos* were ordered to remain in the rear as reserves.

The Juáristas had only one cannon when the attack started, but they were hopeful of capturing more from enemy forces. They overran two Imperialist batteries and turned them on other parts of Matamoras held by Mejia's soldiers. Within an hour of the first cannon shot, the Liberals had a precarious hold on half the town—the half that included the city government building and Dupin's prison.

Creed rode beside Newhouse at the head of his company. They met no resistance as they entered the town and made straight for the jail. Some sporadic gunfire could be heard in the streets, but none of it was aimed at the cavalry unit. The Imperialists in this part of Matamoras were in full retreat.

The gate to the compound was wide open when Creed and Newhouse rode up to it, and no prisoners were anywhere in sight.

"Looks like all the birds have flown the coop," said Newhouse as he scanned the area. "Either our boys already let everybody go, or the guards shot their prisoners before they ran off." He noticed the concern on Creed's face and added, "Don't see any dead men lying about, so I figure they must've gotten away clean."

"But where to?" asked Creed.

A rattle of gunfire drew their attention.

"Let's see what that's all about," said Newhouse.

They kicked their mounts into motion and rode for the stables behind the government house. There they discovered that several Mexicans had taken up positions in the city building and were firing at some men—presumably French—in the horse barn. Newhouse and Creed were about to join the fight on the Mexican side when they heard the familiar sound of Texas English being yelled at them from the stable.

"Those your people, Creed?" asked Newhouse.

"Sounds like them," he replied.

"Well, hold on while I put a stop to this," said Newhouse. He spurred his horse and rode into the government building. In a minute, the shooting stopped, and he came out again. "They say your boys are taking their horses."

"Not very likely," said Creed. "Most likely, they're trying to take their own and get the hell out of here."

"My thoughts exactly," said Newhouse. "You go tell your boys to get mounted, and I'll see that no one takes any potshots at them while you all ride off."

Creed leaned over and offered his hand to Newhouse. "I want to thank you, Frank, for all your help. When I get back to Lavaca County, I'll look for your people there and tell them about what you're doing down here."

"I'd appreciate that, Creed," said Newhouse, shaking Creed's hand. "Now you get back to Texas and take those troublemakers with you."

Creed laughed, then said, "God bless you, Frank Newhouse."

"I thank you for that, Slate Creed. Now go on and get out of here."

Creed kicked Nimbus and rode for the barn. Inside, he found Jake Flewellyn, Bill Simons, and the Reeves brothers, each armed with a pair of Colt's revolvers and an Enfield rifle. A cloud of gun smoke hung heavily in the air.

"Mount up, boys," said Creed. "We're getting shed of this place as fast as we can."

"What about them greasers over yonder?" asked Flewellyn. "They ain't real congenial about us taking our own horses out of here."

"Those Mexicans," said Creed, emphasizing the name, "won't be shooting at you anymore. That man you saw with me is an officer in their army. He's ordered them to leave you be, so let's get out of here while we can."

"No need to tell me twice," said Simons. He leaped into the saddle and added, "I'm ready, Clete."

Creed drooped and said, "The name is Creed now, Bill."

"Whatever," said Simons.

Flewellyn and the Reeves boys mounted up and indicated that they were also ready to ride.

"Good enough," said Creed. "Let's get the hell out of Mexico while we've still got our hides on tight." He spurred Nimbus, and the five of them galloped into the barnyard.

Good to his word, Newhouse kept the Mexican soldiers from firing on Creed and his friends as they emerged from the barn and rode past. Creed waved his hat and gave out a Rebel call as they raced by the government house and made for the street that would take them west and away from Matamoras.

In a very few minutes, the five Texans had ridden beyond the edge of the town and were approaching Tres Palmes. Creed looked at the hacienda longingly—but only for a moment. A mental image of Silveria in his arms flared up in his brain, but it soon dissipated and was replaced by another vision, one of Texada, her eyes filled with love for him and trust that he would never betray that love. He forced himself to look away from the home of the dusky beauty with whom he had come so close to sharing his passion, then stared at the lonesome road ahead, the road to Texas and—

Home? He wasn't sure right now. He would figure that out later.

30

The Texans crossed the Rio Grande at the first ford above the town and decided to rest their horses for a spell before going any farther.

"How'd you boys get out of that jail?" asked Creed as they walked along a road that led to the east.

"Them Mexicans that was shooting at us let us out," said Flewellyn.

"What happened to your guards?" asked Creed. "Wasn't Kindred and his gang guarding you?"

"Them cowards ran off when the first cannonball landed in the courtyard," said Flewellyn. "The Frenchies put up a little fight, then they ran, too. The Mexicans came in and let us all go. There was a few Mexicans in with us, and they joined the fight right away. We grabbed up all the weapons we could find and made for the barn to get our horses and get the hell of there, but this one Mexican started arguing with us about taking them. I didn't understand a word of what he was saying, but Bill did. As soon as he told me what that Mexican wanted, I told him to tell that Mexican that if he tried stopping us he could kiss his ass good-bye. Damn fool tried to stop us, so I shot him." He grinned and added, "In the ass. Got both cheeks with one ball. Dumb son of a bitch jumped a foot in the air, came down holding his ass in both hands, and ran for cover. So did the rest of them. We saddled up and were just about to ride out of there when they started shooting at us from the courthouse. Then you showed up just a few minutes later.''

Creed was smiling. ''Tell me you didn't really shoot him in the ass,'' he said.

''Sure did,'' said Flewellyn. ''Wasn't easy though. He was so skinny I had to turn him sideways to do it.''

That brought a guffaw from Creed. ''Wish I'd been there to see that,'' he said.

''Yeah, you should've been there,'' said Simons.

Turning serious, Flewellyn asked, ''What about Kindred and his gang? You still planning to go after them?''

Creed thought about it for a second and said, ''I don't think so. Not now, anyway. You said they hightailed it out of there when the shooting started, didn't you?''

''That's right,'' said Simons. ''They rode right past the jail, and that was the last we saw of them.''

''One of the Frenchies told us they had deserted,'' said Flewellyn. ''Said they'd be shot if they came back.''

A smirk curled the corners of Creed's mouth as he said, ''It'd serve the bastards right if they were shot by the French.''

''So what are you going to do now, Mr. Creed?'' asked Simons, using the name a bit derisively.

''I don't rightly know,'' answered Creed. ''I can't exactly go home, can I? As much as I'd like to, though. I sure miss . . . everyone back there.''

''You mean Miss Texada, don't you?'' teased Clark Reeves. He playfully elbowed his brother walking beside him, and Kent jostled him back.

''Yes, I suppose I do,'' said Creed honestly, letting his emotions have a brief moment. ''I sincerely wish things were different, boys. I'd marry that gal in an instant if that Yankee noose wasn't waiting for me back in Hallettsville.''

He fell silent as he thought of what that meant.

"Then what?" asked Simons.

"Then I'd take up ranching, I guess," said Creed. "That's what I was intending to do before Markham and those other Yankees decided that I'd led that raid in Mississippi."

"But you can't do that now," said Simons. "So what are you going to do?"

"You could sneak back into the county and bushwhack those goddamned Detchens," said Flewellyn. "No one would miss them."

"No one except their maw," said Kent Reeves, nudging his brother in the ribs.

"You got that right," said Simons. "No one except Sophia Campbell would miss those two coyote pups of hers, and that's trouble enough for any man. If anyone hurt her precious boys, she'd get her ounce of flesh and then some in revenge. You can bet on that."

"Bushwhacking is too good for them," said Flewellyn. "We ought to string them up by their balls and let them hang there until they rot."

"Which do you mean?" asked Clark. "Them or their balls?" He and Kent got a particularly big kick out of that one as both laughed raucously.

Creed smiled at the joke, then said, "I don't know, boys. These past few weeks I've sort of lost some of the hate I had for Kindred and the Detchens. Being down here, I've had plenty of time to think things over, and I'm beginning to wonder if it's all worth it. I mean, killing Kindred and his gang and killing the Detchens won't bring back Jess and Dent. They're gone for good, and I've been wondering if we ain't put a black mark on their memory by killing all these men."

"That's all well and good," said Flewellyn, "but you're forgetting something here. We're all forgetting something here."

"What's that?" asked Simons.

"Crit and Charlie Golihar. They've taken a blood oath to kill the man who killed their brother."

"And that's me," said Creed.

"Yeah, but where are they?" asked Simons. "They left Lavaca County before we did, and we didn't see hide nor hair of them anywhere along the trail down here. If they were so het up to avenge their brother, why didn't they show up in Matamoras looking for you?"

"Who knows that they didn't?" asked Flewellyn.

"I do," said Creed. "If they'd shown up in Matamoras looking for me, the French would have thrown them into jail right alongside of you boys, figuring they were friends of mine, too, and could be used as hostages the same as they were using you. No, the Golihars didn't make it to Matamoras."

"Which means they're still in Texas," said Flewellyn.

"Most likely," said Creed.

"So what do you intend to do about them?" asked Simons.

"Well, I'm sure as hell not going to look for them," said Creed. "I've got enough trouble with the Yankees already."

"Which brings us back to my first question," said Simons. "What are you planning to do now?"

"Like I said before, I don't rightly know. Maybe I should ride up to Tennessee and look for those boys who really were in that raid, and when I find them, make them tell the truth that I wasn't a part to it."

"That seems like a sensible thing to do," said Flewellyn.

"Maybe," said Creed, "but what if the Yankees won't believe them? Then I'm back to where I started. With a noose waiting for me in Hallettsville."

"You could go west," said Simons. "Sneak back to Hallettsville and get Miss Texada, then the two of you go to California or somewhere."

"No, that won't do," said Creed. "I'd still be wanted by the Yankees, and I couldn't ask Texada to live a life where we'd always be worrying about when someone would find me and take me in to be hung. No, that's no life for a woman."

"I'm glad I'm not in your boots," said Simons.

Creed knew what he meant but decided against allowing the conversation to continue in this vein. Instead, he said, "I wish you were in my boots, Bill. Then you're feet would hurt and maybe mine wouldn't. Come on. Let's mount up and get the hell away from here."

31

Shortly after the five Texans remounted their horses, the skies that had been threatening most of the day darkened even more and let loose with one of those torrential rains that were so prevalent along the Gulf Coast. The men dismounted again and donned the slickers that were standard gear for vaqueros.

"We'd better get out of this rain," said Creed.

"And quick," said Flewellyn.

The road soon vanished in a sea of mud, slowing the men to a near standstill. Visibility was down to a few hundred yards, and the light of day was fading fast. Heads down, horses and riders plodded onward not really knowing which direction they were going. Two hours dragged by, then Simons spotted a square of yellow light in the distance.

"Ranch house?" queried Simons, shouting over the roar of the rain.

"Looks like it," said Creed. "Come on. Let's find out."

They rode closer to the light and soon discovered that they had been mistaken. Instead of one light, they found two: one from an adobe ranch house as they had suspected and the other from the doorway of a cantina, also of Mexican architecture. The house and saloon were the principal buildings of a settlement known as Olmito. The only other structures around were two outhouses, a chicken coop, a covered farrowing pen, and a wooden horse barn.

"Let's get our horses inside first," said Creed. "Then we'll see if that saloon has anything to warm our innards."

"Sounds like a surefire plan to me," said Flewellyn.

They led their mounts into the barn. Someone had left a lantern lit and hanging from a center post. Once the last man and horse were inside, Creed turned up the flame, and much to their surprise, they found the place to be full already. As soon as he shook off the rain, Creed counted sixteen horses, three in stalls and thirteen still saddled and tied to a picket line along one wall. That there were so many animals in this small place was odd enough, but that nearly all of them were saddled and ready to ride was completely strange.

"I wonder who these belong to," asked Simons.

"Probably a bunch of Mexicans who came in to get out of the rain the same as we did," said Flewellyn.

"Not Mexicans," said Creed. "Not with those trappings."

The other men took a closer look at the saddles and leather accessories on the thirteen picketed horses and came to the same conclusion that Creed had. The owners were not Mexicans; they were Texans. More than that, they were Texans from Lavaca County. Creed recognized the distinctively stamped Flying W on the underside of the cantle as being the trademark of Pete Wroe, a saddlemaker in Hallettsville.

"These boys are from home," said Creed, showing the W to the others. "I wonder who they could be," he added facetiously.

"You reckon it's Kindred and his bunch?" asked Simons.

"Of course, it's them," said Flewellyn.

"But I thought they was only eleven now," said Simons. "Who do these other two horses belong to?"

"My guess is Crit and Charlie Golihar," said Creed. "What do you think, Jake?"

"That's got my vote," said Flewellyn.

"I wonder what they're doing here," said Clark Reeves.

"Same as we are," said Creed. "They came in to get out of the rain."

"Yeah, but why here?" asked Kent.

"How many places do you reckon there are around here?" asked Simons. "This area ain't exactly like home, you know, where we got lots of roads and houses and people living in them. This is border country, where there ain't a whole lot of anything except Mexicans and rattlesnakes, and I'd bet the snakes complain that there's too many Mexicans."

"What are you thinking to do about this?" asked Flewellyn.

"I don't know," said Creed. "It's a cinch we can't go into that cantina right now, and I sure as hell ain't going back out in that rain to walk over to that ranch house. So for the time being, I guess we'd better make ourselves to home right here. We'd better post a guard and bar the doors so no one tries to come in here without letting us know about it first. And I think we'd best get some rest."

"Whatever you say," said Simons. "I'll stand the first watch if you want."

"Thanks, Bill," said Creed. "Let's take care of the horses, then we'll think about what we're going to do once the rain stops."

Simons barred the twin doors as Creed suggested, then for the next two hours he kept watch on the cantina and the ranch house through a chink in the barn wall. No one left or entered the saloon. Likewise the house. At least, no one that he could see through the murky night.

Creed, Flewellyn, and each of the Reeves brothers took turns keeping watch, and they all had the same result. No one entered or exited the two buildings. The light in the ranch house went out during Creed's watch, and the cantina went dark while Clark Reeves was on duty.

About an hour before sunup, the rain stopped. Simons was on his second watch. The first glimmer in the east brought the rooster out of the henhouse, and soon after his initial crow, a glow in the ranch house window followed by a steady stream of smoke coming from the chimney said someone was stirring about and preparing for the new day. Through the still of the morning air, the creak of a door with metal hinges announced the exit of someone from the house, and Simons spied out the shadowy figure of a tall man in a wide-brimmed soft felt hat making his way to the outhouse in back.

Won't be long now, thought Simons, and the ball will begin. Better wake Clete or Creed or whatever fool name he wants to call himself these days.

Simons shook Creed and whispered, "Rain stopped, Clete. Almost daylight, too." The cock crowed again, almost as if he'd been cued. "We got someone up in the ranch house. Better get up now and keep a step ahead of those boys in the cantina."

"I hear you, Bill," said Creed softly. "Wake the others, and let's figure what we're going to do this morning."

Simons awakened each of the other three men, and after they all urinated in a stall, the five of them huddled together in the middle of the barn's bare dirt floor to discuss their situation.

"I say we rush the cantina," said Flewellyn, "and shoot every last man in there."

"Jake, you've said some stupid things before," said Simons, "but that's about the stupidest thing I've ever heard you say. Shoot every last man in the place. What's wrong with you, son?"

"You got a better idea?" spat Flewellyn angrily.

"I do," said Creed. "As far as I'm concerned, the only man in there that I want dead now is Jim Kindred. But to be honest about it, I'm not so sure I want him dead. Maybe when I see him again I'll want him dead because he's responsible for Dent's death. The others? I don't know. They were led by Kindred, and I can't see killing all of them now for being so stupid as to follow a man like Kindred. Enough men have died already.''

''What about the Golihars?'' asked Flewellyn. ''You think they'll just go away or something? They came all the way down here to kill you for killing their brother. And what about Kindred's gang? I don't think they'll let us just walk in there and take Kindred without putting up some sort of argument.''

''You could be right about that, Jake,'' said Creed. ''His bunch could make a fight out of this, but I kind of have my doubts about that because I'm planning on telling them they can go free. The only man I want now is Kindred, and I think when they hear that, they'll hand him over to us, and that'll be that.''

''Even so,'' said Simons, ''what about the Golihars?''

''I'll try to reason with them,'' said Creed.

''And if that don't work?'' queried Simons.

''Then I guess I'll just have to shoot it out with them,'' said Creed.

''You mean we'll have to shoot it out with them, don't you?'' said Flewellyn. ''After all, we didn't come all the way down here to let them shoot you full of holes.''

''Jake's right,'' said Clark. ''Them Golihars will have to shoot us, too.''

Creed smiled at Clark and said, ''Thanks for the thought, Kent, but that won't be necessary, I don't think.''

''I'm Kent,'' said the other twin.

''And I'm Clark.''

''Whichever,'' said Creed, ''I thank both of you.''

''So what's your plan?'' asked Flewellyn.

''We'll go into the cantina and try to get the drop on

them," said Creed, "and if we do, we'll take Kindred out and hang him."

"And if we don't get the drop on them?" asked Simons.

"Then we'll see what happens from there," said Creed. "Any more questions?" He looked from one man to another, and once he had looked at each one, he said, "All right, let's load up, and get this over with."

They checked their weapons, making certain the powder was dry and the caps were in place. Satisfied that they were all set for a real fight—if it came down to that—Creed went to the twin doors, removed the bar, peeked out, and saw no one but noted that the sun was less than a few minutes from rising. He motioned with his head that the time had come, then started across the open ground between the barn and the saloon with his four friends close behind him.

At this same time, the man that Simons had seen going to the outhouse had finished his morning constitutional and was now headed back to the ranch house. He spotted the five men marching toward the cantina, stopped, and stared at them through the faint yellow light of morning.

"Hey!" he shouted, his accent definitely Texas drawl by way of Tennessee. "Who are you? What do you want here?" He started to move toward Creed and the boys. "Hey, I'm talking to you!" He couldn't see the revolvers they carried at their sides.

Creed halted and said over his shoulder, "Jake, go shut him up. Don't hurt him. Just make him shut his big mouth."

"You got it," said Flewellyn as he left the group and went to intercept the tall man. He covered the distance between them in a few seconds.

"Hey, mister," said the lanky fellow, "what are you doing here?" He still hadn't seen the Colt's in Flewellyn's hand.

Flewellyn raised his pistol to eye level, cocked the hammer, and aimed it at the man's nose. "We got business in that cantina over yonder,'' he said, ''and we'd appreciate you keeping your mouth shut until we're finished.''

The rancher stopped short of bumping into the muzzle of Flewellyn's Colt's, his eyes narrowed and filled with fright as they pinpointed on the gaping hole. Then like a true frontier Texan, he still had to have his say. ''Now lookey here, mister. This is my property, and I'm the law around here, too. My name is Jack Dare, and I own that saloon. I don't know who you boys are, but I do know I don't want no trouble around here. Now what business you got with that bunch in my saloon?''

Flewellyn studied Dare for a moment, noting the man's height, his white mustache and hair, blue eyes, ruddy complexion, prominent nose, and hard-set jaw. He looked like he'd understand what they were about, so Flewellyn said, ''Mr. Dare, I am Jake Flewellyn from Lavaca County. So are my friends. There's a man in that cantina—name's Jim Kindred—who led a raid on a cattle drive that resulted in the murder of two good friends of ours. One of our number is the brother and best friend of the two who were killed. All we want to do is take Kindred out and string him up proper. As for the others, they were in on the killing, but we figure they ain't worth hanging, so we're letting them go. And there's two fellers in there—names of Crit and Charlie Golihar—who came down here looking for a fight. If they still want one, we're willing to oblige them, but we'd just as soon not have to kill them, too. There you have it, Mr. Dare. We don't mean you no harm nor do we want to hurt anyone who wants to stay out of our way. If you get my drift.''

''I hear you,'' said Dare. ''Hanging, you say?''

''That's right.''

''Just one man?''

''Just one polecat,'' said Flewellyn, putting things into perspective for Dare.

"Well, it ain't exactly the way I'd like to start my day, but if you promise no one else will get killed, I'll stay clear of you."

"I give you my word we don't want to hurt no one else, including those two who mean to gun down my friend."

"All right, go ahead and do what you have to, but mind what I said about hurting any of my people here. There ain't many of us, but we're all there is in these parts."

Flewellyn put his gun back on safety, lowered it to his side again, and said, "Yes, sir." He turned and walked back to Creed and the others, who had been waiting patiently for him to finish with Dare.

"All set there?" asked Creed.

"That's the rancher," said Flewellyn. "Name is Jack Dare. He said he's the law here and he don't want us making no trouble. I told him what our business was here, and he agreed to let us be as long as all we do is hang Kindred. He don't want no one else hurt here. I promised him we wouldn't hurt no one who didn't get in our way."

"Fair enough," said Creed. "All right, let's get this over with and be on our way."

They hadn't taken two more steps when a pistol shot from the cantina suddenly shattered the stillness. Without being told what to do, the five veterans of the War Between the States scattered for protective cover, which wasn't much and was widely spread. More shots came from the saloon. A few of them kicked up mud around Creed's feet as he raced for the corner of the house opposite the entrance to the drinking establishment.

As soon as he was hunkered down along the side of Dare's home, Creed began shouting orders. "Bill! Get around back and see that they don't come out that way! Don't anyone shoot until after I talk to them!"

Simons ran between the corral and the cantina and posted himself at the corner of the split-rail fence. Flewellyn found protection behind the only tree in front of the house, and the Reeves brothers retreated to the barn.

Dare came up behind Creed and said, "Hey, feller! That other son of a buck promised there wouldn't be no trouble."

"We didn't start it, Mr. Dare," said Creed.

"And who are you?" asked Dare.

"My name is Slate Creed."

"And I suppose you aim to finish what them men there have started. Is that it?"

"That's about the size of it, Mr. Dare. Now if you'll excuse me, I'd like to get on with this."

"Go ahead, but you'll pay for any damage you cause."

"Yes, sir," said Creed, "but first things first." He turned toward the saloon and shouted, "You boys in the cantina! Hold your fire and let's talk!"

The shooting stopped and Creed got an answer.

"This is Crit Golihar talking. Are you the one who's calling himself Creed now?"

"I'm the one."

"Then you're the one I intend to kill for killing my brother Champ. So why don't you save us all some time and a lot of lead by stepping out into the open where I can plug you clean and get this over with?"

"Can't do that, Golihar. I've got other business to tend to before you. You got Jim Kindred and his gang in there. We don't want all of them. Just Kindred. As for the rest of his bunch, you can go about your business, and I promise that I won't bother you anymore for taking part in murdering my brother. Just send out Kindred and you can be on your way."

"What do you plan to do to him?" demanded Golihar.

"I'm going to hang him for killing my brother and trying to steal my cattle."

"You ain't the law, Creed."

"I am when it comes to avenging my brother and my

best friend. Did you know Jess Tate, Golihar?''

''Not too personal, but I knew him.''

''The Detchens murdered Jess, and they were in cahoots with Kindred to steal my cattle. As far as I'm concerned, Kindred's partly responsible for Jess's death, too.''

There was a moment of quiet before Golihar shouted, ''I'll tell you what I'll do, Creed. I'll give you Kindred if you promise to meet me and my brother out front here after you're done with him, and we'll settle this matter of you murdering our brother Champ.''

''Your brother drew and shot first, Golihar.''

''Is that why you shot him in the back?''

''He turned and ran like all the yellow cowards who rode with Kindred when they killed my brother.''

''So you shot him down like a dog.''

''Not like just any dog, Golihar. Like a chicken-thieving yellow cur.''

Charlie Golihar burst through the doorway of the saloon onto the wooden porch, fired a shot at Creed that zinged harmlessly overhead, and screamed, ''You murdering son of a bitch! Come out and fight like a man!'' He let fly another ball, which also missed its target.

Flewellyn took careful aim at Charlie and squeezed off a round that hit Golihar in his left boot heel, knocking his leg out from under him and sprawling him on the boardwalk.

''Crit, I'm hit!'' cried Charlie as he grabbed at his foot. He wasn't really hurt. The ball had slammed into the boot just a few centimeters above the heel but hadn't penetrated the leather. Even so, the force of the bullet put a real sting in him that radiated up his leg like the electric shock of banging a funny bone.

''Hold your fire, Jake!'' shouted Creed. ''Crit Golihar, tend to your man if you like.''

''And have one of your boys shoot me down, too? No, thank you, Creed.''

"Your man shot first, Golihar."

"Help me, Crit! I'm hurting bad!"

"Aw, get up, Charlie," snarled Crit. "You ain't hurt. You ain't even bleeding."

Charlie looked down at his foot, didn't see any blood, then scrambled back inside the cantina.

"Well, how about it, Golihar?" called out Creed. "Are you going to send Kindred out or not?"

"I think not, Creed. You'll have to come in and get him."

Creed turned away and said, "Dammit all to hell!" He looked at Dare and asked, "Have you got people in there, Mr. Dare?"

"My brother and his wife live in the back," said the rancher. "They got two younguns, too."

"I was afraid of that. Well, sir. Have you got any suggestions on what I should do next?"

32

Jack Dare did have a few suggestions for Creed. He started to express them by stepping out into the open.

"You men in the saloon," shouted Dare. "I want you to send out my brother and his family. They got no business in there with you now. Send them out, then you and this bunch out here can have at each other. Just remember this: the men that survive will have to pay for the damage you all cause to my property. You hear that?"

"We heard you," answered Crit Golihar.

"Mr. Dare! This is James B. Kindred. I am a deputy sheriff for Lavaca County. These men with me are my posse. We have come down here to arrest the man you know as Creed. His real name is Clete Slater, and he's an escaped prisoner from the Federal authorities who convicted him for raiding an army supply train and killing several soldiers after the war was over. The other men with him helped him escape and are also wanted by the Federal authorities. I understand you are the law in these parts, Mr. Dare, and as a fellow peace officer, I call upon you to do your duty to assist us in apprehending these men."

Creed cringed. Damn that Kindred! That lying son of a bitch! He looked at Dare, who was looking back at him.

"Is he telling me true, Mr. Creed?" asked Dare.

"I won't lie to you, Mr. Dare," said Creed. "Some of what Kindred says is true. He was a deputy sheriff for Lavaca County until he and that bunch with him robbed a freighter named Teddy Johnson. They were set free on bail, then ran off to Mexico, where they joined up with the French for a while. When the Mexicans attacked Matamoras yesterday, they ran off again."

"What about that part where he said you were an escaped prisoner?" asked Dare. "Is that true?"

Reluctantly, Creed said, "Yes, that little bit is true, but I was tried and convicted by an army court for a crime I didn't commit."

Dare studied him a moment, then asked, "You fight for the South during the war?"

Creed had a hunch and played it. "Yes, sir, I did, and so did my friends here. But none of them in there did. They stayed home and hid from the law that wanted them to serve."

"Draft dodgers?"

"That's right," said Creed. "Except for Kindred. He was the enrolling officer for Lavaca County then."

"One of them enrolling officers, eh?" said Dare. He turned back toward the saloon and yelled, "James B. Kindred, I figure you for a liar. Now send out my brother and his family or I'll come in there and throw you out here myself."

"The hell you say!" shouted Kindred.

"You heard me right, mister."

"Then come and get them," said Kindred.

Dare nodded with resignation and started walking toward the saloon. A gunshot from the doorway splattered the mud in front of him.

"Don't come no closer, Mr. Dare," said Kindred. "You do and I'll shoot you down for interfering with the law."

Dare put his hands on his hips and said, "We'll see about

who's interfering with the law, mister." He turned and stormed off toward his house.

Kindred fired again, this time hitting Dare in the back of his right leg and knocking him down. The rancher rolled over and grabbed his wounded limb, wincing severely with the pain in his calf. He sat up and glared back at the saloon.

"You'll pay for that, Kindred!" shouted Dare. He struggled to his feet, then hopped into his house. A few seconds later he was back at the door with a Henry rifle in hand. "You in the saloon!" he shouted. "I will kill the first man to come out of there, and I will kill the second, the third, and every man after that unless you send out my brother and his family unharmed and then send out Kindred for Mr. Creed and his friends to deal with. Do you hear me?"

"We heard you, Mr. Dare," said Crit Golihar. "But we ain't sending out no one. If you want to side with Creed, then you go right ahead. We'll shoot you down, too." To back up his words, Golihar fired a round at Dare that chipped off a little adobe beside the door.

"You son of a bitch!" screamed Dare. He fired back, his bullet zinging through the cantina doorway but hitting no one inside. He cocked the rifle again and started to squeeze off another shot but was stopped.

"Mr. Dare!" shouted Creed. "Hold your fire! Remember your brother and his family are in there! You might hit one of them!"

Dare held back, realizing that Creed was right. "Yeah, you're right. The son of a bitch made me so angry, I almost forgot about Randall and his family. Thank you, Mr. Creed, for reminding me."

"My pleasure, Mr. Dare," said Creed. "You got any more suggestions now?"

Dare looked a little sheepish and said, "I guess we'll have to wait them out for now."

"My sentiments exactly, Mr. Dare."

The impasse between Creed and his men and the outlaws inside the saloon continued through the noon hour. The outlaws refused to allow Jack Dare's brother Randall and Randall's family to leave the cantina, and Creed and Dare were helpless to do anything to dislodge the outlaws.

Finally, Creed came up with an idea when he noticed the smoke rising lazily from the chimney of the saloon. "We'll smoke them out," he told Dare. "I'll climb up on the roof and throw something over the chimney. That will force the smoke back into the cantina. They won't be able to stand that for very long, and they'll have to come out."

"How are you planning to get up there?" asked Dare.

"I'm not sure," said Creed. "Got any ideas?"

"You'll need a ladder. There's one in the barn. You can put it against the blind side of the saloon where there ain't any windows. Just be careful not to bang the ladder against the building."

Creed nodded his understanding and said, "Tell Jake over there what I'm up to so he doesn't shoot me by mistake."

"I'll do it, Mr. Creed," said Dare. "I'll get you an old blanket to use."

Creed took the blanket from Dare, then dashed to the barn, where he quickly explained what he was doing to the Reeves brothers. He found the ladder Dare had told him about, slipped out the back of the barn, and dragged it across the corral to where Simons had stationed himself. He told him the same thing that he had told Kent and Clark, dragged the ladder across the open ground to the saloon wall, and carefully stood it against the building. Slowly, he climbed to the roof.

Before he could step on top of the cantina, Creed glanced at the road that ran north from Olmito and didn't like what he saw. "Dammit all to hell," he swore under his breath. Quickly, he scrambled down the ladder and ran over to Simons. "Come on, Bill. We've got to get out of here.

There's a column of Yankee cavalry heading this way.''

"Yankee cavalry?" queried Simons.

"That's right. Let's get to the barn and get saddled up. They'll be here any minute."

"What about Jake? He's out front there. How do we let him know we're leaving?"

"I'll take care of that," said Creed. "Come on. Let's go."

They ran through the corral to the rear of the barn. Simons went inside, while Creed slipped around the side and made the dash back to the house.

"My friends and I have to get out of here," he told Dare. "There's a column of Yankee cavalry headed this way."

"From which direction?" asked Dare.

"North. Why?"

"Well, if you're trying to avoid the army, you'd better take the west road."

"West?"

"That's right," said Dare. "The south road goes straight to Brownsville, and that place is running over with Yankees right now. The west road goes back to the Rio Grande. You can either cross into Mexico or you can take the river trail and stay on our side of the Rio Grande."

"Where does that go?"

"Northwest to La Paloma and southeast to Rancho San José."

"Rancho San José? Isn't that Juan Cortina's place?"

"That's right," said Dare. "Murdering Mexican bastard. I'd stay clear of his place, if I were you."

"You don't have to tell me," said Creed. "I know Cortina all too well."

"Well, then you best head to La Paloma or cross the river. Choice is yours, but either way you go I wish you luck."

"Thank you for that, Mr. Dare," said Creed. He looked

back to the barn and saw Simons signaling that they were ready to ride. "Do you think you'll be all right with us gone?"

"The army don't scare me none, Mr. Creed," said Dare. "I'll be just fine. You take your boys and go on now."

Creed waved to Simons to come on with the horses. The barn doors flew open, and Simons and the Reeves brothers came out on the fly, leading Nimbus and Flewellyn's horse.

"What's going on, Clete?" shouted Flewellyn.

"I'll explain later," said Creed. "Right now, we got to get the hell out of here." He grabbed his mount's reins and leaped into the saddle.

Flewellyn did the same with his horse, and before the outlaws inside the cantina realized what was happening, Creed and his men were off at a gallop, heading west toward the Rio Grande, the same direction from which they had come the day before.

33

"They're running away!" said an incredulous Crit Golihar.

The other outlaws ran to the windows and doorway to see if Crit was telling them true. He was.

"Where do you think they're going?" asked Charlie Golihar.

"It's a trick of some sort," said Kindred.

"No, it ain't," said Crit. "They're leaving."

"Let's go after them," said Charlie.

"What about Dare?" asked Kindred. "Was he with them?"

Looking over at the ranch house, Crit said, "Nope. He's still over yonder with that rifle. Mr. Dare!" he shouted across the way. "You still want your brother and his family let go?"

"You bet I do," Dare hollered back.

"Then you let us ride out of here," said Crit, "and you can have them."

Dare rubbed his leg where Kindred had shot him. It hurt; the wound as well as his pride. He debated with himself for a minute before answering Golihar. "All right," he called out, "you can ride out of here right now, and you'd better hurry because the army's coming this way."

"The army?" queried Charlie.

223

"That's what the man said," replied Crit.

Kindred smiled and said, "Good. We can tell the army about Slater and they can go after him."

"The hell you say!" swore Crit. "I swore on my brother's grave that I'd get the son of a bitch that killed him, and I aim to keep that oath. As for you, Jim Kindred, I'd be worried that the army don't lock me up for fighting on Maximilian's side down in Mexico. Seems to me they're a might friendlier to them Mexicans than they are to the French."

Golihar made sense, and Kindred knew it. The army wouldn't look too kindly at him and his gang. Maybe it would be best to get the hell of there and go after Slater now. After all, counting the Golihars, they were now thirteen against five. Those were fairly good odds.

"All right," said Kindred, "let's go after them ourselves."

Crit smiled and said, "Now you're talking and thinking right, Jim. Let's do'er, boys!" He leaned through the doorway and yelled out, "We're coming out, Mr. Dare, and we're going to saddle up and ride out of here. We're going to take your brother's two younguns with us for a piece, then we'll set them down and let them go. That's just to get us a good head start and so you won't be tempted to shoot any of us or tell the army to follow us. You understand all that, Mr. Dare?"

"I hear you," he shouted back. Then under his breath, he said, "I sure as hell don't like it, but I hear you." Louder he added, "You better come on now. The army can't be more than a mile away."

Crit gave the command, and Kindred's gang ran for the barn, leaving the Golihars and Kindred in the saloon to watch Randall Dare and his family until the horses were saddled and brought out of the barn.

The cavalry troop was less than a quarter mile away. Dare

worried that if they got too close then the outlaws would do something foolish and harm his kin or the soldiers might take out after them and mistakenly hurt the children. Either scenario was no good. He had an idea to prevent any such calamity.

"Golihar!" he called out. "Send my brother over here."

"What for?"

"So I can send him out to stop the army from getting too close," said Dare. "They'll be here before you can skedaddle on out of here unless we stop them out there somewhere."

"Makes sense, but why don't you go?"

"I'm hurt too bad to walk," said Dare.

"All right," said Crit, "I'm sending him over."

Randall Dare came out of the saloon and hurried over to the house. He was tall like his older brother with almost the same looks but younger, black hair and black whiskers instead of white. His head was bare, and he wore only boots and pants over his gray long johns.

"Those dirty sons of bitches!" he swore when he was close enough to the house so that only his brother would hear him.

"There's no time for that now," said Jack. "You got to go out and meet them soldier boys heading this way and stop them."

"What'll I tell them, Jack?"

"Tell them the truth. Tell them there's outlaws here holding your wife and younguns hostage and that they're leaving and taking the younguns with them for a piece down the road. Tell them not to interfere and everybody will be safe. You understand, Rand?"

"I got it," said Randall. He looked over his shoulder at the cantina and said, "And as soon as the kids are safe, I'm going after those bastards myself."

"They hurt you or Emma or the younguns?" asked Jack.

"No, but—"

"But hell!" snapped Jack. "You go stop those soldiers now, and we'll talk about the rest later. Now get!"

Randall ran out the north road to head off the cavalry and met the Federals a few hundred yards away from the settlement.

Riding at the head of the column was Top Sergeant Horatio Hooks. As soon as he saw Dare running toward him, Hooks halted his detachment, suspecting something was amiss in Olmito.

In his excitement to reach the cavalry, Dare didn't notice the coloring of the soldiers' skins until he was almost upon them. Then he noticed it too well. Breathlessly, he studied Hooks and his men, then said, "Ain't you got a white officer leading you darkies?"

As blandly as he could, Hooks said, "No, we don't."

Dare was obviously disgruntled when he said, "Well, why not? We got trouble here, and we need real men to handle it for us."

Hooks knew Dare's kind; he'd kowtowed to them when the slave laws said he had to, but not since Mr. Lincoln had set his people free. Not since and not now.

"These are real men, mister," he said coldly. "Now what seems to be the trouble here?"

"Well, I suppose we'll have to make do with what we got," said Dare, frowning. "Outlaws. Lots of them. There was five other ones here a while back who was wanting to shoot it out with the thirteen who are fixing to ride out of here right now and take my children with them."

"They're taking your children?" queried Hooks. "We'll put a stop to that." He turned to give a command but was interrupted by Dare.

"Now hold on here," said Dare. "You niggras will just muck it up if you go riding in there now."

"How's that?"

"There's men coming out of the barn, Top," said Private Bailey. "They's on horseback."

Dare turned to look, and Hooks craned his long neck to do the same. Kindred's men were coming out of the barn. They rode over to the saloon, leading three horses for the Golihars and Kindred, who then came out of the cantina carrying the Dare children and mounted up.

"We can't stand by and let this happen," said Hooks.

"You got to now," said Dare urgently. "They said they'd ride down the road a piece and leave off the younguns unhurt as long as no one tries to stop them. My brother's the law around here, and he says that's what we're going to do, so don't you niggras get in the way now. You hear?"

Hooks sat back in the saddle and said, "All right, we'll just wait here until they're gone, then we'll ride out and bring back your children."

"No, you won't," said Dare. "I'll fetch them back. You just stay out of this."

Hooks nodded and said, "Suit yourself."

Dare walked back to the settlement, watching the outlaws ride away with his offspring. He still had thoughts of getting his rifle and going after them, but his brother had other ideas.

"Those soldiers look like niggras from here," said Jack.

"They are. They wanted to go after the younguns, but I said no, that I would do it."

"You ain't going after them outlaws, Rand."

"And who's going to stop me?"

"I am. I might only have one good leg, but that's all I need to stand on to whup your ass."

Randall Dare knew his brother was right about that. Although they had very similar physical features, the resemblance stopped there. Jack had all the character of an oldest child, while Randall had the backbone of a jellyfish. When push came to shove, Jack would kick and slug until he was too tired to move; whereas Randall would simply back off and accept defeat without so much as a punch in the shoulder.

"So who's going after them then?" asked Randall.

"Them niggra soldiers, that's who. They're the army, ain't they? So let's let them do their job." He hobbled out into the road and signaled the cavalry unit to come on.

Hooks gave the command to move out at a walk, and the column rode into Olmito. The sergeant halted his men between the saloon and the ranch house and right in front of the Dare brothers.

"Sergeant, I am Jack Dare. I own this land around here. This is my house, and this is my saloon. My brother says he's already told you about our trouble here."

"Not in any detail, sir," said Hooks, reciprocating the courtesy that Dare seemed to be extending to him.

"Then maybe I'd better tell you what's happened here."

34

Creed didn't know it, but he and his men were being pursued by the outlaws; and the outlaws didn't know that the cavalry was chasing them. None of the three groups of horsemen knew that there was a surprise waiting for all of them at the Rio Grande.

The battle for Matamoras had gone badly for the Juáristas after Creed and his men left the town. Imperialist General Mejia led a counterattack that drove the Liberal army from the city for the time being, and Colonel Dupin, after discovering that he had been sent on a wild goose hunt, returned to Rancho Abeytia and surrounded the hacienda, trapping Hunter and his company of cavalry. Newhouse attempted to free his friend by attacking Dupin's rear but was repulsed with ease. Thinking to head off a total disaster for the Liberals, Newhouse took a squad and rode for their real camp upriver. Cortina was supposed to be waiting there with his reserves but wasn't. Before Newhouse could think of what to do next, the storm broke, forcing him to remain there until the next day when the skies cleared.

All through the night Newhouse had wondered where Cortina could have gone. Knowing that Cortina had more larceny in his veins than patriotism, he was willing to bet the Red Robber had gone off on a little raid on the American side of the Rio Grande; then when the storm hit, he probably made tracks for Rancho San José. Even if he hadn't gone on a raid in Texas, Cortina was more than likely at the ranch sucking up to Juárez, who had gone there to await the outcome of the battle for Matamoras. Whether Cortina was there or not, Newhouse figured he should go to Rancho San José and confer with *el presidente*.

Cortina did go to his ranch to suck up to Juárez, but the Mexican president wasn't interested in his general's flattery. There was a battle in progress, and that was all that mattered for the moment. Juárez was already angry with Cortina for leaving the camp on the river, but when the news of General Escobedo's retreat arrived at the same time the rain began, *el presidente* became furious. "As soon as this weather clears," he screamed at Cortina, "you had better remove yourself and your men across the river and aid General Escobedo or . . ." He didn't need to say any more. Cortina knew what the consequences would be if he failed to obey. When the rained ceased, Cortina began assembling his followers to return to Mexico.

Creed and his men were the first group to reach the Rio Grande that early afternoon. The storm had caused some flooding, and the river was flowing over its normal limits, although it was now in the process of receding. Even so, the river trail that Jack Dare had advised Creed to take to the northwest was presently inundated and definitely not traversable. As he contemplated their next move, Newhouse appeared on the other side and hailed him.

"Who's that?" asked Flewellyn.

"Frank Newhouse," said Creed.

"The one who helped us get out of Matamoras?" asked Simons.

"That's him," said Creed

"Well, what's he saying?" asked Flewellyn. "I can't make out a word of it."

"I can't either," said Creed. He tried yelling back at Newhouse, but it was no use. The distance between them was too great, and the rushing of the river was too loud.

"He's waving for us to come over," said Simons.

"No, he's not," said Flewellyn. "He's telling us to stay here and wait for him to come over."

"I think you're right, Jake," said Creed. "But I don't think he's coming over here right away, and we can't wait too long for him because the cavalry might be coming after us."

All of them looked back at the road behind them but saw no one coming—for the moment.

"And we can't go upriver because the road's under water," said Creed. "We could go back and take the other way, but that leads to Rancho San José, and I don't think we'd be too welcome there either. I guess we'll just have to wait here for a while, but I don't want to get caught flat-footed. Bill, you ride back up the road and keep a look out. If you see the cavalry coming, fire a warning shot, then get back here as fast as you can."

"Then what?" asked Simons.

"Then we ain't got no other choice," said Flewellyn. "We swim for it."

"That's about the size of it," said Creed. "We'll have to try crossing. We won't have any other choice." He looked at each man, then said, "You better get going, Bill."

Simons rode off at a gallop.

Creed urged Nimbus into the swift current, wading out until the water was knee-deep on the horse. This brought him twenty or so yards closer to the other side. He yelled across at Newhouse to do the same but wasn't heard. Even so, Newhouse got the idea and did likewise on his side of the river. Finally, the two men were within shouting distance.

"What are you doing back here?" asked Creed.

Newhouse laughed and said, "I was about to ask you the same thing. I figured you'd be halfway back to Lavaca County by now or at least out of Cameron County and riding north."

"Ran into some old enemies at a little place called Ol-mito, just up the road a piece," said Creed. "We were having a Mexican standoff when the cavalry came along and broke it up. What about you?"

"I'm looking for Cortina. We need his reserves for the battle, and he's run off from the camp. My guess is he went home to his ranch to see President Juárez. It's just like him to run off when we need him."

"How is the battle going?" asked Creed.

"Not good. At least it wasn't when I left yesterday to find Cortina. General Escobedo was retreating from town, and John Hunter was surrounded by Dupin's cavalry at the Abeytia ranch. I don't know what's happened today so far, but if I know John Hunter, he hasn't surrendered. He'd go down fighting first. As for Escobedo, he'll attack again and again as long as he has the men to do it with. He's determined to take Matamoras and restore the government to Mexican soil." He paused, then added, "It's Hunter I'm worried about. Escobedo is going up against his own kind in General Mejia and Imperialist Mexican troops. Hunter's facing that French bastard Dupin and his Contre-Guerrillas. They're a mean bunch, but they're the best the Imperialists have got. I don't know how long John can hold out against them."

"It doesn't sound good," said Creed.

"Say, Creed. I know you ain't too fond of Cortina, but you wouldn't consider doing me a favor and riding down to Rancho San José and telling him what's up, would you?"

"I was afraid you'd ask that," said Creed. "I'll be honest with you, Frank. I'd rather be thrown in a pit of rattlesnakes than ride into Rancho San José to see Cortina, but if I don't,

I won't be able to look myself in the eye ever again. Not after what you and John Hunter have done for me.''

"Then you'll do it?"

"Did you think I wouldn't?"

Newhouse laughed and said, "To be honest with you, Creed, I knew you'd at least try."

Before Creed could make another reply, a single gunshot rang out in the distance. The signal from Bill Simons that the cavalry was coming.

"Dammit all to hell!" swore Creed.

"What was that?" asked Newhouse.

"Signal. The cavalry's coming. We got to get out of here."

"What about Cortina?"

"Got any suggestions?" asked Creed.

Newhouse thought for a moment, then said, "Get your boys into the shallow water and ride downstream a few hundred yards, then head through the brush for the road. It's only a few hundred yards from the river down that way." He pointed to the southeast. "You can make it to Cortina's ranch in less than an hour from there."

Creed turned and looked back to see if Simons was coming. He was. Then to Newhouse, he said, "All right, we'll give it a try. For John's sake." He turned Nimbus around and returned to Flewellyn and the Reeves brothers. Quickly, he explained what he was planning to do, and they agreed that it was as good a plan as any. Together, they waited for Simons to join them.

When he was within a hundred yards of them, Simons began yelling, "It ain't the cavalry! It ain't the cavalry!"

Creed and Flewellyn exchanged quizzical looks and said simultaneously, "It ain't the cavalry?"

As if he'd heard them, Simons answered their question. "It's Kindred and the Golihars!" He reined in his horse and gasped, "It's Kindred and Golihars coming, not the cavalry. It's the whole gang coming this way.''

''Dammit all to hell!'' snapped Creed. ''Why now?''

''Why not now?'' asked Flewellyn. ''We can be done with them in a few minutes, then be on our way.''

Creed glared at Flewellyn and said, ''John Hunter saved my life, and he helped me get you boys out of Matamoras, too. I owe him. We owe him.''

Flewellyn blushed, lowered his eyes, and said, ''Sorry, Clete, I forgot. You're right. We do owe him.''

''Forget it, Jake.''

Before Creed could say anything more, the outlaws came in sight.

''No sense in trying to run now,'' said Creed. ''We get out in that water, and we're all so many ducks on a pond. We'll have to make a stand right here.'' He drew his Colt's and checked the chambers to make certain the powder was dry and the caps were in place. ''Better get ready, boys.''

The others did likewise, and the five of them prepared to fight it out with the outlaws.

35

They waited. Creed, Flewellyn, Simons, and the Reeves brothers, Clark and Kent. Guns drawn. Prepared to kill, if necessary. Preferring not to shoot anyone.

Except maybe Jim Kindred. He was the only one Creed really wanted dead. The others? They could go about their business. Most of them were losers anyway and would soon enough meet some unnatural end without his help. But Kindred needed help to die because he was one of those lucky bastards that seemed to escape justice all the time.

If there had to be shooting, Creed wanted Kindred to be the first one dead. He would aim his Colt's with that in mind as the outlaws came riding toward him and his men.

Upon seeing Creed and the others at the river's edge, Crit Golihar signaled his bunch to hold up. They were still a good three hundred yards away. Golihar studied the situation, smiled, then said, "Come on. There's only five of them and thirteen of us. We'll go up and talk a bit first, and if Creed don't come out to meet us alone, we'll just have to kill all of them."

"What about those cavalry coming our way?" asked Kindred.

"What about them?" replied Golihar. "They ain't in sight yet, so that means they stopped to pick up those young-uns and went back to Olmito, don't it?"

"It might," said Kindred.

"It do," said Charlie Golihar.

"Quit worrying about them bluelegs, Kindred," said Crit. "You best concern yourself with Creed. He's still aiming to kill you, you know."

Kindred swallowed hard to summon up some courage, then said, "To hell with him. Come on, let's get this over with." He urged his chestnut horse forward as if he were leading the pack.

The Golihars exchanged evil grins, then followed. Kindred's men spread out in a line with the Golihars and took up the same deliberate pace as their leader. Before they had all ridden a hundred yards, Kindred had slipped back between the Golihars, almost as if being between them offered some sort of safe passage for him.

The outlaws continued forward until they were within twenty-five yards of Creed and his men. Crit halted them there and began to parley with Creed again.

"Look here, Creed," said Crit. "My fight is with you and you alone. I don't want to have to kill your friends just to get to you. You ride over there with Charlie and me," he pointed to a spot upriver a piece, "and the three of us will shoot it out. Then when Charlie and me are through with you, we'll let your friends ride back to Lavaca County with us."

"Golihar, we've been through this before," said Creed. "I have no interest in killing either you or your brother—"

Charlie piped up, "You sure had enough interest in killing our baby brother, you yellow son of a bitch!"

Those were fighting words to most Texans, but most Texans didn't have Creed's ancestry and heritage. He maintained the same serene facade that he usually presented in the face of danger and continued speaking.

"Like I've said before, the only low-down son of a bitch among you that I want dead is Kindred. You boys just move away from him, and I'll do the rest. Then you boys can go on your way because we've got business back in Mexico to attend to."

"And what business would that be?" asked Kindred boldly. "Running from the law, Slater?"

Before Creed could reply, Frank Newhouse led his squad of men into the river as if they were planning on crossing to the American side. The Golihars saw them, and their nerves twitched a mite.

"Who's that coming across the river?" asked Charlie in a low voice that only Kindred and his brother could hear.

Kindred looked and said, "Mexicans in the Liberal army. They're probably coming to help Slater."

"Why would they do that?" asked Crit.

"Because he was on their side," said Kindred. "Come on. We'd better get out of here." He started to turn his horse, but Crit stopped him by grabbing the reins.

"Hold on, Kindred," said Crit. "You ain't going nowhere. Leastways, not yet." He nodded toward the river and said, "Them Mexicans are only bluffing. They can't make it across the river now. It's running too fast."

Kindred reevaluated the situation, smiled, and said, "I think you're right, Crit."

Golihar smiled back at him, released the reins, and said, "I know I am."

Creed noticed that the outlaws seemed to be worried about something behind him. He glanced back and saw Newhouse and his men in the water, then nodded to himself as he looked back at the outlaws.

"Those are friends of ours, Golihar," said Creed. "Sort

of changes the odds, don't you think?''

"A fat lot of good they're doing you over there," said Crit. "They don't change nothing."

Then it was Creed's turn to look off in the distance. He saw Cortina and his contingent of so-called patriots coming down the road toward the ford. "But they do," said Creed, nodding toward the oncoming Mexicans.

Almost as if cued by some omnipotent stage director, the rising rumble of horses' hooves on the road behind them warned the outlaws of the approaching Mexicans. They turned to look, but their mounts wouldn't allow it, every one of them being spooked by the increasingly thunderous din.

General Juan Cortina knew practically nothing about military tactics. He didn't know that any army on the march in what could be considered even slightly hostile territory should post scouts to ride ahead, to each side, and to the rear of the main body in order to give warning if anything out of the ordinary should occur. Cortina didn't do this when he led his *bandidos* from Rancho San José to the ford on the Rio Grande. Had he done so, he wouldn't have been surprised to find two groups of gringos blocking his path.

Cortina halted his men to study the situation. Who were these men? he wondered. They appeared to be Texans. They could be that or they could be some of Dupin's Contre-Guerrillas. Didn't the French colonel have a company of former Confederates in his legion? Yes, they could be Contres. And if they were, was he riding into a trap? Yes, quite possibly. Should he retreat? No, this wouldn't be good, not for him, not for his men. After all, what were they? Should he attack? Out of the question! He had no idea of what he was up against. Stand still then? Yes, that was it. Stand still and wait. Maybe send out a few scouts to each flank, just to see if this was a trap.

Crit Golihar steadied his horse in time to see Cortina's scouts ride off, and he figured that the Mexicans were preparing to surround him and his fellow outlaws, all of whom began to sweat—profusely.

"Give it up, Golihar," called out Creed. "You give me Kindred like I want, and I'll tell General Cortina back there to let the rest of you boys go free. Either that or I'll tell him Kindred and his gang were working for the French up until yesterday and now you're riding with them."

"Hey now, Creed," said Crit. "That ain't the way it is, and you know it. We just run into this bunch yesterday at Olmito. We was there first when they came in out of the rain. We hardly even know them."

"Yeah, that's right," said Charlie.

"Then give me Kindred," said Creed, "and you can ride out of here, and we can go about our business in Mexico."

"He's all yours," said Crit.

"No, I ain't!" said Kindred. He spurred his horse and made a break for the brush.

Crit drew his six-gun and fired at the fleeing Kindred. The ball missed its intended target but still accomplished its goal of halting Kindred by hitting the outlaw's horse in the rump, causing the animal to lurch, then stumble and fall, throwing Kindred to the muddy ground.

Cortina witnessed this little scene, and many of the questions that had caused him to pause were instantly answered. This was no trap. These were real Texans, fighting among themselves, and that made them fair sport for his men.

"*Vamanos, muchachos!*" said Cortina. He and his band began to move forward. He drew his side arm and gave other commands, the gist of which were to surround *los Tejanos*.

"Dammit all to hell!" swore Creed. "Now I've got to deal with that bastard again."

36

After rescuing the Dare children and sending them back to their parents in Olmito behind two of his men, Sergeant Hooks led the rest of his company in pursuit of the outlaws. The cavalry unit was less than a mile away when Crit Golihar shot Kindred's horse from beneath him. None of the soldiers heard the blast of the gun over the pounding of their horses' hooves, but they didn't have to hear it because they could already see Cortina's men ahead of them.

The Mexicans surrounded the Texans as Cortina ordered, and the general rode defiantly and victoriously toward Creed, who put his Colt's back in its holster for the time being. The others followed Creed's example.

"Señor Creed," said Cortina, "we meet again."

"I guess it was just meant to be, General," said Creed in a mild attempt at jocularity.

"Yes, I agree," said Cortina. He waved his hand at the outlaws and said, "Who are these men? Friends of yours?"

"Yes, General, they are," said Creed, lying but attempting to keep his word to Crit Golihar that he would tell the Mexicans to let them go free.

"If that is so, why did that one shoot the horse of that one?" asked Cortina, indicating Crit and Kindred respectively.

241

"That son of a bitch with the mud all over him isn't my friend," said Creed. "He's a murdering, thieving bastard that I intend to hang for killing my brother."

"I see," said Cortina. "But didn't you once say that you came down here to Mexico to find a group of men who had killed your brother while trying to steal your cattle?"

Creed couldn't recall ever saying that to Cortina, so he wondered how the bandit general knew about his purpose for being there, but he didn't ask him about it. Instead, he said, "He was with a bunch of other men, but they were killed yesterday in Matamoras when General Escobedo attacked the town."

Cortina scanned the outlaws, then turned back to Creed. "I think you are lying. I am not certain of the truth here, but I do know that you are lying, Señor Creed. But it makes no difference. You are an enemy of Mexico, and I think all of these other men are also enemies of my country. For that, I think I will have you all shot."

"Hold on, General," said Creed. "We aren't enemies of Mexico. Just ask Frank Newhouse over there." Creed motioned with his head to the Mexicans on the other side of the river.

Cortina frowned when he saw *el capitan norteamericano*. There was no way he could shoot Creed with Newhouse present because Newhouse was too close to *El Presidente* Juárez. Before he could think of an alternate plan, his thoughts were interrupted by the arrival of Sergeant Hooks and his cavalry troop.

Hooks left his men outside the ring of Mexicans surrounding the Texans and rode up to Cortina. He saluted the general and said, "I see you've caught them for us, General Cortina."

"Caught them for you?" queried Cortina. "I do not understand, Sergeant."

"These men kidnaped some children back in Olmito,"

said Hooks, indicating the outlaws. Then nodding toward Creed and his friends, he added, "And we've been told that those men are wanted by the army for breaking their paroles from the war."

Before anyone else could respond to the charges, Kindred picked himself up from the mud and started toward Hooks. "Hold on there, Sergeant," he said. "I ain't a part of this. I'm a deputy sheriff from—"

That was as far as he got before Crit Golihar lashed out with a booted foot and kicked him square on the jaw, knocking him back into the mud and this time unconscious.

Hooks drew his Savage Figure 8 cap-and-ball revolver and aimed it at Golihar's head. "I don't know who you are, mister, or why you did that to that man, but you make one more move like that and I'll shoot you myself."

Crit glared at Hooks but said nothing.

Not so Charlie, who said, "Put a blue uniform on a monkey, and he's still a monkey."

Hooks pulled back the lower ring trigger that cocked the hammer on his Figure 8 and shifted his aim to Charlie. "The same goes for you, white trash!"

Charlie flinched but kept his mouth shut.

"Sergeant," said Cortina, "these men are my prisoners. They are enemies of Mexico in the service of Maximilian."

"General Cortina, I mean no insubordination or disrespect," said Hooks, pointing toward Creed with his weapon, "but I was there when that man was sent back to Mexico on a mission for President Juárez. How could he be an enemy of Mexico if he's working for your own president?"

Creed smiled inwardly. Hooks was a sharp one, and Creed was glad of it. That was on the one hand. On the other, Hooks meant to take him in, and that meant the rope for him. Maybe it was time for him to jump into the conversation.

"Sergeant," said Creed, "I am not a violator of my

pardon and neither are my friends here.'' He waved a hand at Flewellyn and the others. ''As for those men over there, I don't know anything about any children being kidnaped, and I don't think they do either. We are not enemies of Mexico as General Cortina has said. He must have us confused with some other Americans. As you already know, I was sent on a mission to Mexico by President Juárez, and I completed it satisfactorily, as Captain Newhouse over there can attest to. My friends and I were on our way home yesterday when the storm struck and we were forced to spend the night in a barn in Olmito.''

''I know all about what happened in Olmito, mister,'' said Hooks. ''Mr. Dare was kind enough to tell me about all of you men, including the fact that you are an escaped prisoner from some place north of here.''

''I don't know where Mr. Dare got that from—''

''He got it from Kindred,'' said Crit Golihar.

Creed ignored the interruption and went on, saying, ''But Mr. Dare is wrong. My friends and I came down here looking for that man over there because he's responsible for killing my brother. While we were in Mexico, we got involved in their war, did our part for President Juárez, and we were headed home.''

''And when you saw us coming,'' said Hooks, now aiming his gun at Creed with a little more intent, ''you hightailed it out of Olmito as fast as you could go. Why was that?''

''I won't lie to you, Sergeant,'' said Creed. ''You're Federals, and frankly, we don't get along too well with you boys just yet.''

''I see,'' said Hooks.

''But that's not important right now,'' said Creed.

''Oh, no?'' queried Hooks. ''Then what is?''

''The battle for Matamoras,'' said Creed. ''You probably haven't heard the news, but it's not going too good for General Escobedo's army. To make matters—''

"The battle for Matamoras ain't my concern," said Hooks. "But you are, and so are your friends. I'm taking all of you back to Brownsville, where Captain Becker can sort it all out." He waved his Colt's and added, "Come on. Let's get going. Daylight's wasting." To the Golihars, he said, "Get that man on a horse and bring him along."

"General Cortina," said Creed, "are you sure you want to let him do this?"

Cortina glared at Creed and said, "Why should I stop him?"

"Because we can make you the hero of the battle for Matamoras, General."

37

Juan Cortina had an immense ego, and Creed had struck the right chord in it.

Cortina quickly convinced Sergeant Hooks that the Liberal Mexican army needed the Texans to reinforce General Escobedo in the battle for Matamoras. Hooks wasn't so sure that he should let them go, but he knew that it would be a real mistake to deny the Mexicans at this point in time, when they were so desperate to recover their country from the Europeans. Hooks agreed to allow all but Kindred and Creed to go.

"But I need Creed more than anyone," said Cortina.

"Why?" asked Hooks.

"Because I know the area better than anyone," said Creed.

"Better than the Mexicans?" queried Hooks.

"Better than the rest of the *norteamericanos*," said Cortina.

"All right, he can go with you, General," said Hooks, "but the other man stays."

"Now hold on here," said Crit Golihar. "Who says we want to go to Mexico to fight for a bunch of greasers?"

"I do," said Creed. He looked at Hooks and said, "Sergeant, if I could confer with my fellow Texans alone, I'll get this all straightened out."

"All right, go ahead."

Creed took the outlaws aside and said, "There's a man down there right now who saved my life recently, and he's in big trouble. We need every gun we can muster to save him."

"Like I said, we ain't fighting to save no greasers," said Crit. "Leastways, that goes for Charlie and me."

"The man I'm talking about is a Texan fighting for Juárez," said Creed.

"A Texan?" queried Crit.

"That's right. His name is John Hunter, and—"

Golihar's eyes lit up as he interrupted, "John Hunter. I knew a John Hunter during the war. He saved our asses from the Heel Flies once. Could this be the same man?"

"This John Hunter is from Hopkins County, and—"

"Must be him then," said Crit. "A bit on the short side, is he? But a tough little devil?"

"That's him," said Creed.

"Well, hell's bells, Creed. Why didn't you say so in the first place? We'll go to Mexico to fight. Won't we, Charlie?"

"Sure thing, Crit."

Creed glared at the men in Kindred's gang and said, "And what about you boys? Any of you too yellow to fight on the right side now? If you are, then General Cortina has other ways of dealing with those who fought for Maximilian." None of them spoke up. "That's what I thought. All right, we're all in this."

"What about Kindred?" asked Crit. "He shouldn't get out of this, the yellow-belly."

Creed smiled and said, "You got that right." He went back to Hooks and said, "Sergeant, I think you should let Kindred go with us, too."

"I get the impression he don't want to go anywhere with you, Mr. Creed."

Creed smiled and said, "You're quite observant, Sergeant, but I'm willing to give him the chance to redeem himself for killing my brother. All he has to do is fight bravely like a real soldier and prove to me he's not the low-down yellow coward that I think he is, and then I'll let him go."

Hooks studied Creed for a second, then said, "All right, take him with you. Hell, he don't mean nothing to me anyway." Then, to Cortina, he said, "All right, General, they're all yours. I wish you luck in the battle. Actually, I wish I was going with you. We ain't been in a good fight in a while." He saluted, then turned back to Creed. "Mr. Creed, I don't really know you from Adam, but I do know you're wanted by the army for something. I'm letting you go because General Cortina needs you and for no other reason. If you happen to live through this battle, my advice to you is to stay in Mexico. Because if you come back to Texas and I see you again, I will do my duty, Mr. Creed. You understand that?"

Creed looked him straight in the eye and said, "I would expect no less from a first rate soldier in the United States Army, Sergeant."

Hooks felt the sincerity in Creed's voice, and suddenly, he wished to himself that he should never see Creed again—at least not in the line of duty. He saluted Creed and said, "Anyway, I wish you luck in the battle, too." Before Creed could thank him, Hooks spurred his mount and rode back to his company.

Creed turned to Cortina and said, "Well, General, how do you propose that we get across this river?"

Cortina looked at the swollen *rio* and said flatly, "We swim across. *Vamanos, muchachos!*"

"You heard the general, boys," said Creed to the Texans. "Throw Kindred on his saddle, and let's ride."

As soon as the Reeves brothers got Kindred tied into his

saddle, Creed put spurs to Nimbus, let out a real Texas yell, and made a dash for the river. Flewellyn, Simons, and the Reeves brothers—with Kindred secured between them—were right behind Creed, and the outlaws, led by the Golihars, brought up the rear.

The Rio Grande was still in flood but at a less dangerous level now, allowing Cortina's army to cross without incident.

Including the Texans and Newhouse's company, Cortina had almost two hundred men at his command, but he didn't have the slightest idea about how he should deploy them for a battle or even which enemy he should engage: Mejia in Matamoras or Dupin at Rancho Abeytia. He called a meeting of officers—which included Creed—as soon as everyone was safely on the Mexico side of the river.

"*Capitan* Newhouse, what is the latest news from Matamoras?"

"Well, General, it ain't good," said Newhouse. "Escobedo, er, General Escobedo has retreated from the town and has taken up a position to the southwest. He expects Mejia to attack him there sometime tomorrow. Captain Hunter is still surrounded by Dupin's Contres at Rancho Abeytia, but Dupin is cut off from Matamoras by General Escobedo's forces."

"I see," said Cortina, "and that means Dupin is between us and General Escobedo, yes?"

"Well, not exactly, General," said Newhouse. "We could go around Dupin without too much trouble to get to General Escobedo, but that would put us in the same boat with him."

"I do not understand," said Cortina.

"I think Captain Newhouse means we'd be trapped between Dupin and Mejia," said Creed, "the same as General Escobedo is now. Am I right, Frank?"

"That's right, Creed."

"Then you are suggesting that we attack Dupin?" queried Cortina. "Is that it, *Capitan*?"

"Well, General, the decision is yours to make," said Newhouse, "but if it was up to me, I'd try to relieve Hunter before joining up with General Escobedo. With Hunter's men and ours, we could make quite a difference to General Escobedo."

"I see," said Cortina. "And how do you feel about this situation, Creed?"

"I'm not sure that I go along with Frank," said Creed. "Dupin's Contres are very good troops from what I've seen of them. I'm not sure we have enough men to take them on alone. I think we'd need reinforcements first."

"And where do suggest we get them?" asked Newhouse.

"From Hunter," said Creed.

"From Hunter?" queried Newhouse.

"I was thinking that we could attack Dupin's rear," said Creed, "while Hunter mounted an attack from within the hacienda."

"That is all very good," said Cortina, "but how do you propose to contact *Capitan* Hunter and involve him in your plan?"

"That's easy enough," said Creed, smiling. "I'll just ride up to the hacienda and tell him about it."

38

Cortina thought Creed was crazy, but not so Newhouse. The latter knew Creed was a Texan, and that was that.

Colonel Dupin had three companies of Contre-Guerrillas at his command, with each unit numbering approximately ninety men. The men in the French and European companies were all mounted and armed with sabres, long knives, and breech-loading, single-shot Enfield rifles. Only their French officers carried handguns: Beaumont-Adams cap-and-ball .45-caliber revolvers. The American company under Captain Frank Moore was equally as dangerous as the Europeans but in a different way. The former Confederates were also armed with sabres and Enfield rifles, but unlike the other Contres, they carried Griswold & Gunnison .36-caliber revolvers, giving them an extra weapon in close combat.

When Creed scouted the Contres, he discovered that Dupin had divided his forces into three groups: one each to the east, west, and south of the hacienda with the Rio Grande bordering the north side. Also, Dupin had placed his command post with the French company just south of the road that ran past the hacienda.

Familiar with the lay of things, Creed circled around the American company to the west and rode straight for Dupin's camp. He was well aware of the danger that he was facing,

especially since he had been the major participant in the
ruse that had tricked Dupin away from the hacienda, thus
allowing General Escobedo to launch his first attack on
Matamoras. Creed figured Dupin was quite likely to shoot
him on sight, but that was the chance he would have to
take.

To show the sentries that he was coming in peacefully,
Creed stuck the reins between his teeth and raised his hands
high over his head. He still had his weapons, but they were
hidden about his person, both handguns in his pants at the
small of his back and a knife in his right boot. Two guards
aimed their Enfields at him and motioned for him to move
ahead. A sergeant appeared, then an officer. They led him
to Dupin.

"Ah, Mr. Creed," said Dupin with an evil smile on his
lips, "how nice to see you. I had begun to give up hope of
ever meeting you again. Pray tell me, sir. What brings you
back to Rancho Abeytia? Is it the lovely Señorita Silveria
Abeytia?"

Creed still held his hands over his head as he said, "As
a matter of fact, Colonel, that's part of it."

"And what is the rest of it, may I ask?"

Creed glanced at his hands and said, "Could I take my
hands down first?"

"Why certainly," said Dupin. "How rude of me! Please.
Dismount and join me in my tent for a bit of refreshment."
He dismissed the officer and sergeant of the guard, then
held the tent flap open for Creed. After following Creed
inside, he said, "Please sit down and allow me to pour you
a glass of wine. I hope you like Bordeaux. Red, of course.
I prefer the red myself because it reminds me of . . . blood."

"I haven't had any French wine since I was last in New
Orleans," said Creed nonchalantly, after sitting down in
one of two folding wooden chairs, "and the only reason I
drank it then was that you can't get decent beer or water in

New Orleans. But I did like it, so I'll try your wine, Colonel."

"Good! Good!" Dupin opened a chest and removed two crystal wine glasses and a bottle of claret. He popped the cork with his thumbs, then sniffed the wine's bouquet. A smile of satisfaction spread over his lips as he gazed heavenward, enjoying the aroma. "A '59. An excellent year. I think you will like this vintage." He poured the wine, then served it.

Creed had picked up enough etiquette in New Orleans to know that one holds a wine glass by the stem and inhales the wine's bouquet before sipping it; then instead of swallowing the wine immediately, one washes it over the palate in order to totally appreciate the delicate flavor. Dupin observed Creed carefully and was duly impressed by his proper demeanor, especially when Creed remarked, "As you said, Colonel, an excellent year."

Dupin drank his wine in a similar manner, then sat down in the other folding chair and said, "Ever since we first met, Mr. Creed, I have had the suspicion that you possess more breeding than one would expect from an American frontiersman. Your family obviously comes from good European stock."

"You talk about people like they were cattle or horses," said Creed.

"In a way, we are just animals. You have been around these Mexicans long enough that surely you must realize that by now."

"They might not have the manners of European society or even American society for that matter, but they're still people, Colonel, who deserve to be treated like people."

"Is that how you Americans feel about your . . . former slaves?"

"I can't speak for everybody in America, Colonel, but I've always thought of them as being people. I was brought up that way. That's why my granddaddy forbade anyone to beat his slaves. They were people first and chattel second.''

"But they were still slaves," countered Dupin.

"Only in the legal sense of the word. Our slaves were fed well, clothed, and given good houses to live in. They even wore shoes. And we didn't break up families either. When our slaves married, they stayed with us, children and all.''

"But they were still slaves. Bound to you by law.''

"No, by honor," said Creed. "Our slaves were allowed all the freedom they wanted. Granddaddy gave them passes that allowed them to go anywhere they wanted to go, and they honored that by returning to Glengarry when they said they would.''

"Yes, of course," said Dupin, somewhat perturbed that he was losing the argument, "but we are getting away from the point of your visit here. I assume that this is just a visit, is it not?''

"Well, I couldn't come this close and not stop by and say hello," said Creed with a friendly smile. "But I wasn't planning on staying too long.''

"No, of course not," said Dupin, waggling a finger in the air. "You said something about Don Bernardo's daughter being a part of your reason to be here. Would you mind elaborating on that statement a bit further?''

"Sure thing, Colonel," said Creed, setting his empty wine glass on the little camp table that served as Dupin's desk.

"More wine?" asked Dupin.

"Don't mind if I do, Colonel.''

Dupin poured the wine and said, "You were about to explain the reason for your visit.''

"Well, Colonel, it's like this. General Cortina has you surrounded, and he's about to attack you with a thousand men armed with machetes and the Enfield rifles he got from the Federals in Texas. Now I know those odds don't scare you, Colonel, so you'll fight instead of retreating. Am I right?''

"Go on," said Dupin, thoroughly intrigued by what Creed was telling him.

"We both know that you'll have to storm the hacienda and use it like a fort to hold off Cortina. If you do that, some innocent people might get killed, namely Miss Silveria, her father, and your wife and her sister."

"So? Every war has its innocent casualties."

"I realize that you don't care a whole helluva lot about them, Colonel, but I do. And I've convinced General Cortina that he should allow them to leave the hacienda before he attacks you and you attack the hacienda."

"Out of the question," said Dupin bluntly. "If they are killed, then so be it. I am fighting a war here, Mr. Creed, and I have no time to think about civilian casualties."

"Even if one of them is your own wife?"

"Even if one of them is my own wife," said Dupin coldly.

"Even if one of them is your own . . . mistress?"

Dupin's ramrod back suddenly stiffened, not very noticeably but just enough so that Creed saw it. "The army is my mistress, Mr. Creed."

"What about your wife's sister? Aren't you two having an, uh . . . How did that Cajun whore in New Orleans say it? A *l'affaire d'amour? Une liaison?*"

"I do not know what you are talking about," said Dupin, obviously uncomfortable with this turn in the conversation.

"Come on, Colonel," said Creed. "The whole household knew what was going on. Your wife, too. Maybe."

The colonel was quiet for a moment as he considered Creed's words. Then he said, "If I let you go in there, what will you do then?"

"I'll bring out the ladies and Don Bernardo and take them

through Cortina's lines. From there, I assume they'll want to go to Monterrey. That is a safe place for them, isn't it?'' Then as an afterthought, he added, ''Cortina will provide them with an escort, of course.''

''And while you are in the hacienda,'' said Dupin, ''you will tell the Mexican commander that I am about to attack him. Is this not so?''

''Of course, it is,'' said Creed. ''I'll warn him of what's about to happen. Why shouldn't I? He'd figure it out anyway because I'd be taking away his hostages.''

''Do you guarantee they will be safe?'' asked Dupin.

''Absolutely, Colonel. You have my word on it.''

Dupin studied Creed for a few seconds, then said, ''You have my permission then.'' He drained his wine glass, then set it down so firmly on the table that Creed thought he would break it. He stood, glared down at Creed, and said, ''Mr. Creed, I hope this is the last time we see each other. You are a remarkable young man, and I find you to be quite capable of all the prerequisites necessary to be a good military commander. I wish that you were on my side in this war.'' He turned his back and added, ''Now, go before I change my mind.''

''Thank you, Colonel,'' said Creed, ''but I'd like to say one more thing to you before I leave.''

Dupin spun around and said, ''Yes, what is it?''

''Colonel, if you'd have fought for the South in our recent war,'' said Creed, ''I'd have become a Yankee.''

Dupin knew exactly what Creed meant. His first reaction was to be affronted, but he let that pass instantly. Then he laughed and said, ''You are the audacious one, are you not? I take that as a compliment, Mr. Creed, although I know for certain that you meant it as an insult. Good-bye, Mr. Creed.''

''Good-bye, Colonel Dupin,'' said Creed, pronouncing the name with as much French accent as he could muster.

Dupin called out some orders in his native tongue, and Creed was escorted out of the camp.

And none too soon, because coming into the camp from the other direction was Jim Kindred. On foot. Exhausted. And demanding to see the colonel. Because he had vital information for him. About Cortina. About the Mexicans in the hacienda. About Creed.

39

Once Jim Kindred caught his breath, he became a fast talker, and talk he did. He told Colonel Dupin everything that he knew about Creed's plan for the coming battle, and Dupin believed every word of it, smiled to himself, then started giving commands—all in French, of which Kindred didn't understand a single word.

Creed was just entering Tres Palmes through the front gate when a volley of bullets struck the dirt behind him, kicking up a lot of dust and making Nimbus a bit skittish. His master urged him through the entrance with a squeeze of his legs and simultaneously stroked his neck to reassure him that this was just another noisy day in their lives. More shots rang out, some hitting the wall around the hacienda, others managing to go farther and strike the house, but none of them causing any injury to the besieged defenders.

Captain John Hunter met Creed in the courtyard. "I didn't expect to see you again," he said with a nervous laugh. "What in the hell ever possessed you to come back here?"

"Frank Newhouse," said Creed as he dismounted. "He told me you were in trouble here, so . . ." He let the last fade off.

"So you came back to help," said Hunter, finishing his statement. "Is that it?"

"You saved my life once, John Hunter. I owe you."

Hunter chuckled and said, "I guess you do, but why in the hell did you ride in here, you damn fool? Dupin's got us surrounded, and if the bastard ever charges, we'll be Crockett and Travis at the Alamo all over."

Creed slapped Hunter on the back and said, "Maybe not the Alamo this time, my friend. Maybe this time reinforcements have arrived in time."

Hunter looked at Creed suspiciously and said, "Now what in the hell does that mean?"

Before Creed could answer, a soldier along the wall shouted something in Spanish at Hunter. Creed could only pick up parts of it, but it sounded to him like "the French are coming."

Hunter reacted as if that was what the man had said. "Like I said, if the bastard ever attacks . . ." He let his words trail off intentionally.

Creed looked out across the road and over the chaparral-covered plain that separated the two combatant forces. The French were astir, all right, but they weren't charging. Not yet, anyway.

"John, I'll make this fast," said Creed. "Cortina and five hundred men, including Newhouse and some friends of mine from Texas, are behind Dupin right now, waiting for you to attack him."

"Me attack him?" queried Hunter. "Are you crazy?"

"Maybe, but it worked in Tennessee. You attack Dupin, and as soon as he turns everything on you, Cortina attacks his rear. The idea is to put Dupin in a cross fire."

Hunter thought about it for a second, then said, "It might work, but the bastard's already attacking me. So what do I do now?"

"Get your men mounted up and counterattack." When Hunter didn't move instantly, Creed added, "Now!"

"Yes, of course," said Hunter as if he were coming out

of a daze. Then to his men, he shouted, "*Vayan a los caballos!*"

The Mexicans ran for their horses, most of which were in the stables behind the house. Hunter gave other orders in Spanish, and a soldier brought him his mount. Before putting a boot in the stirrup, he turned to Creed and asked, "You staying here or riding with us?"

Creed reached behind him, pulled out his revolvers, and said, "I'd just as soon stay here, John, but I think you'll need an extra gun or two out there."

Hunter nodded his understanding and watched Creed shove the pistols inside his belt then climb atop Nimbus. "You ready?" asked Hunter.

Creed pulled out his Colt's, checked the caps, then said, "At your command, John."

Hunter mounted up, then leaned toward Creed. With a mischievous smile, he said, "What say we give them Frenchies a real Texas yell?"

"And let's go out over the wall," said Creed.

"You got it, Creed."

Hunter barked out another order, then watched as his men formed a solid line to each side of Creed and him. He drew his sword, held it straight up at the shoulder, then gave the signal to charge, shouting, "*Viva la republica!*"

"*Viva la republica!*" shouted everyone else except Creed as every man spurred his horse, made straight for the wall, and took the low *tapia* in a dashing leap. Hunter and Creed let out their best Texas yells as they led the attack across the road and into the chaparral.

In the distance beyond Dupin's encampment, a cannon boomed, signaling Cortina's men to move forward against the French. Then there was an enormous battle cry as the Mexican army moved ahead, half of them on foot and the other half mounted.

As Hunter's contingent raced across the chaparral plain,

Creed noted that Dupin's company was now ahorse and moving, but Dupin wasn't attacking or even defending. He was withdrawing! Turning aside to join his American company to the west. And coming up fast behind Dupin was his European company of primarily Austrian and Belgian volunteers.

"The son of a bitch is running!" shouted Hunter over the thunder of hoofbeats.

Retreating, yes, thought Creed, but not running. Dupin's was an orderly withdrawal from the field. Nothing more. Nothing less. He would live to fight another day.

The Europeans now swung about, came to a halt, dismounted with rifles in hand, and fired a volley at Hunter's company. Several of his men went down. Seeing this and knowing what crack shots these Contres were, Hunter reined in his horse and gave the order to take cover in the chaparral.

This was good strategy, thought Creed, on both sides. Dupin was covering his rear, and Hunter wasn't going to risk losing any more men that would be needed for an assault on Matamoras.

Hunter ordered his men to open fire on the Europeans, which was another stratagem. His force just might draw the enemy's attention long enough to allow Cortina's charging army to engage them from behind and possibly drive them from the field.

The Europeans continued shooting for only a few more minutes, then, seeing Cortina's rabble racing toward them, they quickly mounted up and rode off to join up with their commander on the road to Monterrey.

Sensing they had won the battle, Cortina's Mexicans gave up their pursuit and began celebrating by firing precious bullets and powder into the air and by dancing up and down and congratulating each other on a battle well fought when actually they should have been thanking their American leaders for outwitting the enemy and keeping their casualties at a minimum.

Although Cortina's men were jubilant, Hunter and New-house weren't. Newhouse led his combined unit of Mexi-cans and Texans after the retreating Europeans, and Hunter ordered his men to mount up and follow them.

A quarter mile down the road, the Legionnaires again halted, dismounted, and fired a volley, this one more deadly than the first because it was concentrated on a group of riders who rode closer together. Several men were shot from the saddle, but most of them were able to ride in among the Europeans, the Mexicans hacking away with their ma-chetes and the Americans firing their revolvers at close range. Some of the Imperialist soldiers tried to surrender, only to be cut down by vengeful Mexicans. In a few very short minutes, the fighting was over. All the Europeans were dead, and so were many of their foe.

Newhouse was for chasing after Dupin and the rest of his Contres, but Hunter vetoed the idea, saying that their duty was to capture Matamoras now and that Dupin was certain to retreat to Monterrey until he could recruit more men.

Creed agreed wholeheartedly. He and Hunter watched the cloud of dust being raised by the Contres as they rode west, and both men had the same question in mind: Why? Why did Dupin leave the field? He wasn't that outnumbered. He could have won the battle with his better trained and better equipped soldiers. So why did he go? Creed especially wanted to know.

As he looked over the battlefield, the answer came to Creed. Lying among the bodies were the ten outlaws who had come to Mexico with Kindred in order to escape justice back home. Every one of them had been too cowardly to fight for the South in the War Between the States, and they had been forced into this affray at gunpoint. Creed felt a little remorse for them. They deserved to be dead for their crimes, he argued with his soul, but it was sad that they had wasted their shortened lives running from themselves. For isn't that what a coward does? Run from himself? Which is impossible. Because no one can hide from himself. Worse than their cowardice was their sheeplike lack of character. None of them would ever have made a leader, but all of them were also poor followers because they chose a cretin like Jim Kindred to lead them. Well, at least they died fighting. That had to count for something when they reached those pearly gates.

For them, yes. But not for Jim Kindred. He wasn't among the dead, Creed noticed, and then he knew why Dupin had left the field. Kindred must have slipped away and warned the French colonel of the plan to attack him. Yes, that was it. It had to be. Why else would Dupin retreat?

40

Creed's deduction that Kindred had escaped and gone over to Dupin was confirmed by Jake Flewellyn, who apologized for letting the little weasel get away. Creed told him to forget it, that Kindred was worse off now than he'd ever been before. Dupin hated cowards as much as he did. The colonel probably had one of his chasseurs shoot Kindred like he would shoot a lame horse instead of wasting the formality of a firing squad on him. So never mind the bastard. They headed back to Tres Palmes with Hunter and Newhouse.

Not all was well at the hacienda when the Texans arrived. Cortina's men were behaving as if they had just won the war and Maximilian and Carlota were on their way back to Austria right now. To make matters worse, they were preparing for an execution—at Cortina's orders, of course.

"*Capitan* Hunter! *Capitan* Newhouse! Señor Creed! How good to see you!" said Cortina when they entered the house and stepped into the parlor. *El general* was seated in Don Bernardo's high-backed Spanish armchair. To his right was Captain Auber and to his left was Claire Mounet. "You are just in time. We are going to execute several traitors." He chortled giddily.

It was obvious that he and his men had broken into Don

264

Bernardo's wine cellar and liberated all the spirits within.

A volley of rifle fire reverberated from the courtyard.

Cortina laughed out loud, then said, "Those were *Capitan* Auber's men." He looked at Creed and said, "You two know each other, don't you, Señor Creed?"

Creed was furious, but he didn't want to show this bastard any emotion. Calmly, he said, "We've met."

"General Cortina," said Hunter, "with all due respect, I must protest these executions."

"And with all due respect, *Capitan* Hunter, I don't care about your protests. They are French, and therefore, they deserve to die."

"What about Madame Mounet there?" asked Creed. "She's French. Are you going to shoot her, too?"

Cortina took Claire's hand and kissed the back of it affectionately. "Señora Mounet is no traitor, Mr. Creed." He looked up at Claire and added, "At least not to me."

Creed noticed something that Cortina couldn't see. He saw the look of hatred and disgust in Auber's eyes. Had Cortina seen it, he might have figured out what Creed knew: that Auber and Claire had been having an affair. And had Cortina learned that, he probably would have put Auber in front of the firing squad with his men.

"You see," said Cortina, "Señora Mounet and *Capitan* Auber have been working as spies for me ever since—" He looked up at Claire and asked, "Since when, my darling?"

"Ever since Maximilian came to Mexico, *mon cher*," said Claire. She raised Cortina's hand to her lips and kissed it, while she gazed wantonly at Creed.

"You see, Señor Creed," said Cortina, "I have known the Señora since the days when her husband was alive, and when the French took my country away from my people, I enlisted her in my service as my eyes and ears in Matamoras. And when her sister and Colonel Dupin came here, Señora

Mounet became a most valuable weapon in our fight to rid our country of the French.''

"Speaking of Madame Dupin," said Creed, "where is she? Are you planning to execute her, too?"

"Of course not," said Cortina angrily. "What do you think I am? I do not make war against women."

Creed looked around the room, then asked, "What about Don Bernardo and his daughter? What have you done with them?"

"Yes," said Hunter, "what have you done with them?"

"They are safe for the moment," said Cortina. "I am saving them for the last."

"The last what?" asked Newhouse.

"Firing squad," said Creed.

"That is right, Señor Creed," said Cortina. "I am going to have them shot last. When *El Presidente* Juárez arrives. As a sort of entertainment in his honor."

Hunter and Newhouse took a turn laughing.

"You find that to be humorous, gentlemen?" queried Cortina.

"You tell him, John," said Newhouse. "I don't think I can stop laughing long enough to do it."

"General," said Hunter, "Don Bernardo and his daughter are on our side." He delighted at how Cortina stiffened at this news. "Yes, General, it's true. Don Bernardo and his daughter have been sending us messages about Colonel Dupin's movements ever since he arrived in Matamoras. In fact, it was Don Bernardo's idea to have Dupin stay here so he could keep a closer eye on him."

"I don't believe you!" snapped Cortina.

"Well, General," said Creed, now also smiling, "I wouldn't be in too big a hurry to shoot them until President Juárez gets here and tells you any different."

41

Cortina refused to allow anyone to see Don Bernardo or Silveria until President Juárez arrived at the hacienda that evening. This was done at Claire's suggestion, of course.

After briefly greeting his president in the courtyard, Cortina led Juárez into the house and offered him Don Bernardo's chair, the one he had sat in earlier that day. *El presidente* accepted the seat, then waited until everyone—with the exceptions of Don Bernardo and Silveria—was assembled before him, scanning their faces, almost as if he were searching for someone in particular.

"General Cortina," said Juárez, "I do not see my good and great friend Don Bernardo or his lovely daughter Silveria. Why are they not here?"

Cortina hesitated to answer, looking down at the floor and clearing his throat nervously. Then urged on by a gentle nudge in the ribs from Claire, he said, "*Mi presidente*, I have them under arrest for betraying the republic."

Juárez's brow furrowed, and he leaned forward stiffly. "What is this nonsense?" he asked.

"It is true, Excellency," said Claire, speaking up. "Don Bernardo and his daughter were servants of the Imperialist party."

Juárez looked at Claire with annoyance and said, "And who might you be, Señora?"

"May I present Madame Claire Mounet, Excellency?" said Cortina proudly. "Madame Mounet has been in the service of our country since the first dark days of the French invasion."

Juárez allowed his brow to roll up his forehead as he said, "Since the first days? Why did you not tell me about her before, General Cortina?"

"I do not know why, Excellency," stammered Cortina.

"And you say my good friends are traitors to the republic?" queried Juárez of Claire.

"Yes Excellency, they are," said Claire. "I have lived in this house since the arrival of the Imperial army and have had the opportunity to watch Don Bernardo and his daughter give aid and information to them at every turn."

Juárez sat back in his chair, leaned to his right, and stroked his lower lip with his right forefinger as he studied Claire for a tense moment.

Quietly, Patrice Dupin slipped into the room from the foyer and stood behind Frank Newhouse. All were so intent on listening to the conversation between Juárez and Claire that no one noticed Madame Dupin's entrance.

"I find this hard to believe, Madame Mounet," said Juárez. "I have known Don Bernardo for many years, and he has never given me any reason to doubt his loyalty to the republic."

"Excellency," said Claire, "with all due respect, I have to say that he has made a fool of you all this time. I can offer you proof of Don Bernardo's duplicity."

"Proof?" queried Juárez.

"Yes, Excellency. Proof. Recently, a surprise attack was led against General Cortina's camp on the river, and General Cortina accused this man"—she pointed at Creed—"of leading the Imperialists to the camp. This man was an innocent placed in harm's way by Colonel Dupin and only made to look like a spy. Don Bernardo told Colonel Dupin where the camp was located and when General Cortina would be there.''

''That is a lie, Mr. President,'' said Patrice Dupin quite calmly. She stepped out from behind Newhouse so Juárez could see who was speaking, and all eyes turned to her. Her hands were hidden in the folds of her skirt. ''She is lying, Mr. President, to cover up her own deceit in these matters.''

Silence. No one stirred or even breathed until Claire stepped forward.

''You cannot trust her, Excellency,'' said Claire. ''She is Colonel Dupin's wife.''

''I am also your sister,'' said Patrice, her face totally void of emotion. She seemed to glide ahead, her dress not even swaying as she moved closer to the center of the room.

''General Cortina,'' said Juárez, ''who is this woman?''

''Excellency, this woman is Madame Dupin, the wife of the French butcher, Colonel Dupin,'' said Cortina, trying to spit the words in disgust but failing.

''And you are also Madame Mounet's sister?'' asked Juárez.

''Yes, Mr. President,'' said Patrice as she continued to come closer to him.

''And you say your sister is lying to cover up her own deceit?'' queried Juárez.

''Mr. President, if you will have General Cortina bring Don Bernardo and Silveria to this room,'' said Patrice, ''I am certain that I can exonerate them from the charges my sister has made against them and I can prove that Claire is your real enemy here.'' She stopped only a few feet from Claire and Cortina.

''General Cortina,'' said Juárez, ''bring my friends here. *Pronto*, señor!'' Cortina turned to order a subordinate to fetch the Abeytias. ''No, señor!'' snapped Juárez, pointing a finger at Cortina. ''I want you to get them.''

"*Sí*, Excellency," said Cortina. He gave a half-bow to Juárez, then left the room. All was quiet until he returned with Don Bernardo and Silveria.

"Don Bernardo," said Juárez, smiling and rising from his chair. He extended his hands and said, "I am so happy to see you again, my old friend."

Don Bernardo walked past Patrice to greet Juárez, while Silveria stopped almost beside the Frenchwoman.

"Excellency, it is an honor to have you in my house," said Don Bernardo.

"My friend, I am so happy to be here," said Juárez, "but I am a bit confused as to what is happening here. Could you help enlighten me?"

Don Bernardo turned, pointed at Cortina, and said, "This fool has accused Silveria and me of being traitors to the republic, Excellency. *Capitan* Hunter and *Capitan* Newhouse have tried to tell him that we have been in your service all the time, but he refuses to believe them."

"Yes, Mr. President," said Hunter, speaking up boldly, "we have been trying to convince General Cortina that Don Bernardo has been supplying us with information about the Imperialist army ever since they came here, but the general has chosen to believe Madame Mounet and Captain Auber instead."

"Captain Auber?" queried Juárez. "Who is he?"

Auber stepped forward and presented himself. "I am Captain Rene Auber, Excellency." He bowed.

"Are you one of our officers, Captain Auber?" asked Juárez.

"No, Excellency, he is not," said Cortina.

"Then who is he, General?" demanded Juárez.

"He is one of my spies, Excellency," explained Cortina. "He was working with Madame Mounet. He often delivered information that she sent to me about the Imperialists. He could do this because he commanded one of Colonel Dupin's companies."

"I see," said Juárez. "So you wish to serve the republic now, Captain Auber?"

"Yes, Excellency."

"Very good," said Juárez. "But let us get on with this matter of Madame Mounet's deceit. Madame Dupin, you said you could prove this. Would you please do so?"

"Mr. President," said Patrice, "before our soldiers came here, my sister was married to a merchant who lived in Matamoras. When he died, my sister came to live with me and my husband in Mexico City. Later, we moved to Monterrey, then here. During this whole time, my sister kept up a correspondence with your General Cortina. You see, they had met when she and Antoine lived here in Matamoras before this war. In her letters, she informed General Cortina of military matters, and he wrote back to her, telling her about you, Mr. President. This is how my husband was able always to find you and then to drive you from your own country. General Cortina did not know that he was being used in this way, but he was being used."

"She is lying!" screamed Claire.

Patrice slowly lifted her left hand. In it, she held a small bundle of letters. "These will verify everything I have just told you, Mr. President," she said.

"General, bring me those letters," said Juárez.

Lead-footed, Cortina took the letters from Patrice and walked them over to Juárez. The president opened the first one, read the salutation at the top and the signature at the bottom, then put it back with the others. He glared at Cortina, but to Patrice he said, "Please continue, Madame Dupin."

"When we came here," said Patrice, "she seduced Captain Auber, and he betrayed his colonel."

Cortina was dumbfounded. He stammered, "Claire, is this true?" She didn't answer him.

"Yes, General Cortina," said Patrice, "it is quite true. Is it not, Silveria?"

"Yes, Madame, it is," said Silveria. "I have seen them together many times, Excellency. They are not very discreet."

"What about you and Creed, you little *puta*?" screamed Claire, using a word everyone knew whether their native tongue was Spanish, English, or French.

"*Puta?*" gasped Silveria. Then without another word she struck out at Claire, slapping her soundly across her left cheek, and in another heartbeat, she slapped her again with the other hand on the other side of her face.

Claire stumbled backward into the wall but didn't fall.

"Silveria!" shouted Don Bernardo.

Everyone was aghast at her action.

Creed crossed the room in a flash and grabbed Silveria from behind. She struggled to get away, to get at Claire.

"*Tu eres una perra mentirosa!*" screeched Silveria. "You lying bitch!"

Claire cringed against the wall.

"Silveria!" said Don Bernardo, coming to help Creed restrain his daughter. "*Por favor, mi hija!* Remember that you are a lady!"

As suddenly as she had begun the attack, Silveria ceased to battle Creed, actually going limp in his arms.

Realizing that everyone was watching them, Creed let up on the bear hug he had her in and allowed Don Bernardo to take charge of the scene.

Leaning close to his daughter, Don Bernardo whispered sternly, "Remember your place, Silveria!"

"Yes, Papa," said Silveria, her eyes lowered but not filled with shame or embarrassment; instead, they were ablaze with hate. Then she looked up at the president and said with almost enough propriety, "I beg your forgiveness, Excellency, for my conduct. I am very sorry."

"I can understand your anger, Silveria," said Juárez. "I am not too pleased myself at this moment." He shifted his gaze back to Patrice and said, "Please continue, Madame."

"There is not much more to tell, Mr. President," said Patrice. "My sister used Captain Auber to help her with her masquerade with General Cortina, and she used General Cortina in her masquerade with . . ." Her voice trailed off as she looked directly at Claire. Finally, she said, "She used General Cortina in her masquerade with my husband."

"No, Patrice, no!" cried Claire.

"Yes, Claire, admit it," said Patrice as coldly as a judge pronouncing sentence.

Claire's eyes darted from one person to another in the room, pleading with them all, with Cortina, with Auber, with Juárez, who held her life in his hands. Then she burst forward, past Silveria and Creed, falling on her knees before Patrice, clutching at her sister's skirt.

"Patrice! Patrice!" she cried. "Why? Why are you doing this to me?"

Patrice reached down with her left hand, took Claire by the arm, and pulled her to her feet. "My sister, you have betrayed everyone who has ever loved you," said Patrice once Claire was standing and looking her straight in the eye.

Creed, like everyone else in the room, was immobile, unable to interfere with the drama unfolding between the sisters. Even when he saw a glint of steel within the fold of Patrice's skirt and suspected that something foul was afoot, he was slow to act.

"And you have betrayed me more than anyone," said Patrice, putting her left arm around Claire as if to comfort her. No one saw her right hand, the fingers grasped tightly around a Corsican stiletto, come upward—so powerfully, so swiftly, so deadly—until it was too late to stop the fatal move.

"No, Pa—" gasped Claire, her eyes bulging, her breath trapped in her throat. She felt the pain, looked down at its source, and saw the blood gushing from beneath her ribs and over Patrice's hand. Then, looking up at Patrice again, her brow crinkled over her nose, and her eyes begged for an answer.

"Yes, Claire," whispered Patrice. "Because you are so very evil, you must die."

Creed rushed forward and pulled Patrice away from her sister.

Claire slumped to her knees, holding her hands over the wound below her heart, her eyes still pleading.

Now everyone saw the knife in Patrice's hand. And the blood. On Patrice and spilling through Claire's fingers. Pooling on the tile floor. They gasped in disbelief.

Claire fell forward. At Patrice's feet. Dead.

42

No one was more shocked by the murder of Claire Mounet at the hand of her sister Patrice Dupin than Creed. Women—at least, not Texas women—didn't kill people, least of all someone of their own blood. Even if they did deserve it.

If nothing else, Madame Dupin saved everyone a lot more grief. Left alive, Claire would have managed to foul the air about her in some manner or another. Captain Auber and General Cortina were both truly in love with Claire. Sooner or later, she would have broken one or both of their hearts, Cortina's in particular because he would have been forced to order Claire's execution for her role as a spy for the Imperialists. Once the jolt of Claire's death had passed it was generally agreed that she wouldn't be missed.

Although the battle for Matamoras was far from over, Creed had had enough of Mexico and its brand of civil war. He gave the Golihars one hard look, and they agreed to let bygones be bygones; after all, they were outnumbered now that Kindred had run off and the rest of his gang was dead, and besides, killing Creed wasn't going to bring Champ back to life. Between themselves, Crit and Charlie figured Creed wasn't the kind to go shooting a feller in the back—leastways, not without good cause, which made it all right then. They asked Creed if they could join up with him and his four friends for the long ride home, and he was agreeable to that notion.

The morning after Claire's murder Creed figured there was nothing left for him in Mexico except to say his farewells. He started with President Juárez, saying he was glad that he could assist him in his noble cause but declining to do anything more because he had his own cause back home to do something about first. Juárez expressed his disappointment at losing such a good man but said he understood. John Hunter and Frank Newhouse thanked him for his aid in the battle for the hacienda, and the three of them agreed to meet again back in Texas once the Mexican war was successfully concluded. Don Bernardo thanked Creed for saving his home from sure destruction and said the doors to Tres Palmes would always be open to him.

Cortina refused to leave his room, and Creed could have cared less except that they had some unfinished business to complete. He burst into Cortina's room and told him that they had agreed that the noncombatants would go free, originally meaning the Abeytias, Claire, and Madame Dupin. Now that Claire was dead—a subject that brought tears to the Red Robber's eyes—and the Abeytias had no need of safe passage, the only one left was Madame Dupin. Creed demanded a promise that she would be escorted to Monterrey, where she could rejoin her husband, and reluctantly, the general agreed to do it.

Creed intentionally left Silveria for last. They walked in the garden for one last time.

"When you left before," said Silveria, "I thought that I would never see you again."

"You wouldn't have either," said Creed, "if we hadn't run into that storm and been forced to meet up with Crit and Charlie like we did. We were on our way home and would have kept on going right past Olmito, and right now we'd be a hundred miles north of here."

"But you are here now."

"Not for long. We're riding out as soon as I finish saying what I've got to say to you."

"Please do not say it," she said, turning her face away from him.

"If I don't, you'll always wonder and so will I." He stopped, took her by the arms, and made her face him. "That night you first came into my room . . . I wanted you . . . to lie down beside me . . . so that I could make love to you." He swallowed hard, then went on. "I've wanted you more and more each time I've seen you. I've felt a great . . . need . . . in my heart for you."

"You are making this so very difficult for me," she said as she put her hands on his chest.

"It's hard for me, too. Especially because I've got a girl back in Texas waiting for me."

"And now I have no one."

"We didn't really have each other, Silveria. I know I wanted to have you, but it just wasn't meant to be, I guess."

"And now you will go home to your girl, and I will only have a memory of what might have been."

"Yes, I guess that's the way it'll be. But I'll often think about you. Everytime I see a beautiful girl with raven hair and soft skin I'll think of you, and I'll remember your kiss and touching you and wanting you, and I'll be a little bit sad because I don't have you in my arms right then and there. I'll probably dream about you, too, Silveria. And when I do, I won't want to wake up and find you aren't lying beside me."

"But you will forget about me once you marry this girl back in Texas."

"No, I don't think I'll ever forget you. No, never. In fact, I'll probably wonder what it would be like to stay here with you and maybe ask your father for—"

She wrenched herself away and said, "No more! Please,

say no more!'' She turned away from him, tears streaming down her cheeks. ''Please, Creed,'' she said hoarsely, ''go now. Go and let me be. I have too much pain already.''

Creed reached out and touched her shoulders, but Silveria squirmed away. ''All right,'' he said, ''I'll go, but I won't say good-bye. I won't say good-bye because we'll see each other again. In our dreams. I'll see you in our dreams, and there . . . there we'll make love . . . and we'll be in love . . . and there won't be anything to keep us apart ever again.'' He wanted to touch her one more time but didn't. He turned and walked away.

Silveria peeked slowly over her shoulder when she heard his fading bootsteps, and softly she said, ''Yes, *caro mio*, I will see you in our dreams.''

WESTERNS!

àt least a savings of $3.00 each month below the publishers price. Second, there is never any shipping, handling or other hidden charges—Free home delivery. What's more there is no minimum number of books you must buy, you may return any selection for full credit and you can cancel your subscription at any time. A TRUE VALUE!

Mail the coupon below

To start your subscription and receive 2 FREE WESTERNS, fill out the coupon below and mail it today. We'll send your first shipment which includes 2 FREE BOOKS as soon as we receive it.